M. A. H... ...ries since a
young age and ...cied the idea of trying to write one.
That dream became a reality when One More Chapter signed
The ...

Born in Darlington in the north-east of England, Hunter grew up in West London, and moved to Southampton to study law at university. It's here that Hunter fell in love and has been married for fifteen years. They are now raising their two children on the border of The New Forest where they enjoy going for walks amongst the wildlife. They regularly holiday across England, but have a particular affinity for the south coast, which formed the setting for the series, spanning from Devon to Brighton, and with a particular focus on Weymouth, one of their favourite towns.

When not writing, Hunter can be found binge-watching favourite shows or buried in the latest story from Angela Marsons, Simon Kernick, or Ann Cleeves.

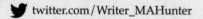 twitter.com/Writer_MAHunter

Also by M. A. Hunter

TRAFFICKED

The Missing Children Case Files

M. A. HUNTER

One More Chapter
a division of HarperCollins*Publishers*
1 London Bridge Street
London SE1 9GF
www.harpercollins.co.uk

HarperCollins*Publishers*
1st Floor, Watermarque Building, Ringsend Road
Dublin 4, Ireland

This paperback edition 2021
First published in Great Britain in ebook format
by HarperCollins*Publishers* 2021

A catalogue record of this book is available from the British Library

ISBN: 978-0-00-844332-0

Printed and bound in Great Britain by
CPI Group (UK) Ltd, Croydon CR0 4YY

Content notices: suicide, domestic violence, paedophilia, sexual assault, drug abuse, child abuse.

*Dedicated to all who have
struggled during the lockdown.
We're all in this together.*

I shall choose the target
His arrow deserves;
I shall trace and mark it
In scarlet curves.
Small and bloody
As a fallen sparrow
My own dead body
Shall receive his arrow.

— *Lucifer Sings in Secret*, Elinor Wylie

Chapter One

THEN

Poole, Dorset

The concrete burned her feet, even though the sun was already starting to disappear behind the hills in the distance. She couldn't say how long she'd been moving in this direction, and somewhere in the back of her mind she knew sticking to a straight line was not the best method of keeping out of sight. But the quickest distance between two points is a straight line, and her need to find help was stronger than the panic of what *he* would do if he caught up with her.

She wanted to scream, as another sharp stone dug into the rough skin of her heel, but any momentary stop to check whether it had drawn blood would have meant slowing her escape.

Escape.

It had been merely a pipe dream for so long; so much so that she couldn't even be sure she was out in the open now. For all she knew, she was still in that dingy hole, and this was just another cruel dream from which she'd be painfully woken at any moment. It wouldn't have been the first time.

Regardless, she had to keep striving onwards. To fail now would be to waste the best chance she'd ever had to flee that musty, windowless room beneath the ground. With no watch, she had no frame of reference for how long she'd been stumbling along the road, though her grumbling stomach told her she would be gobbling up the scraps right now if she hadn't made for the unlocked door.

What if this was all part of his plan? Just another torturous trick for which she'd be forced to pay a heavy price. Promise freedom, only to snatch it away. How many times had he told her he loved her one day, only to violate her the next?

She tried to shake the thought from her exhausted mind, and just focus on putting one foot in front of the next. She had to come into contact with somebody – anybody – soon, if she could just keep going; but this was the most exercise she'd had in years. She couldn't even say for certain that she wasn't walking around in circles now. She'd tried to keep the dying sun's glow ahead of her the whole time, using it as a fixed point to aim towards; through the forest, low branches scratching at her cheeks and bare arms as she'd torn through it.

That part had been a surprise. With no clue where they'd been living for all these years, she hadn't expected to come out of the hole into such a wild and unyielding monster of trees and undergrowth. The few occasions he'd brought her up, he'd kept her blindfolded; less trouble if she was disorientated. She'd fallen at one point, a thicket of thorns drawing blood from her right palm, and she'd been certain that's where he'd catch up to her, and drag her back by the ankles. She hadn't allowed herself to wait for that; tearing off even faster, ignoring every bite, scratch and sting as her barely clothed body bore the brunt of the forest's clutches.

The nightdress was practically glued to her skin, such was the expulsion of sweat as she persevered, vowing to take just one more step. Cars had passed, but she hadn't allowed any of them to stop and check if she was okay. Every time a set of headlights neared, she'd try and cower out of sight, uncertain whether it would be him out hunting for her. Again, for all she knew, he had friends out here who would also be only too willing to watch him take her back as his prisoner. She'd come too far now to allow him to catch up with her.

Another stomach grumble, and she was consciously cursing herself for trying to get away on an empty stomach. The scraps he gave her each day were barely enough to satisfy the smallest of appetites, but it had to have been at least twelve hours since she'd devoured the stale crust for her breakfast. It had been enough for then, but had she known how the day would play out, she would have saved some for this journey. Last night he had promised her chance would come, but she hadn't wanted to believe it when he'd told her he loved her. How could something so forced be love? Even as she'd found the door ajar, and had felt the cool breeze filtering through the gap, she'd been sure he would appear and force her back down the narrow tunnel to her cell.

She'd moved unsteadily forward, unwilling to believe the possibility, her heart racing, as she tugged on the tiny edge, and felt it move beneath her broken fingernails. She'd pulled it open just wide enough so she could peer out, half-expecting him to be there, ready to kick it in and send her stumbling, but all she'd seen was the darkness of the wooden boards lining the dirt floor. Opening the door wider, she'd dared to step out, again expecting to feel the pain of his anger that she'd dared to defy him, but he didn't emerge from a secret hiding place to punish her.

Keeping her foot in the gap between the door and the entrance to her makeshift room, she'd reached into the darkness, feeling the cool air blowing from above, but then she'd rushed back into the room. It was too good to be true, and she'd learned from her mistakes. She'd been about to push the door closed and allow it to lock when something had stopped her. Was it possible that he had been telling the truth? That he would grant her the freedom she'd so desperately craved?

Taking one final look at the room she'd called home for so many years, she'd taken a deep breath, and headed out of the door, crawling on hands and knees, certain the wooden boards would whine and groan beneath her frame and reveal that she was revolting against her captors. Yet she'd made it to the top of the tunnel without hearing him coming for her, and as she'd leaned into the door at the top, expecting to find it closed, it had swung open, and she'd felt the gust of fresh air wash over her. She hadn't waited a second longer, tearing out, refusing to look over her shoulder in case he was there waiting to pick her off with his hunting rifle.

When she'd made it to the edge of the forest, where a grey strip of road divided the woods in two, she'd turned onto it, and tried to keep her feet and legs moving in tandem, despite the agony it caused. That felt like hours ago now, but with the terrifyingly slow pace it probably was less than an hour. He could still be on her trail; watching and waiting.

The dark of the bordering forest swallowed up the route she'd come by, and the road continued to twist and wind. She couldn't believe she hadn't come across any kind of habitation where she could seek shelter.

Another set of headlights appeared in the distance, hurtling towards her at some speed. Looking around, she could see nowhere to duck and cover. She'd yet to come across a property, but there was now a barbed-wire fence along the line of trees, and she didn't have the strength to get over it without inflicting further injury. If this was him, she had no means of escape.

Stumbling forwards, she crashed to her knees, yelping as her right wrist buckled beneath her weight, breaking her fall. Exhaustion had set in, and no amount of will power and fear could get her back to her feet. All she could do now was wait for him to come and find her, and take her home.

Lying perfectly still, save for the deep lungfuls of breath she willed into her body, she waited for the headlights to pull over, but as they neared, and her pulse quickened to breaking point, they continued past.

It wasn't him; or at least, if it was, he hadn't seen her.

Rolling onto her back, she stared up at the ever-darkening sky. She had a simple choice: lie here and wait for death to take her, or continue the journey; the former felt like the easier option, but she was too resilient to give up. He'd told her as much last night.

When the time is right, you'll know it. You can do this!

Rolling over, she pressed her left hand against the ground, and forced her legs to lift her back up. Over her shoulder, she could see the tail lights of the car that had passed, now long gone, and too far for the driver to see the lurching figure now continuing along the potholed road.

Another five minutes passed before she came across a sign

on the edge of the road, but whilst she recognised the words, she couldn't say for sure what they meant. She'd always been good at reading at school, but her eyes were too tired to focus properly. The fading sun was to her right, such was the nature of the bends in the road. The only way to right the course of her journey would be to scale the wire fence, and head back through the trees, but the path of the road could easily correct itself if she just continued along it. Breathless, she strode onwards, leaving it up to fate to determine her future. If her escape was to be completed, then the road wouldn't lead her straight back into his waiting arms.

I love you. Let me prove it to you.

She just had to keep believing.

And that's when she saw it. A large building, at least four storeys high, and with a mismatch of lights glowing from windows in its sides. It reminded her of one of the crossword puzzles he'd once allowed her to attempt. He'd offered to set her free if she could complete it, but she hadn't come close. Another of his sick games.

Rubbing her eyes, as her legs threatened to give way once more, she again questioned whether what she was witnessing was real or the final embers of the dream. This side of the building burst into flashes of blue as she neared, and her heart raced harder at the prospect of what she'd finally stumbled upon. She had to get inside; that much she knew. It would be just like him to be parked up somewhere, revelling in the glee in her face suddenly being torn away when her eyes fell on him. It would be the cruellest of tricks, but if she *could* just get inside, she would be safe; of that she had no doubt.

Gripping the handrail of the staircase directly in front of her, her toes scraped across the hardened concrete steps as she dragged her feet up them, until she arrived at the set of automatic double doors. Nobody seemed to notice her at first as she stepped through and was immediately struck by a wave of cool, conditioned air. So bright inside too that she could barely keep her eyes open and focused on finding that one person who might tell her she was safe after all these years.

A man's face appeared in her immediate vision, and for the briefest of seconds she thought it was *him*, dressed in some kind of brown shirt and sweater, but as the spirit left her body, and she collapsed into the man's arms, relief washed over her. The man was now shouting to others, calling for help as far as she could tell, but she didn't care. In that moment, she would have happily allowed death to take her in his embrace.

She was out.

She was free.

Chapter Two

NOW

Uxbridge, London

I s there anything worse than being trapped inside when you can see how warm and clement the sunshine looks through the poky window, which doesn't even open wide enough to allow a draft in? The whirring electric fan on top of the filing cabinet is doing little to cool the stuffy atmosphere inside the box room where Jack and I have been sitting for the best part of two hours; me with my eyes buried in a typed report, and Jack hunched over his laptop.

'You're doing it again,' he says now, bringing my attention back to the desk.

'Doing what?' I ask, frowning.

'Staring out of that tiny window. You know, if I didn't know better, I'd say you're secretly working on the plot of your next novel, rather than concentrating on Jemima Hooper.'

His tone is playful; teasing; he isn't criticising, and yet I still invoke a stern face for my reply.

9

'Plotting is for fiction writers, Jack. We both know that my work is stranger than fiction.'

He smiles thinly, nodding as he does. 'You can say that again. If I hadn't been with you when you found Cassie Hilliard, I never would have believed the story in *Ransomed*. And as for where Natalie Sullivan's suicide led you six months ago...' He pauses. 'You have a talent for reading between the lines, Emma, a *real* talent; you see things that others don't.'

I can feel the heat rising in my cheeks, but rather than arguing against the compliment as is my default setting, I hold my breath and count to five. 'Thank you, Jack, but we never would have found Cassie if it weren't for your help too.'

He pulls a wounded face. 'You came so close to just accepting a compliment there, and then at the last second, you rejected it. I wish you could see just how brilliant you are.'

I have to look away this time, because I can see in my periphery that he knows he's said too much, as his five o'clock shadow has taken on a beetroot hue.

'I should get us both a fresh drink,' he says, quickly standing, and avoiding eye contact. 'You want tea? Coffee?'

I know that tea is supposed to be able to help regulate body temperature, but I'm certain that a hot beverage is only going to crank up the temperature in the already stuffy box room. 'Water, please.'

'I'll run the tap to get it as cold as I can,' he says with a nod, leaving the room without another word.

I push myself back in the hardened plastic chair, picking up the typed page I was failing to read, and wafting it near my chin like a fan. After a fairly soggy spring, they are predicting one of the hottest summers on record, and even though it's early June, it already feels like we are more or less breaking records. The thin cotton dress I'm wearing is clinging to my front and back, and with Jack out of the room, I take the opportunity to peel it away, and give my skin a breather. Jack will have wandered to the small kitchen near what was once Uxbridge police station's canteen, and, knowing him, he'll stop for a natter with any of his colleagues floating about, meaning I have at least two minutes until he will be back, though more likely closer to five. I don't blame him for wanting a different view, as it almost feels like these four walls are moving steadily closer to the table.

It was quite a surprise when Detective Chief Superintendent Jagtar Rawani reached out and invited me to come and work with Jack in the capacity of Public Liaison. Jack's role as cold case review officer has evolved in light of the files discovered on Arthur Turgood's hard drive, and Jack has been tasked with identifying every child's face on the images and videos Turgood had produced or downloaded during his years running the St Francis Home for Wayward Boys. In prison, but in poor health, Turgood will likely be dead long before his sentence expires, which is why the Crown Prosecution Service has decided against bringing further charges for being in possession of indecent images of children. 'Not in the public interest' is how they officially described it. Jack told me off the record that prosecuting Turgood further would be a waste of taxpayers' money, which I can understand, even if I don't like the thought that he is getting away with more crimes. It is bad enough he wasn't captured and tried for the abuse he inflicted on Freddie Mitchell and the others until he was eighty years old. After a long life evading prosecution, he will likely serve less than a quarter of his sentence for his crimes.

It still rankles; especially as my missing sister Anna was one of the victims in the footage. That is why I accepted DCS Rawani's invitation to support Jack. Not only will identifying these victims help in some way to bring closure for their families, deep down my motivation for helping is far more selfish: I hope that somehow we'll find the pattern that tells me what became of my sister. It's twenty-one years now since she walked from our family home in Weymouth to visit our maternal grandmother, never to be seen again. If it takes me the rest of my life and every resource at my disposal, I will learn the truth about what happened to Anna and why she never made it to her destination less than five minutes up the road.

For now, though, my attention must remain focused on Jemima Hooper, the eleven-year-old girl who wandered off while waiting with the family Beagle outside Greggs six years ago. This was in Gateshead, so I wasn't overly familiar with the story until Jack presented me with the file yesterday morning. Since then, I must have read nearly every report filed by the investigative team in Northumberland. As far as they're concerned the case was closed the moment Jemima's body was found dumped just inside the gates of a public park on the outskirts of Tamworth eighteen months later. The image of her blue and broken body – covered in fresh welts, and left tangled in nettles – is permanently engraved on my long-term memory.

The Jemima in that final picture looked nothing like the innocent freckled-faced girl with ginger plaits who stares back at me now from the desk. It is this image that facial recognition software estimates as a seventy-six per cent match to the girl in the still captured from the horrific video footage. I'm grateful that I don't have clearance to see the video in full, as I don't think there'd be any way back for my subconscious if I was subjected to it. Jack has seen it, and the haunted look he wears whenever he has to reference the footage tells me everything I need to know.

That is why we are determined to find out as much about Jemima Hooper as we can, to confirm whether the software match is correct. There is a part of me that really hopes it isn't, as I don't want to think of her being tortured in such a disgusting manner for other people's gratification. Security camera footage taken from the Greggs shop shows Jemima through the shop window, standing patiently, talking to the Beagle, when something catches her eye off camera. The lens is trained to take in as much of the shop as possible in an effort to capture potential thieves, and so when Jemima wanders out of shot while her mum is paying for the two sausage rolls and bag of doughnuts, it is impossible to know where she goes next. The Greggs is next to a jeweller's which had its shutters down following a break-in the week before, so we don't see Jemima again until she and the Beagle wander past the front of the butcher's, only this time she is holding the hand of a figure in a baseball cap and denim jacket. He or she is approximately five feet ten, slim build, but the face is never captured on camera. A team of trained detectives watched every frame of every security camera feed and dash cam for the hour before and after Jemima wandered off, and the footage at the butcher's is the only one where the figure is seen.

Who this person is, is anyone's guess. For some reason, Jemima walked away with him or her willingly, and even released her grip on the Beagle's lead somewhere before the railway track, where he was found tied up, whining. That strip of track isn't even five minutes from Greggs, and yet the Beagle wasn't found for nearly an hour, by which point there was no trace of Jemima. In those fifty-five minutes that sweet eleven-year-old girl became just another statistic.

Frantic with worry, Jemima's parents made a television appeal for the return of their daughter, and despite an initial onslaught of online abuse (aimed at Mrs Hooper for taking her eyes off Jemima for the three minutes it took for her to order and pay for the sausage rolls and doughnuts), neither parent was ever in the frame for being involved in the abduction.

Fast forward eighteen months, and a jogger training for The Great North Run spotted what she thought was a distressed animal trapped in the nettles beside the park gates. It was only on closer inspection that she realised just how wrong her initial impression had been. A hurried DNA test confirmed Jemima's identity, and the Hoopers – who had still believed they would find their daughter – were dealt the cruellest heartbreak.

Post mortem examination of the body confirmed she had been the victim of sexual assault, kicking, scratching and whipping. I can't even begin to imagine how terrified she must have been throughout such a painful experience, and in many ways death was probably the kindest fate that could have befallen her in those circumstances. I've met with victims of abuse and the mental scars never heal. At least Jemima is at peace now, even if she probably experienced more cruelty than any one of us will ever have to face.

I won't allow my mind to consider how Anna would have coped with such terror. No body has ever been found, and I'm in two minds about which fate I'd rather have come her way. Surviving such abuse feels almost as cruel as having to go through it in the first place; and yet I desperately long for the day when I might be reunited with Anna.

A knock at the door is followed by Jack entering and resting a mug of water on the desk beside the file. There are light brown stains inside the mug where years of tea and coffee have left their mark. I don't doubt that the water will provide the refreshment my overheated body is craving, but it's less than appetising.

'Sorry,' Jack offers, 'best I could find. Say, do you fancy getting out of here? Maybe grabbing a drink or a bite to eat somewhere? I know we have the video call with Jemima's parents in a bit, but how is it going to look if they see us melting in here? There's a café up the road, and I'm sure we'd both benefit from a breath of fresh air.'

He doesn't have to ask me twice. Peeling myself off the plastic chair, I grab my satchel and follow him out of the door, before he locks it behind him.

Chapter Three

NOW

Uxbridge, London

The fresh air has done wonders to wake my flagging mind, though I really wish we could just stay outside in the glorious sunshine. There is a slight breeze here in Uxbridge, and sitting outside the café has brought back memories of being a carefree student, and skipping lectures with my best friend Rachel so that we could head to the Student Union and spend our student loans on bottled drinks. Hardly appropriate for a writer with a mortgage, but the memory brings a much-needed dose of endorphins.

When we are buzzed back through the police station, even the corridor feels like an oven, and any refreshment the outside breeze had brought is swiftly swallowed up. At least for the duration of the video call with Jemima Hooper's parents we won't be trapped in the box room. Instead we're in a purpose-built suite usually used for reviewing security camera footage during a live investigation. Jack has reserved the room, as it is

17

soundproof and will enable the two of us to perch in front of the laptop's digital camera.

We have to tread very carefully with Mr and Mrs Hooper, as they don't know the reason for our call. Their local contact at Northumberland Constabulary has notified them that Jemima's case notes have been requested by the Metropolitan Police as part of a wider investigation, but they know little more than that. They don't know that we believe Jemima to be one of the victims in the footage found on Turgood's hard drive; and I don't know how they will react to such news.

'Are you ready?' Jack asks, straightening the tie he's just put on to create more of a professional look. I do feel for him; I'm melting in this thin cotton dress, but he must be baking in the wool-blend trousers and buttoned polyester shirt.

I give him a muted nod. The truth is, I'm worried about what conclusions the Hoopers will jump to if they happen to recognise my face. Since the publication of *Monsters Under the Bed* – the non-fiction book that finally exposed Arthur Turgood, Geoffrey Arnsgill and Timothy MacDonald, as well as catapulting my writing career – I've struggled with being recognised by total strangers who assume they know who I am just because they've read and empathised with my words; but that isn't who I am.

I've spent the last twenty-seven years of my life trying to find my place in the world, and understand who I am, but I don't feel any closer to the answer. I wish I could be the confident and sophisticated extrovert my agent Maddie expects me to be. If the Hoopers do recognise me, their first thought is bound to be that I'm planning to write about their daughter's situation, which couldn't be further from the truth.

At the same time, I don't want to admit to them that my interest in their daughter is for my own selfish gain.

Jack logs onto the laptop, and fishes in his pocket for his notebook, in which he has scribbled Dave Hooper's email address. I take the seat furthest from the screen, hoping that their focus remains more on Jack than me. He then sits and types in the address; the computer whirs, and beeps as the call is connected.

'Good morning, Mr and Mrs Hooper,' Jack begins, offering a sincere but dispassionate smile. 'I trust you are both still comfortable with us talking this afternoon?'

'Aye,' Dave Hooper replies.

He's much older than I was anticipating, given Jemima's relatively young age when she disappeared. The man before us with strawberry blond hair that has all but faded to grey has tired eyes. Even though it's been years since Jemima's discovery in Tamworth, it's clear grief still has a firm hold of him, as it does his wife. She looks a few years younger than her husband, her hair much darker, though it's possibly dyed, and difficult to tell from the grainy image being projected onto the screen. Despite the obvious pained expression, I instantly see where Jemima inherited her freckles from.

'Firstly, please accept my condolences on what I'm sure is still a very difficult series of events to process. My name is Police Constable Jack Serrovitz, and I'm the officer who requested access to your daughter's case file. This is Miss Em—'

'Have yous found the bastard who killed her at last?' Dave Hooper interrupts, exhaling a sigh of pent-up frustration.

'Not exactly, Mr Hooper. Our interest in Jemima's case isn't to directly investigate how she died, but to—'

'So the bastard is still out there then, free to abduct and rape and murder other tots.'

I don't like to assume that I can understand what they are going through. Every family that experiences a disappearance or an abduction deals with it in different ways, and just because the pain of Anna's disappearance is still fresh in my mind, I cannot begin to imagine what the Hoopers have been through. But I can see how frustrated Dave Hooper is with the system he feels has failed him in the worst possible way. Not only did the authorities not manage to bring Jemima back, they have also failed to prosecute the person responsible for all their devastating pain.

Jack doesn't respond to the challenge, instead allowing Dave Hooper to fill the silence with the anger and rebukes he's kept bottled up. Jack doesn't flinch once, accepting full responsibility even though he played no part in the failings the Hoopers experienced. Carol Hooper remains silent, but her lips tremble as she grinds her teeth, feeling every word her husband spits.

'Ah, wha's the point in any of it, like?' Dave Hooper exclaims, waving a hand dismissively at the camera, before standing and disappearing off screen.

This certainly wasn't how either of us had thought the call would go, and we haven't even broached the topic of what was found on Turgood's hard drive.

Carol Hooper has remained where she is, and has made no effort to end the call.

'I am truly sorry for your loss, Mrs Hooper,' Jack tries again. 'Please know that nobody here takes your feelings for granted, nor feels anything but the purest sympathy for your loss. I have a young daughter myself, and I cannot even begin to imagine how I would deal with things if anything bad ever happened to her. I truly am sorry.'

She nods for him to continue, but lights a cigarette in the process.

Jack takes a deep breath. 'There's no easy way for me to say this, Mrs Hooper. We believe we have found a video of Jemima produced while she was missing. The video is of a sordid nature, and would perhaps account for some of the injuries Jemima sustained prior to her death.' He takes a deliberate pause to allow the gravity of the statement to sink in.

Carol Hooper's expression doesn't change. I had expected shock, anger or for her to lash out at the cruel world, but she remains silent, the only sound coming through the tinny speakers on the laptop that of her inhaling and exhaling the cigarette smoke. For a moment I'm wondering whether she even heard what Jack said, or whether her mind has refused to hear any more negative news about her daughter.

'Figures,' she finally says, when Jack isn't forthcoming.

'The video is one of several recovered from the hard drive of a suspect in a different case, but we do not believe that that suspect was responsible for the production of the video, or involved in any aspect of Jemima's abduction or murder.'

'What d'you wanna know from us, like?' Carol asks, blowing smoke at the camera.

'I know you were probably asked lots of different questions at the time Jemima was taken, and I promise you we have reviewed every report linked to the original investigation, but what we are trying to establish is whether Jemima was targeted by the people responsible for the video.'

I desperately wish we'd made the journey to Gateshead to visit the Hoopers in person. Conducting such a sensitive and personal interview by video call feels so intrusive and clinical. I want to reach out and hug Carol Hooper and assure her that we will do whatever we can to bring her daughter's abusers to justice, but those kinds of platitudes sound so false when delivered via digital means.

'Yous think she was chosen.' It's a statement rather than a question, but the truth is Jack and I have no idea; it's a theory we're developing.

'Can you remember anyone at the time taking a particular interest in Jemima?' Jack continues. 'Anyone you can now remember watching you when you'd collect Jemima from school; maybe someone who didn't look quite right when you took her to the park?'

Carol Hooper shakes her head, stubbing out the cigarette in an ashtray off screen. 'We went through all that at the time. I didn't see anything out of the ordinary, like; but we was so busy back then – so stressed out with the business folding – that it was always like we was chasing our tails.'

The Hoopers' local IT company was in financial straits at the time of Jemima's abduction, and at one point questions were raised about whether the abduction had been staged for monetary gain. The accusations were levelled during the onslaught of abuse that the Hoopers experienced on social media, but it soon became apparent to the Senior Investigating Officer and his team that the parents weren't involved.

'What about clubs and things, Mrs Hooper? Did Jemima attend any after-school activities?'

'She had swimming lessons at the local pool every Wednesday at five, but that was it, like.'

Swimming pools are notorious for perverts looking to cop an eyeful of barely clothed children, but swimming lessons are generally delivered when pools are closed to the public; at least they are where I'm from. I haven't seen any mention in the case file of security footage at the swimming pool being viewed to see if anyone matched the description of the person in the baseball cap, but I'd be surprised if that angle wasn't covered. I make a mental note to speak to Jack about it after the call; at the very least we should follow up with someone on the original investigation team to double-check they considered the possibility.

'This video with our Jem on it,' Mrs Hooper begins, lighting a second cigarette, 'you're certain it's her?'

'Honestly, not one hundred per cent, but there is a strong possibility. We are in the process of trying to identify as many of the victims as we can in order to establish if any kind of pattern exists that might help lead us to those involved. It's going to take time to piece together, but I do appreciate you making the time to speak to us this morning.'

I don't know whether it's Jack's reference to *us*, but Carol Hooper is suddenly staring at me. 'You look really familiar. Did we meet when our Jem was taken?'

I shake my head. 'My name is Emma Hunter; I'm providing civilian support and oversight to the investigation,' I say evenly.

Her expression remains blank; either her mind hasn't made the connection with my name, or the world of celebrity has no place in her life.

'Have you got kids?' she asks.

'No,' I say with another shake of my head.

'Aye, yous probably too young yet. Don't let our misery put you off though. In spite of all that happened, I wouldn't hesitate to do it all again; I think I'd just make more of an effort to appreciate what we had before it was snatched away.'

I doubt there's a single person alive who wouldn't echo that sentiment in some way. None of us realise what we have until it's gone.

Chapter Four

THEN

Poole, Dorset

Waking to the sound of beeping and whirring, she couldn't believe she'd managed to sleep through such a cacophony until that point. She hadn't woken to anything but silence for as long as she could remember, and that was the first indication that something wasn't right. Her entire body ached, as she tried to shuffle her legs in bed, and as her other senses started to sharpen, she suddenly became aware of the strong chemical aroma of cleaning products, but not the fruit-scented varieties she had become accustomed to. These lacked any kind of sweetness.

Her throat felt so dry, and as her memory tried to kick into gear and recall whatever her last action was, she suddenly felt a bubble of bile building in the back of her throat, and before she could prevent it, she knew what was coming. With no time to push the sheets back and race to the toilet, she leaned as far out of the bed as she could and retched; only with nothing in her stomach, it was dry and painful.

'Whoa, whoa, whoa,' a voice said from somewhere in the darkness, and was followed by a pair of cool, smooth hands supporting her arms.

Her shoulders tensed with the contact and, fearing a backhanded strike, she promptly finished retching and shuffled back into her pillow, her throat raw from the exertion.

'There, there,' the voice said again, but the tones were softer than she was expecting. It wasn't *him*.

Her eyelids felt as though they were glued shut, and she had to strain to get them to part even slightly, and when she did, the explosion of light forced her to clamp them shut again. Why was it so bright in her room? And who was this woman with soft hands and kind words?

Finally, her short-term memory engaged, and was suddenly filled with recollections of her finding the door unlocked, and making a break for it through the dark forest, until she found that road, and eventually, just when she'd thought she couldn't go any further, she'd stumbled into the hospital, and collapsed into a janitor's arms.

That had to be where she was now: hospital. And that would, therefore, make this woman a nurse of some kind.

The woman's voice spoke again, but the unfamiliar words flowed too quickly for her to interpret what they meant, so she remained silent, and tried to open her eyes for a second time. Lifting her right hand, she tried to shield her eyes from the light, but as the arm came out from beneath the sheet, it felt heavy, as if weighed down.

'Easy, easy,' the nurse's voice came again, as she took control of the right arm, and rested it back on the bed.

She tried to lift her left arm instead, but something pulled at it, as she did.

'Easy, easy,' the nurse said again, followed by the words, 'hospital… broken… doctor.'

It was no good, she would have to open her eyes, and so bowing her head slightly she focused all of her energy on opening just her left eye, blinking several times to allow it to adjust to the large white light coming from somewhere to the right side of whatever room she was in.

Her vision blurred and focused as fluid filled and cleaned her eye, and there was a slight crackle as her sleep-covered eyelashes fluttered open and closed. She was in some kind of private, very white room. She was lying in a bed, with a metal frame around the sides, and as her eye fell on her right arm, where the nurse's gloved hands held it in place, she realised it was the thick plaster-cast bandage that had been weighing it down. A flash of her falling to the ground as the car had sped towards her filled her mind.

Focusing her attention on her left arm, she saw a thin plastic tube poking out of the crook in her arm, behind her elbow. The tube led off the bed to a metallic stand and into a blue box, which was whirring and occasionally beeping with bright LED numbers.

Finally, she looked into the face of the nurse; such a pretty and angelic face that for a moment she questioned whether she'd actually died in that janitor's arms, and this was some form of purgatory she'd been thrown into until she could justify her life to St Peter. Not much hope of being able to justify anything, she silently chastised herself.

The nurse tilted her head, and said something else, ending with, '…feeling?'

She tried to say she was thirsty, but the words wouldn't make it past the burning in her throat, and so she pointed at her neck, and mimed drinking from a glass.

The nurse nodded, and moved around to the other side of the bed, reaching for a transparent plastic jug on the stand just behind it, and proceeded to fill a beaker of water, before dropping a paper straw into it. The nurse held it out for her to drink from, but it was difficult to swallow the lukewarm liquid.

'Sip,' the nurse instructed, but it was lost on her.

She eventually spat out the straw, and waved for the nurse to return the beaker to the stand. Looking back at the tube in her arm, she tried to determine what cool and clear liquid was being pumped into her arm, but as she tried to move it closer to her eyes, the nurse prevented her from doing so, shaking her head, and saying something else she couldn't understand.

The woman in the bed pointed at the large square window off to the right and then at her eyes, grateful when the nurse seemed to pick up on the subtlety of the mime, moving across to the window and drawing the blinds, casting a shadow where the brilliant light had once been. With the room suitably dim, the woman prised her right eye open, the dried goop crackling as it broke apart.

The room was larger than the space she was used to sleeping in. Back at home, the inflatable mattress she slept on was built into a narrow coffin-like recess in the wall, and she felt overwhelmed by all the space around her now. Her room beneath the ground had comprised little more than the bed and a distance of twenty heel-to-toe steps by fifteen heel-to-toe steps. She could no longer recall the sheer panic she'd felt the first day he'd forced her into the room; in fact she could remember little of any life prior to the hole. The occasional shard of memory would penetrate – usually while she slept: images of wide, open beaches; of the sea; of a long boat crossing the sea; of a mother's hand holding hers. Yet whenever she tried to recall anything about her parents, her mind's eye would lose focus, and the memory would fracture into a thousand shards.

The nurse was speaking again, but the woman didn't even attempt to decipher what was being instructed or asked. It was clear she must have broken her arm or wrist, and that was why the plaster cast had been fitted around her right arm; but she had no idea why there was a tube in her arm.

Holding out her hand, the woman cut off the nurse mid-sentence and lifted her left hand, flattening it palm up against the sheet over her legs, before using the fingers of her right hand to mime a pen, and the action of writing. The nurse reached into a pocket at the front of her tabard, pulled out a small notebook and biro, and passed them over. The woman dropped the notebook to the bed, and tried to hold the pen in her right hand, but the plaster between her thumb and index finger made gripping the pen impossible.

The nurse proffered a hand, but the woman shook her head, instead picking up the pen with her left hand and attempting to write, but the letters were jumbled in her mind, and she quickly tore up her first attempt, opting to draw what she wanted to say. The pen was unwieldy, and slipped from her grasp several times, but she finally finished, and handed the notebook back.

The nurse's eyes widened as they focused on the picture, and she hurried from the room, returning with a tall, thin bespectacled man in a white coat.

'Bonjour,' he said, the words echoing in her mind.

She tried to return the greeting, but her throat was still too scratchy.

'Comment vous-appellez vous?' the man asked.

Her name? Why was that important? Hadn't the nurse shown him the drawing? Didn't he realise why she needed to speak with him?

The man in the white coat continued to consider her, exchanging silent glances with the nurse.

Pressing a hand to his chest, he spoke again. 'Je m'appelle Monsieur Truffaut. Je suis médecin.'

So, he was a doctor; that made sense given his white coat and presence in the hospital. His eyes were still waiting for her to answer his initial question, and she tried to speak, but her throat was so hoarse. She coughed before raising the four fingers of her left hand.

He frowned as he studied the gesture. 'Quatre? Four? No, what is your name?'

She extended her hand further, gently waggling the four fingers. 'Four,' she croaked.

'Four what?' the nurse tried.

'Four,' she croaked again.

'Wait, your name is Four?' the doctor tried. 'Vous appelez vous Quatre? Four?'

The woman nodded.

That was what he had called her for as long as she could remember; whenever he wanted something, he would call her 'Four'; whenever he was angry he would shout 'Four'; whenever he was sorry, he'd whimper 'Four'. Why were they struggling to understand?

'Your name is Four?' the nurse asked.

She nodded.

Another silent exchange between nurse and doctor, followed by mumbled words that they needn't have spoken so quietly, as Four could not have understood anyway.

'Ou habitez-vous, Four? Where do you live?'

Another pointless question! Even if she'd wanted to tell him where he'd kept her, she had no way of providing an address, and her memory of last night's trawl through the forest and along the road was quickly fading into the recesses of her mind. She had to have been walking for at least an hour but that was merely an estimate. It could have been less than an hour, but certainly felt far longer.

They weren't getting the message. Four pointed at the notepad that was still being clutched by the anxious-looking nurse.

'This?' the nurse asked, passing the pad back.

Four snatched the pad, and gesticulated at the picture of the monster she'd drawn. It was a crude sketch of a large figure chasing a stick version of herself, but surely they could see what she was trying to tell them?

'Man,' she croaked. 'Bad man… coming.'

Chapter Five

NOW

Ealing, London

'Did you see her face when you mentioned the video?' I ask Jack when the call is over, and he's driving me back to Rachel's flat in Ealing where I'm currently sleeping on her sofa bed.

'She didn't look surprised,' he comments, pulling out at the roundabout.

'I know, right? I swear there was no change in her expression at all. Not shock, not anger, not even denial. Just acceptance. Can you imagine what they must have been through to reach such a place devoid of emotion?'

'It's every parent's worst nightmare,' Jack concludes. 'I meant what I said to Carol Hooper on the phone: I don't know what I'd do if anything ever happened to Mila. I never expected I could ever feel so strongly about another human being, but I swear I would literally lay down my life for that girl.'

I try to meet his gaze, but he's too focused on the road ahead. Traffic from Uxbridge to the entrance of the A40 is nose-to-tail, as mums and dads and nannies battle through rush-hour traffic to collect and return children to the safety of their homes; most probably oblivious to the pain the likes of Carol and Dave Hooper are going through every second of every day. There's no school pick-up for them; not any more. I bet they never thought they'd see the day when they would miss this daily circus. So many take it all for granted.

Not that I have any right to comment on the thoughts, feelings and motivations of parents, as I'm not one, and because of that I probably will never truly know what it feels like to lose a child. I can listen, I can question, I can understand and I can sympathise; but I'll never truly know until I have a child of my own to be thankful for.

It's funny: until now I've never really thought about having a child of my own. It's not that I'd be against the idea – not if the circumstances were right. With my twenty-eighth birthday only a couple of months away, I suppose I'm reaching that age where I'm questioning where I want my life to go next. With *Monsters Under the Bed* and *Ransomed* both selling well in the charts, and *Isolated* out for pre-order, I've never been in a better position financially. Maddie arranged for the mortgage on my flat in Weymouth to be paid off with the advance of *Isolated*, and apart from everyday bills, my outward expenditure is very small. I suppose all that's missing now really is the certainty that I do want a child of my own one day.

At university, Rachel and I would talk about a future where her son or daughter would happily play in the park with my offspring; how we'd take them to pre-school and then head off for brunch somewhere fancy. I know that's not really how mums behave, but we were naïve twenty-somethings who still believed life would be as easy as it had been until that point. Neither of us considered exactly how much work would be involved in just getting a child ready for school.

'You've gone all quiet,' Jack says, leaning over. 'Is it because I mentioned Mila?'

The question throws me. 'No, why would you think that?'

Jack shrugs nonchalantly. 'Forget I said anything. What are you thinking about?'

'Just about how dark a place a mind would have to go to not to react to the news that your daughter had been filmed for graphic entertainment before she was murdered.'

'Yeah, but in light of the scars and injuries identified during the post mortem, I suppose it was fairly obvious she'd been mistreated during her disappearance. For the Hoopers, it's probably been two years of their imaginations picturing the worst possible scenarios. I'm sure that's why Dave Hooper was so angry at the start of the call. He wants someone to blame for the injustice, and we've failed to deliver the guilty parties.'

There he goes again, shouldering the responsibility for his colleagues up north, even though he had no involvement in how things turned out.

'Why do you do that?' I ask now, my nose scrunching involuntarily.

'Do what?'

'Say that *you've* failed them. There is nothing you could have personally done to change the circumstances surrounding Jemima Hooper's abduction and death.'

'Because I have absolutely no doubt that the men and

women who worked that case gave it their all to find her. I've worked on missing child cases before and those in the job go above and beyond what is humanly possible to get the right result. It's not just the hours and hours of overtime, the lack of sleep, the lack of regular breaks; it's *everything*. It devours the human soul, and on those occasions when the missing child is discovered alive and well, it feels like we've done our job.' He pauses, eyes focused back on the road. 'But when it does end badly... that's when the real torture kicks in. Every second of every passing day is spent thinking *what more could I have done?* As a profession, we take the wins when they come, but boy, do we also take the blows; harder than you can begin to think.'

Jack and I have never really talked about his career prior to taking on the cold case review project that saw him voluntarily relinquish his detective's grade, just so he could play a more active role in Mila's upbringing. I sense now that there is a lot more going on behind those soft brown eyes than I'll ever know about; not that I'm not curious, but because Jack isn't the sort to unburden. His experiences are *his* cross to bear, and he will do everything in his power not to show the strain of the weight.

'So, are we to conclude that the girl in the video is definitely Jemima Hooper?' I ask glumly.

'The software said it's a seventy-six per cent match, which is pretty strong given we never see a full frontal shot of the girl's face. I don't know. What do you think?'

'I must have looked at the still shot from that video a hundred times in the last few days, as well as the image the Hoopers shared with the press during the appeal for information, but I still can't say for certain. I don't want it to be her, because that family have already been through so much without having to now accept more. Let's say it is confirmed that Jemima was the girl in the video, what does that mean for the Hoopers?'

'We're not at that stage yet. You and I need to continue to review the case file, and speak to the original investigative teams. The tech boffins are doing what they can to sharpen the image from the video to see if there's any way to get a greater or weaker match percentage.'

'Okay, but after that? What happens if we conclude that it is more likely Jemima than not?'

'Then we will pass our findings up the line, and probably I will have to go up and visit the Hoopers and share the findings and ask them whether they can positively ID their daughter from the still. This might all take weeks or months, and the purpose of today's call was just to notify them of the work you and I are doing. If their daughter is a part of something much wider, then they have the right to know.'

The truth is, as much as I *don't* want the girl in the video to be Jemima, at the same time, I don't want it to be any other girl either. Today's call was hard enough without having to repeat it with some other family who have no clue what their child has been put through.

'Right now,' Jack continues, 'I think there's a strong likelihood that we have identified our first girl. I didn't think we'd do that so quickly, but there are so many other victims in similar videos from that hard drive. This is only the beginning, Emma, and I would totally understand if you've had second thoughts about being civilian liaison on this project.'

I know he doesn't mean to suggest that he doesn't think I

have the stomach for such work, but I can't say I'm not a little offended about his tone.

'Do you know why I accepted DCS Rawani's invitation?' I challenge, feeling tears pricking at my eyes.

'Because of my sparkling personality?' he says sardonically, maybe aware of how his last statement might have come across.

I can't mirror his smirk. 'It's because I want to do something to help. That's why I wrote *Monsters under the Bed*; it's why I accepted Lord Templeton Fitzhume's request for me to find his granddaughter; it's why I couldn't ignore Natalie Sullivan's request before she jumped from that building... In twenty years I have been helpless in my quest to locate Anna, and for all I know I'll never get any closer to discovering what really happened to her all those years ago. But right now – in this moment – there are others I *can* help, and I would be selfish not to try.'

'Look, I'm sorry,' he says, resting a hand on mine. It seems weird feeling his warmth against my skin, but I don't reject it. 'You are a brilliant investigator, Emma, you *really* are. I only wish there were more selfless detectives like you in the force today.'

I'm blushing, and forced to look away.

'I'm not blowing smoke up your arse, here, okay? I mean it. When the DCS told me you'd agreed to help, I was over the moon; not just because it allows me the opportunity to watch you in action, but it means the victims in those videos have a better chance at being identified.'

Silence descends, and I can't bring myself to meet his stare. 'Are you seeing Mila tonight?' I ask, keen to lighten the mood.

'No, not tonight,' he sighs in resignation. 'She's at a schoolfriend's birthday party, so her mum suggested I have her tomorrow night instead. That suits me fine, to be honest, as I'm not sure I'd be very good company after today. What about you? What are your plans for tonight?'

I shake my head. 'Nothing planned as far as I'm aware. Need a good night's sleep as my agent Maddie is taking me to meet with my publishers in the morning, so want to make sure I'm together and don't make a bad impression.'

I look out of the window, as traffic begins to flow as we exit the A40. I miss home. I've been in West London for four days straight, and I long for the sound of the waves crashing against the sand, the seagulls squawking and waking me in the morning, the taste of sea salt in the air. London, with all its culture and modernisations, isn't even in the same league as Weymouth. Life never seems to stop in the capital, and I don't know how anyone manages to get a break from the stress and toil of a city that never sleeps. I'm supposed to be here until Friday night, and then I'm booked to board the late afternoon train from Waterloo, back along the south coast, and I can't wait!

Jack is silent until we pull up outside Rachel's flat, but in the window's reflection he keeps glancing at me. I don't know why he looks so nervous.

'If you don't have any plans, do you maybe think we could...' he begins. 'What I mean is, I know it's still early, but neither of us ate much when we went to the café... Are you hungry?'

I've had no appetite since the call with the Hoopers. 'Not really. Sorry.'

'Okay, no worries,' he says with forced casualness. 'Listen, I'm sorry if I offended you by what I said. I know you're braver than maybe I gave you credit for, but I wouldn't think any less of you if you didn't want to continue. It's no easy job.'

I finally rest my eyes on his face, and press my hand to his cheek to show there's no lasting damage. 'I want to help you, Jack. You're my friend – I think – and you shouldn't have to do this work on your own. As you said earlier, it'll eat your soul.'

He presses his hand against mine, and then pushes a kiss into the palm of my hand. 'We are friends,' he confirms.

I turn my head to look for the door handle, and as I turn back to say goodbye, his lips are suddenly heading towards me, and I freeze in panic, meaning his kiss ends up on the bridge of my nose.

'Um, sorry, I meant that to be—'

I don't allow him to finish the sentence, pulling on the door handle, grabbing my satchel and darting from the car, racing up the stairs to the communal entrance of the converted townhouse, in through the door, and only daring to breathe again when I am inside Rachel's flat, with my back against her closed door.

What the hell was that? Jack just tried to kiss me, I think, but why? I didn't think he felt that way. We're just friends, aren't we? I know that Maddie and Rachel have said they thought Jack was interested, but until now he hasn't let on that he sees me as anything more than a friend or co-worker.

'Everything okay?' Rachel calls out from the sofa, hunched over her laptop.

'Fine,' I lie, taking several breaths to compose myself.

'The kettle's just boiled if you fancy a brew,' she adds, without looking up.

I feel like I need something a lot stronger than tea to settle my nerves, but I resist. Pushing myself away from the door, I move into the open-plan kitchen and find my mug on the draining board, the adrenaline finally starting to dissipate, leaving me with a sense of regret; not because Jack just tried to kiss me, but because I didn't kiss him back.

Chapter Six

NOW

Ealing, London

'Are you sure you're okay?' Rachel asks, finally sitting back from the laptop when I've joined her in the living room-cum-bedroom for the night.

I can still see Jack leaning in towards me, puckering up, his eyes closed. If he'd offered even a hint of what he was going to do, at least I would have been prepared, but the lurch caught me totally off-guard. How long has he been harbouring these feelings?

'I'm fine,' I lie, trying to mask how flustered I really feel. 'What are you working on? Big story?'

She tilts her head. 'Kind of; it's about these two women who agreed to act as trustees for a charitable foundation, funded by an eccentric billionaire. Only, one of the women seems to be spearheading the bulk of the work.'

My cheeks redden instantly. For Rachel to confront me directly about my lack of effort with the foundation's recent workload means that she's unhappy, and probably has been for some time.

The Anna Hunter Foundation, a charitable organisation we set up to support the families of runaways, has been in place since Lord Templeton Fitzhume offered to fund it in an effort to buy my silence about what really happened with his missing granddaughter. By the time he realised I was going to share the truth with the world, it was too late for him to wind up the foundation's activities. The purpose of the foundation is to provide support and guidance to those families suffering the sudden disappearance of a loved one. We have a website which contains links to a variety of sources of useful information about police protocols, dealing with social media trolls, and coping strategies. But in addition to that, families who are struggling financially – for example, a mother unable to work because of the effort required to keep searching, and keeping the home ticking – can submit a request for financial support. There isn't an unlimited pot of money to accept every request – and we've had a few chancers too – so we can't agree all requests, but we try where we can.

'I'm sorry,' I say quickly, wracking my mind for any kind of justification for why I haven't been pulling my weight, but the truth is I have no excuse. 'I know,' I say in surrender, 'and you're right.'

Rachel looks away. 'Oh look, I'm sorry too. That wasn't fair; I know you're busy with work too, but I'm worried that the two of us running things part-time just isn't working. Maintenance of the website alone is taking the best part of a day per week. My IT skills are pretty average, and maybe if one of us understood html it would be swifter, but I haven't the time to learn a new language. Then there's the emails received through the website. Some are sweet messages of thanks, but even they need to be acknowledged. This week we've received forty emails; maybe a quarter of those were in gratitude, half were requests for funding and the rest a combination of requests for information already on the site.

'The thing is, Emma, I have a full-time job too, and whilst I really do believe in the work of the foundation, I can't give any more of myself, and the part I can give just isn't enough.'

I can see she's struggling to talk about her true feelings, and it wouldn't surprise me if things are a lot worse than she's letting on. When Fitzhume first mooted the idea of the foundation, I thought it was a brilliant idea: a resource that I wish had been around when Anna first went missing. I wish I'd known how the police would respond, what tactics they would deploy, and that there are other people experiencing a similar situation. Naively, I hadn't realised exactly how much work would be required to make the foundation work.

It isn't that I've been avoiding my share of the responsibility, but between writing, supporting Jack in an effort to find connections to Anna, and dealing with my own mother's rapidly deteriorating Alzheimer's, there just hasn't been the time to do more than refresh the inbox occasionally. It doesn't help that every request we receive for financial support sounds more believable than the last, and had Rachel not suggested we retain a private investigator to scrutinise each requestor, I probably would have agreed to all of them, and the foundation would be close to wrapping up.

'You're right,' I tell her, reaching out and taking her hand in mine. 'I need to do more, and I will, I promise.'

She turns her head to meet my gaze. 'I don't think even that is enough.' Her other hand wraps around mine. 'I've been thinking long and hard about this all day, and what I think we need to do is hire an administrative assistant. I know the money will have to come out of the foundation's coffers, but I think it would be an investment in the future.'

Rachel knows how I feel about using the foundation's money on anything but the families it was set up to support. Initially, I was reluctant to pay an annual subscription for web hosting, until she convinced me that we needed a place where people could find us. Neither Rachel nor I have taken a penny for the work we've done in the last six months, but we would have to pay an administrative assistant, and I can already feel myself squirming at the prospect.

'I know what you're thinking,' Rachel says reassuringly, 'and that's why I did some research before pitching the idea to you. Realistically, hiring someone is likely to cost between twenty-five and thirty thousand per year—'

My eyes widen at the figure.

'—but it will be money very well spent,' she concludes, her voice rising to counter any argument I might offer. 'At the moment, it's impossible to see the wood for the trees. Let me ask you a question: when the foundation started, what was your priority?'

I open my mouth to speak, before stopping and allowing the time to truly consider the question. 'To help those families most in need.'

'Exactly! If I told you the foundation currently has forty-three requests for financial support, which of those would you say is the priority?'

She knows I can't answer, so I shrug. 'That's why we hired Derek – to investigate each of them.'

'Derek is just one man, and what if I told you he has only

managed to file reports on eight of the forty-three, but that all eight came back as legitimate enquiries? Which of the eight should be the priority?'

'I don't know without reviewing them.'

'Exactly! Have you really got the free time to review those eight? Maybe you would over the next three to four days, but their need is only going to worsen in that time. If we had someone who could handle the emails, liaise with Derek and only bring high-priority situations to our attention, think how much smoother things would run. He or she would act as a filter to all the noise, allowing us as trustees to focus on the important decisions.' She pauses, reaches for a printed sheet on the coffee table and slides it across to me. 'I drafted this, this afternoon. It's a job advert, detailing the skills I think we'd be looking for. Give me the nod, and I'll upload it to a recruitment website.'

I read the sheet of paper, but I can't escape the feeling that I'm losing control. Rachel has every right to make such a suggestion, and I know that as co-trustee – and my best friend – she has the best interests of the foundation at heart. Even with the best will in the world, I know I can't commit to any more than a couple of days a week, and even those would be snatched moments between publicising *Isolated*, meeting with Pam Ratchett at Mum's home and continuing to investigate Jemima Hooper's possible appearance in that video.

'You really think this will help?' I ask, handing the page back to her.

Her anxiety breaks into a wide smile. 'I *really* do. You shouldn't feel bad about it either. When we agreed to act as trustees, we never had any idea just how wide an audience it would reach; we couldn't have predicted we'd be inundated with this level of contact, but what it means is that the foundation is doing what you intended. Hiring some support is the natural next step in the evolution of the foundation.'

I don't want to argue, and if hiring an administrator will improve the support that can be offered to those families, then who am I to stand in the way of progress?

'Okay,' I say, returning her smile. 'Do it, but I will help you with interviewing prospective clients; you shouldn't have to do all of this on your own.'

She thrusts out her hand. 'Deal! And I am sorry about snapping at you when you got in; I was frustrated at my editor, and shouldn't have taken it out on you.'

I reach for my tea. 'What's your editor done now?'

'He wanted me to go down to Poole to follow up on that woman who appeared at one of the hospitals down there.'

My brow furrows.

'Haven't you seen? It was trending on Twitter briefly overnight. They reckon she stumbled in, bruised and beaten, with no identification, and not speaking a word of English.'

'Who is she?'

Rachel shrugs. 'Nobody knows, but with the next round of trade agreement talks with the EU imminent, I don't need to be following up on a human interest story. I told him to send one of the junior reporters.'

Rachel looks tired, and I don't want to point out the dark circles beneath her eyes. Although she might be blaming her frustration on her editor, I know there is something else on her mind she's not so keen to talk about.

'Have you heard from Daniella?' I ask as casually as I can.

Rachel glowers silently on the sofa. 'No.'

Daniella broke up with Rachel right before Christmas, and

although Rachel vowed she would do her best to move on with her life, I've seen the alerts pop up on her phone whenever Daniella tweets, or her name is mentioned in the news. It worries me that Rachel is getting dangerously close to cyber-stalking her ex, but what's worse is that we both saw the tweet that Daniella would be back in the UK for a few weeks in the run-up to London Fashion Week in September.

'Oh, well, I'm sure she's just been busy catching up with family and friends… It doesn't mean she won't ask to see you.'

I'm reaching, but I'm really not sure what else to say.

Chapter Seven

THEN

Poole, Dorset

Four belched as she swallowed the last of the cheese sandwich, and washed it down with more warm water from the straw and beaker. She had been propped up in the bed now, and the tube in her arm had been removed, which had meant she could now feel the weight of the plaster cast around her right wrist. The sensation was uncomfortable rather than unpleasant; certainly not as painful as other trauma she'd experienced beneath the ground.

The French doctor – Mr Truffaut – had spoken to her in her mother tongue, and she'd managed to understand most of what he'd said, but it had been difficult to respond to several of his questions; as if someone had reached in and cut out her tongue. He'd disappeared, promising to return and assuring her that no bad men would be allowed access to the hospital, let alone to her room.

It wasn't men she was afraid of; just one man who would be out looking for her now.

He'd warned her what would happen if she ever got out, that she wouldn't understand the world she'd been away from for so long, and for the first time she could understand what he meant. This room alone was so alien to her. So bright. Was the whole world this infused with light? Despite longing to be free for so long, she now missed the darkness.

It hadn't all been bad; there had been splintered moments of enjoyment. He'd patiently taught her to understand his language; had given her the benefit of language tapes; he'd read to her from magazines with shiny pictures. But then the darkness would swell in his eyes, and that's when it was at its worst.

She rested the plate of breadcrumbs on the weird table on wheels that they had slid over her, and pushed it away. A small television screen blinked and flashed numbers beside her, but despite her best efforts she couldn't make it actually play anything resembling a show. Either it was broken or the technology was beyond her. And that just left her alone with her thoughts.

She didn't want to be alone; not any more.

Pushing back the bed sheet, she swung her legs over the side and daintily pressed her toes onto the ice-cold floor, keeping a tight grip of the mattress with her left hand. She lowered her weight onto one leg at a time, desperately hoping they would be able to support her, and relieved when they didn't turn to jelly. The nurse had showed her a small toilet and basin just beyond the door beside the bed, and as she opened it, she gasped at the figure staring back at her.

From her position in the bed, she hadn't been able to look

into the small bathroom, and hadn't realised the far wall was a floor-to-ceiling mirror. Yet the painfully slight reflection was a complete stranger. Her hair was darker than she'd realised, straggled and greasy, cut to her neckline.

A flash of memory fired behind her eyes. He'd told her it was getting too long, and he didn't like it when it fell on his face. He'd pulled out a pair of shears, grabbed a handful of her hair and cut straight through it. She'd begged him to stop, but he'd lifted the shears towards her eye, and the fight had left her. She'd allowed him to continue chopping without protest, and when he was done she'd thanked him as he'd demanded. Once he'd left, she'd wept as she'd scooped up the discarded locks and thrown them into the bucket in the corner. After that she didn't dare complain when he came at her with the shears; not a battle worth picking.

This was the first time she'd seen what it looked like, as her hole hadn't included a single mirror, yet it was the rest of her appearance that she now found so startling. Where was the ten-year-old girl with freckles either side of her nose? Who was this taller woman staring back at her?

She emptied her bladder and tried to wash her one free hand, before shuffling back to the bed, not daring to look back at the woman who had taken over her life.

A knock at the door was followed by the white-coated Mr Truffaut entering with a short woman dressed in black trousers and a short-sleeved black polo shirt; the radio hanging from her sleeveless jacket indicated she was someone of authority.

'Hello again, Four.' Truffaut spoke in partially accented French. 'I would like to introduce Detective Sergeant Zoe Cavendish. She is a police officer, and would like to ask you some questions. Is that okay?'

Four considered Cavendish: fixed shoulders, legs apart; her petite size belied her obvious upper body strength. This was certainly not a woman you'd want to take on in a fight. And yet her face was soft, probably not much older than Four herself, and as their eyes met, Cavendish offered a simple professional smile.

'Bonjour,' Cavendish said with no attempt at proper enunciation.

'Bonjour,' Four echoed, nodding for the two of them to approach the bed.

'Detective Cavendish does not speak French,' Truffaut explained, 'so I have offered to translate on her behalf. Is that okay?'

Four nodded again, relieved that they seemed to finally be taking her drawing seriously.

Cavendish began speaking in rapid English, and Four could only blink, picking up fewer than one of every six words. She was grateful when Truffaut translated the question.

'She wants to know who did this to you.'

Four frowned. Who did what exactly?

Truffaut looked away for a moment, before fishing into his pocket, pulling out the drawing Four had sketched on the nurse's pad. 'Is this you?' he asked, pointing at the stick figure.

Four pointed at the stick figure and then back at herself with an affirmatory nod.

'And who is this?' Truffaut asked, pointing at the round mass of squiggles.

She stared at the ball of blue scratched hard into the paper. What did a name matter? He was her captor; her master; her everything.

'Bad man,' she tried in English.

'Bad man? He is a person then?'

Four's eyes widened in panic, as she felt the lash of his belt against the still raw welts on her lower back.

The detective was speaking again, asking Truffaut to translate.

'Did you know this man?'

It was such a difficult question to answer. She'd learned what she needed to about him: he came to her at night; he smelt of B.O. and cigarettes; he liked to restrain her; he liked to choke her; he didn't speak much; he preferred the lights off; he said he loved her.

'This man attacked you?' Truffaut tried again.

The way the question was phrased it sounded like a one-off occasion, but not a day had passed when he hadn't tormented her in some way. She couldn't remember ever not living in fear.

Cavendish led the doctor away to the back of the room so they could talk quietly, not that it would have mattered; even if they'd shouted their hushed conversation, she wouldn't have been able to properly understand. He'd brought her books and a candle once, but had then taken them away when she'd displeased him.

Cavendish had removed an envelope from a side pocket in her trousers, and was now showing the contents to Truffaut, explaining what she wanted him to do. He didn't speak, didn't argue, just moved his head up and down.

The pair of them agreed their course of action before returning. This time, though, they parted, Truffaut moving to the left side of the bed and Cavendish to the right. It was the detective who spoke first, pausing to allow the doctor to translate.

'We are going to show you some photographs now; these were taken when you arrived at the hospital. They are pictures of you, and some of the scars and injuries we discovered on your body. Do you understand?'

She took a deep breath, as Cavendish lowered the first photograph to the sheet covering her legs. At first it wasn't obvious what she was staring at, but as Four tilted her head, she could now see it was the back of one of her legs, though she couldn't be sure which. Small, round darker rings pocked the length of the leg. Though all now healed, the burn of the teaspoon had left its mark. That's how he'd coerced her obedience in the early days; she had learned to be obedient.

'Who did this to you?' Truffaut asked. 'Was it the bad man?'

Four closed her eyes and nodded. What if he found out that she'd told the police about him? She couldn't even begin to envisage the pain she would feel for her betrayal.

When she opened her eyes again, another photograph had been rested on top of the first. This time, it was obvious she was looking at her own neckline, though it was larger than she would have imagined. The bruising here was fresher; more recent.

A second flash of memory, this time of him behind her while she was kneeling on the bed. She hadn't understood why he was so angry, and she'd tried to please him, but that had only made the squeezing harder, to the point where the dimly lit room had seemed to spin, and she'd seen a ghostly-white figure beckoning to her.

'Did the bad man cause these injuries too?' Truffaut asked, bringing her back to the private room in the hospital.

A tear escaped as she nodded bravely.

'Is the bad man your boyfriend?'

He'd said he loved her, but what he'd done wasn't love, was it? Certainly not the love she'd read about in fairy tales. Where in Cinderella did the handsome prince beat and threaten his new bride in the glass slippers? Had he thought that was love though? Did he consider himself her boyfriend? She'd never asked, and hoped never to find out.

Four shook her head. 'No. He is… my keeper.'

Truffaut and Cavendish exchanged a silent glance, before the detective returned the remaining images to the envelope and secured them back in her side pocket. She said something to Truffaut, and after a moment of consideration he nodded. The detective reached into another pocket and pulled out a small screen, no bigger than a large matchbox. She tapped on it with her finger before lowering it to the bed.

Four instantly recognised the face she'd expected to see in the bathroom mirror. The freckles either side of her nose, her fair hair plaited in pigtails, and a red and white ruffled dress that stirred a distant memory somewhere in her head. She had no doubt she was staring at a picture of herself, and for the briefest moment all the pain of the recent past evaporated.

'Do you recognise this girl?' Truffaut asked.

Four couldn't take her eyes off the screen; it was as if they had reached into the darkest recesses of her mind and found the one glimmer of hope she'd dared to hold onto for so long.

'We believe this is you,' Truffaut continued. 'We took some blood from you when you arrived to check for drugs and viruses, and when we shared the sample with the police they found you. Your name is Aurélie.'

That sound stirred something else in her head; it was a sound she'd been so familiar with once.

'Do you remember what happened to you thirteen years

ago, Aurélie? Your parents reported you missing when you were ten years old and staying in Worthing along the south coast of England. You were here on holiday; do you remember?'

She continued to stare at the image of the girl in the ruffled dress, not daring to believe any of this was more than a cruel dream from which she'd be forcibly woken at any minute.

Chapter Eight

NOW

Ealing, London

I'm not one of those who necessarily buys into the theory that dreams are the subconscious' way of telling us what our conscious mind refuses to accept. However, it wouldn't take a trained psychologist to see that the dreams of Jack that plagued my sleep last night were a direct consequence of his attempted kiss. The more I think about it, the more I cringe. But what makes me want to cringe more is the prospect of how he will react when we next see one another. A sensible man would immediately bow out with an apology and quickly sweep the incident under the carpet. Alas, I fear Jack is the second type of man, who won't even mention it, and will just assume that nothing has changed, as if it never really happened. At least that would be better than the third type of man – the one I secretly think Jack is – who will want to discuss at length what happened, dissecting *every* minor detail until he is certain he knows why I didn't lean back in and meet his lips.

Oh my God! Is this really what I've become? It feels like I'm fourteen all over again, all padded bras and gloopy makeup residue where I've used too much because I don't know that less is more. I'm a professional writer; no, I'm an *award-winning* professional writer. Why should I care what some guy thinks? I am a strong, independent woman who needs a man like a fish needs a bicycle. I need to get my head out of the clouds and focus on my own priorities, rather than worrying about Jack or his lecherous intentions towards me.

Yet, if I was back in that moment in his car, and I saw him leaning in again, would my reaction still be the same?

I think that's the bit that bothers me most: I can't see past what would have happened had I kissed him back. Would we have given in to passion and been unable to keep our hands off one another? It doesn't sound like me, and I don't think Jack has that level of passion coursing through his veins either.

He's a nice guy, that much I know after the nine or so months I've known him – the multiple conversations we've had, the way he dotes on his daughter Mila, those moments when I catch him looking away and daydreaming about a life that doesn't involve hunting down criminals who have thus far evaded the law. And yes, although I've denied it to Rachel, Maddie and Freddie Mitchell, there is a part of me that thinks Jack is a handsome man – a bit goofy and nerdy at times – but handsome nevertheless. Could I really see myself in a relationship with him though?

'You're doing it again,' Rachel says from the kitchen countertop, removing her glasses and chewing on one of the arms.

'Doing what?' I ask, my mind coming back into the present.

'You're staring into space, eyes are glazed over, and so I'd assume you're daydreaming, but the question is: about what?'

'I was just thinking about the launch party for *Isolated*,' I reply offhand.

Rachel cocks an eyebrow, clearly seeing through the lie, but doesn't verbally question it. We both know I'm fibbing, but we're close enough to both know I'm not ready to come clean yet.

'Aren't you supposed to be going to the police station to meet Jack today?'

When my alarm woke me, and I began picturing that moment I walk into the makeshift office we've set up, and I see Jack, I decided I'm not mentally ready for that confrontation, and was going to message and say I'm not well. So, when Maddie's text message came through, inviting me to brunch with the editing team from my publishers, it was the perfect excuse.

'I'm meeting Maddie at eleven,' I explain to Rachel. 'Agent and publisher brunch apparently.'

'But you hate those things,' she says, her brow furrowing ever so slightly.

'Maddie insisted,' I say, avoiding her gaze. 'Unfortunately just one of those things I can't get out of.'

I can sense Rachel watching me, but she doesn't say anything else, returning the glasses to her face and focusing back on whatever she's reading on her phone.

'What are you reading?' I ask, keen to change the subject to anything but me.

'Oh, it's nothing important,' she says, quickly locking the

phone's screen, even though there's no way I can see what was on it.

I don't want to judge my best friend, but the speed with which she locked her screen suggests it was anything but nothing.

'What are your plans for today?' I ask.

'I'm going to upload that job advert for an administrative assistant, and then head into the office to check on the latest Brexit negotiations updates. In fact, I'll jump in the shower now, unless you want to use it?'

'No, you go ahead, I'd better be on my way to meet Maddie.'

Rachel nods, pocketing her phone, and heads towards the bedroom. As soon as the door closes, I pull out my own phone and perform an internet search for Rachel's ex's name. The first hit is a picture of Daniella Vitruvia, looking glam at a movie premiere in Leicester Square last night. She is one of dozens of famous faces who attended the event, but what is most alarming is the flash-looking footballer with his arm looped through hers.

Given the alerts I know Rachel has set up on her phone, I've no doubt she's seen this image and associated story. It is bad enough Daniella looking so cosy with this guy, but the fact that she must have stayed in London last night and *didn't* reach out to Rachel speaks volumes. I just want to go in and give her a hug, but then she'll know that I know what she's been reading, and it'll cause unnecessary awkwardness. Tackling this problem needs a more sensitive touch.

With this thought in mind, I reach for my satchel and anorak, and head out of the flat in the direction of Ealing Broadway tube station, which is a ten-minute walk away at most. I know this route now, as I've ventured to and from Rachel's flat more times than I can remember in the last year. Although it's cramped when I stay – me crashing on the sofa bed – I think Rachel appreciates the company, though she does also keep mentioning the prospect of the two of us getting something bigger to share. Although I want to remain based in Weymouth, the requirement to be closer to London – for my writing career, as well as hunting the likes of Jemima Hooper from those videos – is becoming greater, and it may soon be time to put some tentative roots down here. It's not like I would give up my flat in Weymouth; that will always be home.

Maddie has messaged to say she will meet me at the restaurant instead of her office, but as always has included the restaurant's full address so I can copy it into the navigation app on my phone; she knows me so well!

Alighting at Moorgate tube station, I find that the restaurant is a short walk away, and a stone's throw from the Barbican Centre, but it isn't what I was expecting. The large glass panels separating the restaurant from the space would have you thinking it was just another tower of office blocks, if it weren't for the large neon sign hanging in the window, and the bar stools just the other side of the very reflective glass. Maddie is waiting for me by the entrance and hugs me as I arrive.

'Great, you found it,' she begins. 'I was beginning to worry I'd get a phone call saying you were somewhere south of the river because you'd got lost.'

I know the dig is meant to be light-hearted, so I don't allow myself to react to it; Maddie knows only too well how bad I am at following directions.

'The publishers are already inside,' Maddie continues,

straightening the collar on the cotton dress I've opted for. 'This is nice; is it new?'

Maddie is wearing her usual ensemble of straight skirt, hanging just below the knee, suit jacket and crisp white blouse. She is the consummate professional, and I've only ever once seen her looking less than pristine. Unfortunately we differ in our opinions of what looks good on me, which is why I deliberately opted to leave my usual array of thin cardigans at home today.

'Yes, it is,' I comment, brushing the pleats. 'Do you like it? I'm not underdressed for today, am I?'

'Relax, there's no dress code, and yes, I think it really suits you. The autumnal colouring brings out your eyes beautifully.'

I try not to gush at the compliment, and as we head into the restaurant, I don't tell her I picked it up in a charity shop in Weymouth. My editor Becky beams as we approach the table, and then it's a flurry of introductions, and air kisses before we all sit.

'I hope you don't mind,' Becky begins, her Dublin upbringing evident in her gentle tones, 'but when I told the office I was meeting you for brunch today, this motley crew insisted on coming along so they could all tell you how much we loved *Isolated*! I have no doubt that by the time this meal is over, we'll struggle to get you out of the restaurant because your head and ego will be so big!' She laughs at her own joke, not realising that hearing virtual strangers enthusing over my work is not my idea of fun; quite the opposite in fact.

With no cardigan sleeve to absently chew on – Maddie always tells me off for that – I reach for the crusty bread roll beside me, and break a bit off to nibble.

The restaurant is packed, and it is difficult to hear what

Becky is saying as she introduces the unfamiliar faces around the table. Despite the relaxed decor and Tex-Mex menu, I instinctively sense that this is the sort of place with a weeks-long waiting list, and even though I know Becky's team will front the bill, my eyes are immediately drawn to the less expensive meal choices.

'… and this is Greg,' Becky continues, as I strain to hear, 'who is our metadata guru; all hail Greg!'

Those at the table echo, 'Hail Greg!' He raises his hands and accepts their accolades. This is clearly some in-house joke that is lost on Maddie and me.

'And then finally, next to you, is Lucy, who is the creative genius behind the amazing covers used on the series so far.'

I offer a friendly smile, whilst inside I'm cringing like mad.

'I loved your book *Ransomed*,' Lucy now tells me, leaning in, her arm brushing mine, 'and I can't wait to read whatever's next! I find myself devouring your books in a single sitting, desperate to get to the end, and then devastated when it ends too soon.'

'Thank you,' I say, my throat suddenly dry, but there's no sign of any water on the table.

'Have you two started sketching out ideas for what you want to do next?' Becky asks, though it is clear the question is aimed more at Maddie than me. In this relationship I am just the one who churns out the words; anything career-related is dealt with by the grownups.

'We have one or two irons in the fire,' Maddie tells her secretively, as if divulging anything could cost lives.

'Well, that's what we wanted to meet you about,' Becky replies, her bright smile and wide eyes in contrast to Maddie's. 'We have an idea we'd like to pitch to you.'

My shoulders instantly tense at the memory of how it was Becky's insistence that my second book be based on the abduction of Lord Templeton Fitzhume's granddaughter. I didn't like my subject matter being dictated to me, when I wanted to focus my next book on my own sister's disappearance, and I don't like the thought that my publishers are in the driving seat again. This trepidation is only tempered by the fact that I managed to reunite Fitzhume's granddaughter with her mother.

'Have either of you heard of Aurélie Lebrun?' Becky asks, her lips trembling in anticipation.

I can see Maddie shaking her head in my periphery, but I do recognise the name. 'She was the ten-year-old daughter of the French Minister for Trade, right? Disappeared in Worthing, if memory serves... what, twelve or so years ago?'

'Thirteen years ago, to be precise,' Becky says, now turning her attention to me, and clearly pleased that I know what she's talking about. 'What if I told you that Aurélie Lebrun has turned up alive and well?'

I drop the bread roll to the table. The reason I recall Aurélie's story is because I saw so many comparisons between her situation and Anna's.

'She stumbled into a hospital in Poole on Tuesday evening and has been undergoing treatment for malnourishment and a broken wrist ever since.'

I now recall Rachel mentioning her editor wanting her to go and report on a story about a woman in Poole, and it can't be a coincidence.

She stumbled in, bruised and beaten, with no identification, and not speaking a word of English.

'She was identified through DNA, but her true identity has

66

yet to be released to the public,' Becky continues. 'We were given the tip-off about it first thing, and I immediately thought of you, Emma. Her injuries would suggest exposure to significant trauma for several years, and could make for an interesting twist on a tried-and-tested format: you could interview the victim and tell her story in her words. What do you think?'

Our meals can't come soon enough; if Aurélie was taken by the same people who snatched Anna, then she could be the breakthrough I've been waiting for.

Chapter Nine

NOW

Moorgate, London

As soon as Becky said she would speak to her contact and try and get me some time to speak to Aurélie Lebrun, I rushed through my portion of the tacos, nachos and breakfast burritos ordered for the table. I've learned over the years that opportunities like this don't come along very often, and so all my feelings of angst and reticence about allowing Becky and her team to choose the direction of my next case are gone.

'It's definitely her?' I check, as I drain my glass of water to quell the thirst brought on by the chilli in what I've just eaten.

'DNA confirmed it,' Becky says, beaming. 'And the best part is, nobody else knows about it. As far as every other media publication is aware, the girl in that hospital room is an unidentified Jane Doe.'

Becky is naïve if she thinks other media outlets won't soon lay their hands on this juicy detail. I bet as soon as Rachel's editor realises exactly who is recovering in Poole, he'll insist

Rachel travel down there. Part of me wants to give my best friend the heads-up to help her get ahead of the curve, but it isn't my place to share Becky's tip. Maybe I can just hint that there's more to the story than Rachel realised, and see if she wants to tag along with me.

'How much do you know about Aurélie's story?' Becky now asks.

In truth my recollection is limited, but I close my eyes and try to picture the notes I wrote at the time of researching it. I'm blessed with the ability to visualise memories. I don't have a photographic memory, and I'm lousy in general knowledge quizzes, but if you asked me to recite the names of every missing-child case history I've reviewed since Anna went missing, I reckon I'd be able to give you better than ninety per cent of the names.

'Aurélie's father – Remy Lebrun – was the Minister for Trade; something of a controversial figure from what I've read. He was a self-made millionaire when he decided to enter politics in France, and was tipped by many to be the next French Prime Minister until all this happened.' I pause, trying to recall any other salient details I'd sketched down. 'Remy Lebrun had come to the UK for talks with our government on renegotiating trade matters that fell outside the EU's capacity, but he brought his wife and daughter with him, so that they could spend a few days together as a mini holiday.

'They were staying in a seafront hotel, and had taken Aurélie down to the beach on what was a particularly hot day. She was paddling at the water's edge when her mother returned to their room to collect a new book to read, leaving her husband watching Aurélie. However, he received an urgent phone call, and looked away for what he claimed couldn't have been more than two minutes, and she vanished. At first they panicked that she'd wandered further into the water and had been swept up in it. A frantic search was engaged, but she couldn't be found. Given his prominence, an investigation was commenced immediately with detectives from the Met sent down to support local investigators.

'A day later, checking of local security camera feeds captured the moment a kicking and screaming Aurélie was placed in the back of a Transit van and driven away. The time on the camera matched the moment Remy Lebrun was heading into the water to look for her.

'It was assumed the abduction was targeted, because of the family's notoriety. The beach that day was packed with holidaymakers making the most of the August sunshine, but despite the hundreds of beach-dwellers interviewed by police in the immediate aftermath, nobody could recall the moment Aurélie was taken, nor did anyone recall a ten-year-old girl being dragged from the beach.'

The table falls silent as we all reflect that there is more to this than just a thrilling story. As someone who has experienced the sudden disappearance of a loved one, I know full well that it is the quiet nights of contemplation that are the most painful to deal with; there is a natural human need to ask what we could and should have done differently, and I have no doubt that both Remy Lebrun and his wife Solange will have criticised their every move that day and in the days before.

If only Remy hadn't taken that call; if only Solange hadn't returned to their room to collect her book; if only they hadn't gone to the beach that day; if only they'd stayed at a different hotel, or in a different town; if only Solange and Aurélie had remained in Paris.

I know because I've asked similar questions of myself every day since I saw Anna wander from our driveway twenty years ago.

'We'll have to move quickly,' I say now. 'If Aurélie is well enough to speak to me, then let's get an interview arranged before anyone else gets wind of the story.'

I'm not sure I've ever seen Becky look as excited as she does right now. 'I'm so thrilled that you're as enthusiastic about this as us. Can you imagine getting to hear first-hand what it was like being taken against her will, and held for so long? There is such a human interest story here that it's giving me tingles. I'll phone my contact now, and get the wheels in motion.'

I nod my agreement, and watch as Becky excuses herself from the table with her phone to her ear. What I haven't told her is that my interest in speaking with Aurélie is less about where she's been held, or how she escaped; I want to know if she ever saw Anna.

Catching the tube back to Rachel's flat in Ealing, I am focused on packing my bag and catching a train back to Weymouth from where I can base operations. I don't see the point in commuting from London to Poole every day. Becky has managed to get me in to see Aurélie first thing in the morning, so there is no point in me sticking around in London when I could be back home listening to the crash of the waves and the seagulls gossiping while refreshing my memory of the events surrounding Aurélie's abduction.

The last thing I'm expecting to find waiting on Rachel's doorstep is Jack Serrovitz. I start when I see the forlorn look he's wearing, and that he's clutching a bunch of flowers surreptitiously behind his back.

'Sorry to just turn up like this,' he says, his usual goofy grin replaced by thin lips drawn into a tight grimace. 'I wanted to apologise for last night.'

I don't need a mirror to see that the heat has rushed to my cheeks. I hadn't even thought about our awkward encounter since Aurélie's name tumbled from Becky's mouth. I just want to go inside, pack my things and catch the next train out of London, but I'm not cruel enough to ignore Jack's effort.

'It's fine,' I say, non-committally. 'Forget it happened.'

He takes a step forward, the plastic veil around the flowers rustling. 'No, it wasn't acceptable. I misread the situation, and I want to apologise for my behaviour. I like you, Emma. You make me laugh, and you challenge me to be a better detective than I think I ever was. *But* the last thing I want is to mess up our friendship and put you off helping me with our investigation.'

I suppose it had been too much to hope he'd buy the excuse of the brunch meeting as a reason for me not to go to the police station today.

'You've not put me off helping,' I reassure him, 'I had a business meeting with my publisher that I couldn't blow off; that's all.'

He studies my face, looking for those tell-tale signs of deceit that I know my body is showing despite my best efforts to hide them. 'These are for you,' he says, thrusting the bunch of flowers towards me. 'I feel awful about what happened, and I want you to know that it won't happen again.'

It's at times like this I wish I lived in Jane Austen's era, where such communication and discussion about feelings were reserved for written correspondence. I'm no good at speaking from the heart when talking about myself. I momentarily picture Jack as Mr Darcy emerging dripping wet from the lake, and it causes me to snicker, but that only deepens his frown.

'What's so funny?' he asks.

'Nothing,' I say, quickly shaking the image from my mind. 'Listen, Jack, you caught me off-guard last night, and had I known—'

'I was out of order,' he quickly interrupts, 'and I promise it won't happen again. You've made your feelings on the matter clear, and I just hope I haven't screwed things up between us. Jemima Hooper and the others need you on this investigation.'

If he'd allowed me to finish, I would have told him that we should postpone discussions about romantic entanglements until after we've identified each of the children on those videos, but I don't have the courage to come out with it now.

'You've not messed anything up,' I say, offering my most encouraging smile. 'Okay? I do need to go back home for a few days though, as something has come up that I need to deal with. I promise it has nothing to do with last night, so don't go reading anything into it. Okay?'

He doesn't look convinced.

'I have a potential lead on Anna that I need to plough my efforts into,' I clarify.

'Really? That's incredible! What's the lead? A location?'

'Not exactly. It's a long shot, but something I need to pursue.'

'Do you need any help? I'm happy to chase anything down that might help; after all, Anna is one of the victims on the video, so it is technically related to our investigation anyway.'

Actually, a few days apart will probably be a good thing for us, I don't tell him.

'Thanks,' I say, 'but I need to check the source first. As soon as I have something more concrete I'll let you know, okay?'

He is still dangling the bunch of white lilies at me, and I sense he won't leave until I take them and formally accept his apology.

'Thank you for the flowers,' I say, accepting the bunch and breathing in the sweet perfume, 'but they really weren't necessary. Everything is fine between us, I promise.'

Jack returns to his car at the side of the road, and I wave as he pulls away, before heading into Rachel's flat to gather my things. Seeing Jack has pushed another question to the forefront of my mind: is it possible that Aurélie Lebrun is another of the children in the videos recovered from Arthur Turgood's hard drive?

Chapter Ten

THEN

Poole, Dorset

She had a name. When Mr Truffaut had first said her real name was Aurélie, the name had sounded wrong, out of place somehow, yet there had been something familiar about the sound of the vowels that had triggered distant memories, memories locked so deep in her consciousness that she hardly dared to believe they were there. But the more he – and the petite firecracker DS Cavendish – said it, the more familiar it became. The sound reminded her of a time when fear wasn't her preliminary response to every occasion; a time when she could play, and explore, and hope.

DS Cavendish had told her she was Aurélie Lebrun, and had been missing for some thirteen years, making her twenty-three now; an entire youth spent in trepidation and darkness, and for what? Now she was out, and lost in a world her fragile mind could hardly contemplate. For the first time, she allowed her mind to wonder what she would be doing now had she not escaped.

Aurélie shook the thought from her mind; it didn't serve any purpose to allow such daydreaming. She had to believe that sometime the grass really could be greener on the other side. And as terrified as she was to be learning so much about a life that was long since forgotten, it didn't compare to the terror she'd lived through. If there really was a Hell, then she'd survived it somehow, and at some point her mind would have to allow her to see that she really had escaped; there was no way *he* would be able to get her, now she was safe with the police.

'I've just spoken to your parents,' DS Cavendish exclaimed, bounding into the room, swallowing the distance between the door and the bed in a few elongated strides. 'They couldn't quite believe we'd found you, but they'll be on the next flight out of Lille, and will probably be here first thing in the morning. Your mother was in tears.'

Aurélie looked down at the photograph of herself in the red and white ruffled dress that Cavendish had now printed out for her. Behind her stood a handsome man she recognised as her father, and a woman whose once youthful features weren't dissimilar to the reflection Aurélie had caught in the bathroom mirror. Memories of these two figures had yet to filter through the fog in her mind, but she had no doubt that she was staring at the faces of her parents. How much they must have changed in the last thirteen years too; would she even recognise them when they arrived? Would they recognise her?

'Listen, it's getting late,' Cavendish now said, nodding towards the dimming sunlight at the window closest to the door, 'and my shift ended an hour ago. If it's okay with you,

I'm going to go now, unless there's anything I can get for you in the meantime?'

Aurélie couldn't understand every word, but managed to get the gist of the question, shaking her head at the offer of further support. She suddenly felt very tired, even though the furthest she'd ventured all day was the bathroom for toilet breaks. Truffaut had said something about shower facilities in another room, but she didn't dare venture out alone. Stifling a yawn, Aurélie fixed her pillow and turned onto her side as Cavendish bowed out, closing the door behind her.

Aurélie closed her eyes, willing sleep to come, yet she also worried that this glorious dream was nearing its end, and that she would soon be woken by *him*, and the dream would be smashed.

She didn't know how long she'd been asleep when a knock at the door disturbed her. In walked a woman with an unfamiliar face. She had to be at least six foot tall, but with a wiry frame that for a moment had Aurélie picturing an icicle. The woman closed the door behind her. Dressed in a khaki-coloured long coat, she didn't look like a nurse or doctor.

Aurélie remained still in bed, squinting as the stranger picked up the medical file clipped to the foot of the bed and examined the contents. Aurélie was already fed up with being prodded and fussed over as various tests had been carried out on her over the course of the day. She hoped that if she remained still, this woman, whoever she was, would leave her be and go on her way. But then the woman in green pulled out what looked like a small camera or phone, and a flash of bright light suggested she'd taken a picture of the medical notes.

Aurélie sat up at this point, startling the woman in green.

'Oh, you're awake,' the wiry woman gasped. 'How are you, Aurélie?'

Aurélie remained silent, an alarm bell ringing somewhere in the back of her mind, instantly sensing danger. Was it possible this woman worked for *him* in some capacity?

'I bet all of this,' the woman continued, rolling her gaze around the room, 'seems a bit mental, right? There's no need to be scared; I'm a friend, and I mean you no harm.'

Aurélie tried to recall what the nurse had said about pressing a button to call for a nurse if she needed to, but she couldn't recall which button to use. She was just reaching for the paddle hanging from the bed frame when the wiry woman moved to that side of the bed.

'My name is Tessa Imbrock; I know your mother.'

Aurélie froze, studying the woman's face, looking for any clue to another long lost memory, but drawing a blank.

'Do you mind if I take a seat?' Tessa Imbrock said, not waiting for an answer before pulling over the chair that Cavendish had left beside the wall, and promptly sitting in it. 'How are you feeling, Aurélie?'

She adjusted her pillows, to allow her to sit up, and continued to look at the woman's face. The skin beneath her eyes was dark and hung lifelessly, almost as if she'd just stepped out of a boxing ring, yet there was no pain or swelling; this was the face of someone who'd burned the candle at both ends for too long. Yet there was nothing threatening about the gentle smile or pixie-cut fair hair.

'Heavens!' Tessa exclaimed. 'Can you even understand what I'm saying to you?'

Aurélie offered a small nod, even though she was barely following the questions.

'Oh, what a relief! As I'm sure it is for your mum and dad. Have you spoken to them yet? Your parents?'

Aurélie shook her head, not trusting her own voice.

Tessa glanced at the watch hanging from her bony wrist. 'Probably too late. Allowing for the time difference, it's well after ten in Lille. I'm sure you'll get to speak to them in the morning. I can just imagine how overwhelmed your mum will be at the news. Poor Solange; she took it the hardest, you know.'

Cavendish had confirmed her parents as Remy and Solange Lebrun, and although she couldn't say how, Aurélie had felt those names were right. So this woman had to be a friend of her mum's; at least that ruled out the possibility she was in cahoots with *him*.

'Do you remember the day you were taken?' Tessa asked next. 'Do you remember being on the beach with your mum and dad?'

In truth, Aurélie couldn't recall a beach, but she'd never forgotten the feeling of terror as her body had been flung into the back of the van, and how she'd rolled and bounced as the vehicle had picked up speed. She'd thought of herself as a sock in a washing machine, until eventually it had stopped, but from that moment, the memory faded until the relentless daily waking in the dark. Whatever had happened in the days and weeks that followed her abduction, those memories had been buried deep enough that they weren't readily available.

'Can you tell me anything about the man who took you? His name? What he looked like?'

Aurélie thought about the crude sketch of the monster she'd scribbled for Truffaut and Cavendish. It hadn't been accurate. Her captor hadn't been barrel-chested or covered in hair. Latterly, he'd been bereft of any kind of hair, as the scent of death had hovered nearby. At times he could be tender, almost allowing her to believe he cared, but those few occasions could never make up for the brutality of the rest. Whatever he'd felt for her, she didn't want to believe it was anything resembling love.

'Aurélie? Did you understand my question? Can you tell me anything about the man who took you?'

She shook her head again, knowing that Cavendish would want answers to similar questions, and feeling as though her unwillingness to provide answers was letting everyone down. She'd learned not to look, not to listen to anything not directed at her; it had taken time and pain, but she'd learned to be obedient.

'What about where you've been for the last thirteen years? Can you tell me if you've been in a house, or a flat, or a basement? Where have you been, Aurélie? Were you in the UK?'

The directness of the questions was starting to grow tiresome, but these were just the tip of the iceberg, Aurélie knew; she would be questioned over and over until she could shed light on the truth of what had happened, of what had happened to her.

'Je ne sais pas,' she offered with a slight shrug. 'Pardon, I not know the words.'

Tessa paused, and considered her. 'Would you mind if I took your photograph? I'm sure your mum and dad would want to see that you're safe and well.'

It seemed such an odd request, but Aurélie didn't know how to let her down, and reluctantly nodded.

Tessa raised the small camera that she'd been clutching the

entire time, and snapped two pictures of Aurélie in the bed, before joining her and taking an image of the two of them together. The flashing of the light hurt Aurélie's eyes, and must have been visible through the closed door, as a moment later one of the nurses opened the door and peered in, instantly losing her temper.

'You shouldn't be in here,' she challenged Tessa, marching into the room, and placing her hands on her hips.

Tessa didn't seem the slightest bit concerned, pocketing the camera and walking nonchalantly towards the door. 'I've got what I came for.' She stopped, reaching into her pocket again, this time extracting something that she swiftly handed to Aurélie. 'If you want to talk, or you want to sell your story, call me first. My editor will pay handsomely for an exclusive.'

Tessa didn't wait for an answer, hurrying from the room under the watchful glare of the nurse.

Aurélie examined the business card, trying to decipher the language, but recognising the red lettering of the logo in the top corner. It seemed Tessa wasn't a friend of her mother's, but a journalist looking for a scoop. Aurélie sank back into her pillows as her eyes watered; maybe life had been easier underground.

Chapter Eleven

NOW

Weymouth, Dorset

Being woken by Maddie calling me at six a.m. is not the most conducive start to what could be a very long day. My alarm had been set for seven, giving me time to wake, shower and gather my thoughts before catching the train to Poole, where I have an appointment to see Aurélie Lebrun at nine a.m. The phone call interrupted a dream I was having about a talking horse who knocked on my door and tried to sell me a magazine; when I refused, he rolled it up and started trying to clobber me with it. As violent as that sounds, it was actually rather entertaining as he couldn't seem to climb the four steps that lead up to my front door. I was just threatening to phone the local vet to have the horse taken away when the ringtone cut through the silence of the bedroom.

'I thought I should warn you,' Maddie begins, not stopping to check whether she's woken me, 'but Aurélie's return is no longer a secret.'

It takes several seconds for my mind to process that I'm no longer dreaming, and a second longer to process this news. 'Oh. How?'

Maddie sounds unusually flustered. 'I guess someone else leaked her identity. I haven't spoken to Becky yet, but I imagine she'll be annoyed. I suppose it was always inevitable that it wouldn't stay buried forever. The story made the first edition of the red tops, and is likely to be picked up by the broadsheets in the next few hours.'

This is going to make things tricky. The curse of the success of *Monsters Under the Bed* is that my face is more recognisable, and I only have to be spotted for rumours to start about my next investigation. In the last three months my name has trended along with such headings as 'The Ghost of Kew', 'The Brandon Hill Park Murder' and 'Jack the Ripper'. The first was as a result of a trip to see the gardens with Rachel; the second because I happened to be signing books in Bristol; and the third because someone with a passing resemblance to me (personally, I don't see it, but Rachel says we could have been sisters!) was spotted looking at gravestones in East London. If I'm seen going into the hospital to meet Aurélie, it won't be long before the truth will out.

'I want you to know I didn't leak the story,' Maddie says next, catching me off-guard.

During the Cassie Hilliard investigation, Maddie leaked details of the story to an Australian blogger, and could have sabotaged my relationship with the family. It angered me at the time, but ultimately helped crack the case indirectly.

'I didn't assume…' I begin to say, before realising the unintended implication. 'I didn't leak it either,' I retort. 'I swear! The last thing I want is more competition disrupting any investigation.'

'Good, well, it's as I thought,' she concludes, pragmatic as ever. 'What time are you due at the hospital?'

'Nine.'

'Oh, well what are you doing up so early?'

I'm about to point out that it was Maddie's call that woke me, but I don't get the chance.

'Never mind. Listen, it's probably worth reviewing the papers before you go in. I don't think the journalist who broke the story – Tessa Imbrock – managed to get too much information. From what I've read on Twitter, there's very little detail about where Aurélie's been for the last thirteen years. Still, it would be good to familiarise yourself.'

I stopped listening at the mention of Tessa Imbrock. It's a name I know on account of her being an acquaintance of Rachel's, and she provided some useful background information about the Hilliards last year. I haven't spoken to Rachel about my meeting with my publishers, or what was proposed, but I do now recall Rachel saying her editor had wanted her to do a piece on the unidentified Aurélie; it wouldn't surprise me if Rachel passed on the tip, and Tessa had taken full advantage.

'I'd better go,' Maddie now says firmly. 'I'm hoping to do 5k before I go into the office. Let's have a call tonight to go over your meeting with Aurélie, and we can start to flesh out the book proposal. Okay?'

She doesn't wait for me to agree before hanging up.

Dropping the phone, I press my head into the soft comfort of my pillow, and pull the duvet up to my chin. I know I won't get back to sleep before the alarm sounds in less than an hour, but there's nowhere else I'd rather lie in wait.

The media circus is in full throttle when I arrive at Poole Hospital. There are video cameras on tripods lined up, each facing a recognisable journalist and a sliver of the hospital in the background of the broadcast. They're all relaying the same titbit of information Tessa shared in her exclusive this morning: Aurélie Lebrun has emerged thirteen years after her disappearance from Worthing beach, and is being treated for malnutrition and osteomalacia as a result of her confinement; wherever she's been held, she has suffered a severe vitamin D deficiency which has resulted in the softening of her bones and muscles.

I bury my chin in the thin scarf I brought in an effort to shield my identity, and dart past the BBC and Sky News vans that have been abandoned at the side of the road, causing no end of traffic issues through the grounds of the hospital. Becky has sent me the name of the ward where Aurélie is being treated, and I'm to locate the police officer now stationed outside her room and show my credentials.

I'm early, as I often am, and stop at the Costa Coffee, purchasing a takeaway tea for myself, and instinctively I also order a hot chocolate. It must be all those years of studying GCSE French at school – being envious of French children drinking bowls of hot chocolate for breakfast – that have triggered the impulse. In truth, I don't know if Aurélie is even allowed to consume anything not on a prescribed diet, but I'm hopeful it will help break the ice.

By the time I have entered the ward, keeping my face covered until I reach the awaiting officer in black, it is two minutes to nine. He holds the two takeaway cups while I reach into my bag and pull out my identification. He looks long and hard at the digital image of me and then at my face, before nodding, and handing back the cups.

'My wife's a huge fan of your books,' he whispers as he holds the door open for me.

I'm about to thank him and offer to sign an autograph, but the door is already closing, leaving me in a dim room, the blinds in the room drawn. When I turn back to the bed, the young woman carefully watching me is partially obscured by the crisp white bed sheet she is holding just below her eyes. As I take a step forward, her legs quickly curl up, like a terrified animal trying to escape the clutches of a predator.

I instantly stop moving and extend my arms in what I hope she will see as a calming gesture. 'I'm Emma Hunter, Aurélie. I'm the writer who has come to interview you.'

Her body remains contorted beneath the bed sheet, and it is only now I think about the fact that she may not have a good understanding of English. Thinking back to those GCSE lessons, I try to recall anything that might explain what I am doing here.

'Je m'appelle Emma,' I begin, plastering on a warm smile. 'Je suis...' Oh God, what is the word for writer? 'Je suis auteur.'

I suddenly feel incredibly nervous, and wish I'd thought sooner about asking Becky to arrange for an interpreter to attend this preliminary meeting. In fairness, the purpose of today is just to introduce myself and audition for the chance to tell her story. Any real investigatory work will occur at a later date, at which point a professional interpreter can be hired.

'I brought you hot chocolate,' I say before trying to translate the phrase in my head. 'Chocolat. Je vous ai acheté un chocolat chaud.' I extend the cup towards the bed, but don't move forwards until she sits up straighter, and nods for me to approach.

'Merci,' she says in a quiet, angelic voice, accepting the cardboard cup.

She is so thin that it's painful to look at her; emaciated doesn't even begin to explain how grey and lifeless her skin looks. It is tight skin; this is someone who has looked this way for some time, and hasn't just suddenly lost weight. Her dark hair is short, and hangs just above the shoulders of the hospital gown that is making her face look even paler. I don't mean to pass judgement, but the jagged edges of her fringe suggest that this hair wasn't cut professionally. I'd even go so far as to say scissors weren't used. If Tessa Imbrock's article is right, and Aurélie has been held beneath the ground for all these years, it's hardly surprising that she's felt the need to draw the blinds and keep out the sunlight; her eyes are probably no longer accustomed to its rays.

For the briefest of moments I see my sister in the bed beside me. For all these years I've been scouring for any kind of clue to what happened to Anna, but for all I know she's suffered irreparable damage, just as Aurélie has. Anna could still be trapped somewhere beneath the ground, with the world oblivious to her pain and terror.

'Can I sit?' I ask. 'Um, puis-je m'asseoir?'

She nods again, and I drag the plastic chair across from the wall, so that I am in line with her now straightened knees.

She lifts the lid of the cup and takes a sip of the hot chocolate, before wincing. 'C'est très chaud.' She places the cup on the small table stand that lies above the bed.

'Comment ça va?'

I can't tell if she recognises that my linguistic skills are limited to basic small talk, but she yawns in response, before wobbling her hand to indicate she's neither good, nor bad.

I'm definitely going to need an interpreter going forwards. Pulling out my phone I open the draft email where I saved my list of preliminary questions, but of course they're all in English. I don't want to bombard her with questions on day one, given that the police have probably already tried conducting interviews with her since she arrived here on Tuesday evening, but at the same time, I don't think that asking her for directions to the museum, swimming pool or library is going to help move things along.

'Do you know who I am?' I ask, pressing a hand to my chest. 'Est-ce que vous savez qui je suis?'

She frowns, and I'm not sure if I have correctly translated the question. 'Êtes-vous journaliste?'

I'm assuming 'journaliste' is a literal translation, but I don't know how to answer the question. I mean, I am a journalist of sorts, but it has been a good three years at least since I last wrote anything significant for a newspaper or periodical. And yet, calling myself an author doesn't sit comfortably either. Some say that writers write, and so by definition I'm a writer either way, but how do I explain that level of nuance and lack of self-confidence succinctly to a stranger, *and* in another language?

In the end I mimic her hand-wobbling gesture. 'Sort of.'

I'm searching for language apps that I can use to translate

my questions when there is a knock at the door, and a tall man in a white coat enters. He is too busy talking to the couple behind him to notice that I am in the room, but when he closes the door, our eyes meet. He opens his mouth to speak, but before he can say anything, the woman behind him gasps, and it is all the grey-haired man beside her – presumably her husband – can do to keep her from collapsing.

'Aurélie,' the woman yelps. 'Mon petit chou.'

I turn to look at Aurélie, and can see her eyes are welling up at the sight of these two older figures. And as my gaze falls back on the woman, who is still being held up by the man beside her, there is just the slightest trace of resemblance between the two women. Instinctively I know I am staring at Remy and Solange Lebrun.

Chapter Twelve

NOW

Poole, Dorset

I shuffle my chair backwards, not wanting to intrude on this reconciliation between mourning parents and disbelieving child. Neither speaks, as Solange hurries to the bedside, reaching for Aurélie's hand, but then stops herself as if any kind of contact might make the illusion end.

'Aurélie? Est-ce toi?' Solange dares to whisper, a small cloud of steam evaporating from her lips as she does.

The tears escape Aurélie's eyes as she nods her head, the glazed look suggesting she can't quite believe she's been reunited with figures who were nothing but a distant, repressed memory.

Solange stretches out a trembling hand and catches one of her daughter's tears on her thumb. And it's as if time has frozen in this room; like staring at a photograph. There is pure love between these two women that elevates them above space and time. In years to come, when people ask me what I recall of my first meeting with Aurélie Lebrun, *this* is the moment I will describe to them.

Solange has now lifted Aurélie's hand in her own, careful not to disturb the cannula, but is handling it as if the skin is a delicate petal on a flower that could fade to dust. She presses her dry lips to the back of the hand, before wiping her own tears with it. No words are spoken but their eyes are locked, and I'm convinced their thoughts are passing telepathically; all those years of talking to each other internally must be a difficult habit to break.

I can't bear to intrude any longer, and lifting my satchel from the floor, I stand up, peeling myself from the chair without a sound. Neither woman turns, but as I reach the two men at the door, Remy Lebrun turns his head to face me.

'Mademoiselle Hunter?' he croaks, before swallowing, and introducing himself. 'My name is Remy Lebrun; I am Aurélie's father.'

I smile sincerely. 'I know who you are, sir. If you'll excuse me, I'll wait outside and allow you all to get reacquainted.'

I open the door and step out, nodding an acknowledgement at the police officer who let me in earlier, but it's only now I realise that my own vision is misting. Quickly reaching into my satchel, I locate a packet of tissues, extract one and wipe my eyes.

'Excusez-moi,' I hear Remy Lebrun say behind me. 'Might I speak to you, Mademoiselle Hunter?'

A wave of guilt washes over me: who am I to be shedding tears at this reunion? I don't know Aurélie, nor her parents, so what right do I have to be sharing in their sadness and joy?

'Certainly,' I reply, swallowing the emotion, and giving my eyes a second wipe, before pocketing the tissue.

Remy leads me away from the room, and we duck in through the door to the next room, which is vacant. The silence inside is eerie, and I'm the first to break it.

'You must be overjoyed to see Aurélie after all this time!' I'm cringing as the lame words tumble from my lips, and if I had my time again, I'd choose something more worthy to describe such a monumental moment.

'It is a miracle,' he replies, his English a hundred times better than my French. Given his senior role in the French government, I suppose speaking English was a requirement for diplomatic events.

I can only imagine how overwhelmed he must be to be reunited with a daughter he probably thought he'd never see again; I can only assume that's why he's decided to speak to me privately, rather than being next door, telling her how much he loves and missed her. I have allowed my imagination to picture the moment I might be reconnected with Anna, but it's difficult to know how she would react to learning that she's had a sister out here searching for her for all this time; that's assuming she's still alive when that day emerges. A writer's imagination can be a blessing and a curse, and depending how I'm feeling on any given day, my future reconciliation can be a joyous one, or tragedy.

When you lose someone close to you as we both have, you spend such large chunks of your life wondering how things might have been had you acted differently at the time. For me, I've replayed the moment Anna walked from the driveway over and over, questioning would things have been different had I just let her play with my stupid skateboard, or had I begged her not to go to grandma's house, or had I insisted on going with her. Had I known it would be the last time I'd see her, I'm certain I would have acted differently, and changed the course of both of our lives forever.

For Remy, he must have questioned whether things would have been different had he not answered his phone that day on Worthing beach; or had he offered to collect Solange's book from their hotel room; or had he insisted that Aurélie stay closer to him, rather than paddling in the sea. He will have blamed himself for the past thirteen years, even though the real culprits are the people who snatched her from that beach and have held her against her will for all this time. In truth, he will never forgive himself, as I won't ever accept that I'm not at least partially to blame for Anna's disappearance.

'I wish we were meeting under better circumstances,' he offers next, and yet such a statement throws me.

What could be better than being reunited with his missing daughter? I suppose maybe his sentiment has just been lost in translation, and in fact what he means is he would have preferred to meet in a more sociable situation.

'I don't want to intrude on your time with your daughter,' I say instead. 'My publisher said I was to meet with Aurélie this morning, but I don't think she knew you would be here too.'

'On the contrary, Mademoiselle Hunter, I was the one who asked that you be here when we arrived. Unfortunately, our taxi from the airport was delayed by traffic.'

I think back to that brunch meeting with Becky and Maddie yesterday, but I don't remember her saying that it was in fact Aurélie's dad who had been in contact. I'd assumed the tip-off came from one of the police officers working on the case.

'Wait, *you* asked me to be here?' I clarify, in case there is another language miscommunication.

'Bien sur, of course. Who better to find out where my

daughter has been than the great Emma Hunter? I want the men responsible for this captured.'

This is not what I was expecting to hear, and the heat rises to my cheeks, as I attempt to compose myself. 'With all due respect, Monsieur Lebrun, that is the job of the police.'

He scoffs. 'It is because of the British police that my daughter wasn't discovered thirteen years ago. Alors, I am not a young man anymore, and I want to see these men caught before I die.'

He covers his mouth with his hand, and coughs, though it isn't clear if this is a nervous reaction, or because of something underlying.

'Monsieur Lebrun—'

'Please, call me Remy.'

'Okay, Remy, it isn't that I don't want to help you and your daughter, but I'm really not who you think I am. The reason I came here today was to meet Aurélie, and hopefully to interview her, and tell her story. I would expect the police to launch a formal investigation into what happened, who took her and where she's been.'

'No, Mademoiselle Hunter, it is *you* who does not understand. The men responsible for this tragedy are not the sort of people who will cave under pressure from the British police. What I need – *what my daughter needs* – is someone who doesn't stop when doors are closed. I know exactly who you are, Emma, and I know what you have done for others. I have read all of your books, both in English and the French translations. I have had my people look into your background, and I am certain you are exactly who we need.'

He isn't listening, and this has to be the worst part of the fame that has come with the success of my books: people seem to believe I have some magic wand that allows me to uncover great mysteries, when in truth I have had more than my fair share of luck with the investigations I've conducted. I wish Maddie or Rachel were here, as they're both far better at arguing their points than me.

'I appreciate you thinking of me, Remy, but—'

'I know your own sister is missing, Emma. *That* is why I know you are the right person to help us. I know about your work with the Anna Hunter Foundation, and if you agree to help us, I will happily make a generous donation to the charitable trust.'

An uneasy feeling coils like a snake in my gut. Lord Templeton Fitzhume made a similar offer when he hired me to investigate his granddaughter's disappearance, even though he was the one behind it. I don't want to leap to conclusions and draw a parallel here, but I can't help it.

'That's a kind offer, but—'

He raises his hand to silence my objection. 'Please think about it. I am going to go and see my daughter now, and you are more than welcome to join us. I am sure she will be equally keen to help you find the men responsible.'

He doesn't wait for me to object again, swiftly opening the door and exiting the room. I follow him back out to the main corridor, but shake my head when he offers to hold the door into Aurélie's room for me. Despite what he's said, his wife and daughter need him, and don't need me gawping at their reunion. Solange is sitting in the chair I vacated, and her face looks drawn as the tears continue to fall. This woman, who was once considered one of the most beautiful women in France, is a shadow of her former self, and those red rings beneath her eyes show the strain of the emotional rollercoaster she's currently riding.

I remain where I am, allowing myself to glance in and watch as he moves quickly to the bed and embraces his daughter. She seems reluctant to accept the contact at first, and as our eyes meet, I see something in Aurélie that sends a shiver the length of my body: she's never looked more scared.

Chapter Thirteen

THEN

Poole, Dorset

On all of the nights when the pain had been the worst – and on one particular night when she'd offered to sell her soul to the devil himself – Aurélie had prayed for the moment when she might one day be reunited with her parents; they would somehow discover where she was being held, kick in the doors and drag her away from the madness, but after so many years of the dream not coming true, she'd begun to doubt it ever would. Yet here she was now, being fussed over by two people she'd once known love for. It was almost impossible to allow herself to believe that they were really here. In all of the dreams of this moment, not one had occurred in a hygienic-smelling room in a hospital ward.

Neither had said much since that writer had left the room, but their tears and faces said all they needed to. It wasn't just Aurélie who was clearly overwhelmed by this recoupling. Her father was perched on the edge of the bed now, trying to talk to her in her mother tongue, but she was only picking up on every third word. It was like a hole had been punctured in the barrier keeping those familiar words from her mind, but more and more of that previous vocabulary was gushing forwards, and it wouldn't be long before she was able to understand most of what he was trying to communicate.

It wasn't just words that were starting to prick at the edge of her subconscious. Flickers and flashes of memory were appearing in fragmented states too: a raised voice; laughter; tearing at wrapping paper; jelly sliding down her throat; splashing water in a bathtub; a bonfire burning nearby; the frosty, sweet lather of ice cream on her tongue. Each memory interspersed with a younger version of either the man or the woman before her, or both together; happy memories of a time before the darkness and fear came.

She'd been happy once, that much she was sure of. What felt like a lifetime ago had been happy, albeit probably tinged with sadder moments that had been totally obliterated from the memory banks; there wasn't room for hurt and pain from that period of her life; all of that had been taken up by fresher recollections of such feelings.

'What can you tell me about the man who took you?' her father asked next.

It was thirteen years ago, and so much had happened since that day on the beach; she couldn't be sure what she could now recall was what had actually happened, or something her subconscious had created to fill in the blanks, and to explain how she had come to be in that bolthole beneath the ground.

Why did he want to know what the man looked like? Did he have someone in mind he was expecting her to describe? Did he know something she didn't? Because as she tried to picture that moment when her world had been turned on its head, it wasn't a man she pictured.

It had been so hot in Worthing on that so-called holiday. It was another of her father's business trips, and he'd spent more time away from Aurélie and her mother than he had with them. Even when he was there, he would often be stopped and interrupted by some strange face or another, desperate for a few minutes with him, and he always obliged. But on that morning he'd promised her mother he would be with them in the moment, and would not allow anything or anyone to get in the way.

Aurélie could still feel the tiny glass-like grains of sand pushing between her toes as she'd stepped onto it; so warm and dusty, but also promising such fun. She'd run on ahead, so she could splash her toes in the cool luxury of the sea's white froth, before rushing back, the bucket and spade swinging from her hand and brushing against her bare leg. The elastic of her one-piece bathing costume chafed at the top of her thigh, but her mother told her to stop fidgeting with it, and just to allow the distraction of play to ease the pressure.

The beach had already been quite crowded when they had pitched the wind barrier into the sand, her father hammering the stakes into the unforgiving ground, before laying on the sand the two towels they had borrowed from the hotel. The pitch was about halfway between the road and the sea, and as Aurélie began to fill her bucket with warm, dry sand, it was already getting hot.

Her first attempt at a sandcastle had failed, the dry sand quickly dispersing, and her father had told her she needed wet sand to make a sustainable structure. He'd taken her hand and led her down the beach towards the much darker variety smothered by the water and had helped her fill two buckets, lugging them back to their pitch for her, showing her how to flip them quickly and tap the edges with her spade before lifting them. Her eyes had been on stalks as he'd revealed the first two towers of the palace she would go on to create with his help.

A new flash of memory peppered her mind: an image of her sitting beside a large sand structure, her father sprawled out behind her, and her mother snapping the shot with a disposable camera. Aurélie wondered now what had happened to that image, whether they'd been brave enough to have it developed.

'What did the man look like?' Remy Lebrun asked next. 'Was he tall or short, fat or thin? Was he English or French?'

Aurélie could remember collecting more wet sand, and when she returned to the pitch, she could see the back of her mother up near the road, ready to cross it. She'd asked her dad where she was going, but as he'd been about to reply his phone had rung, and he'd told her he just had to take the call, and that she wasn't to go far. Aurélie had built a moat around her sand palace, but whenever she tried to fill it with water, it would disappear into the sand, leaving a wet trail. She was certain that if she kept filling it, eventually the water would remain, and so she set off back to the water's edge to fill her bucket.

She remembered there being a lot of people laughing and splashing in the froth; there was a dog barking, and two older boys throwing an egg-shaped ball to one another. She was filling her bucket with water, when a big wave caught her unawares, and she fell into the foaming froth headfirst. The salt had tasted bitter on her tongue and lips, and when she'd looked up to her father for help, she'd been unable to see him or the windbreaker. Confused, panic had rippled at the surface of her mind, and gathering her bucket she'd set off in search of him, fearing that he had followed her mother, and that they'd simply forgotten to take her with them.

'Hello, are you lost?' A woman's voice now stirred in the memory.

Such a pretty young woman, wearing a golden dress that flapped in the breeze. The woman had spoken in French, and as Aurélie now tried to concentrate on the woman's appearance, she could only see Emma Hunter's warm smile where her subconscious filled yet another blank. Shaking her head, Aurélie tried again, but all she could see was that smile, and the feeling that this woman would help her locate her parents.

'I'll take you back to your mum and dad,' the young woman had said, taking Aurélie's hand in hers, and leading her up the beach. Aurélie could recall looking left and right frantically in search of the windbreaker, but couldn't see it, and then they arrived at the edge of the road.

'Your mum and dad went to a café and asked me to bring you to them. They said you can have an ice cream, and they have so many flavours; what's your favourite?'

Aurélie had answered, 'Chocolate,' of course, but the young woman hadn't taken her to a café, instead suddenly grabbing her around the waist and forcing her into the back of a waiting van. Aurélie had been so scared that she'd screamed and wet herself, but no matter how much noise she made, it hadn't made a difference.

'Aurélie, are you okay?' her mother now asked, wiping fresh tears from Aurélie's cheeks.

Aurélie looked her mother in the eye, but couldn't begin to explain the absolute fear she'd felt in that moment, but how she would later come to appreciate that it was merely the tip of the iceberg. Her mother looked so much older, but Aurélie could still see that younger face buried beneath the wrinkles and makeup covering thirteen years of heartache.

Not that Aurélie could remember them ever being that close before that day at the beach. In fact, she could now recall that there had been talk of Aurélie joining a boarding school after that summer, an idea that Aurélie had hated. Snatched snippets of overheard conversations now echoed through her mind; her parents talking, but making little effort to obscure their voices.

'She will thrive there,' her father had said. 'It will give you the time to work more; you are still a beautiful woman, and there is a market for women who have managed to maintain their looks and figure post-childbirth. And with the election next year, I don't know how much I will be around to support you both. The Clairefontaine école will be ideal, and when there is a break between terms, the three of us will make the most of the time we have together. I promise you.'

They had wanted to pack her off so that she would be somebody else's problem. That had been their plan, and no matter how much Aurélie had protested, they had made up their minds. How ironic then that she was taken that day on the beach. She wondered now whether they would have thought twice had they known how events would prevail.

'Can you tell us where you have been, Aurélie?' Remy Lebrun asked.

How could she find the words to explain where she'd been? The last ten years she'd been settled in the hole, but before that she had been ferried from one cell to another. She'd tried to make friends with one of the girls in one of those places – she could no longer recall which one – but had been told in no uncertain terms that it was every girl for herself. When she'd then been moved to the last place, she hadn't known she would be there for so long, nor that the regular turnover of faces would eventually reduce until it was only her and *him*.

She shuddered at the memory of his rough stubble scraping against her cheek; the tang of cigarettes, beer, and wine on his breath; the coarseness of his tongue as it prodded and probed inside her mouth. He'd told her he loved her, and that she was special, but then he would strike her when she was less than compliant. She'd grown accustomed to what he offered: two parts affection to one part aggression. It was all he knew, and she'd learned to accept it.

She shook her head in answer to her father's question. Even if they gave her a map, she'd never be able to pinpoint the exact location of the bolthole.

'Trees,' she offered in French. 'There were lots of trees.'

'A forest?' he clarified.

She nodded. 'Yes, a forest. Very dark. I must have walked for more than an hour to get here.'

Her father pulled out a phone and pressed it to his ear. 'Detective Cavendish? Please come quickly. She is starting to remember.'

Chapter Fourteen

NOW

Poole, Dorset

There is a sudden hubbub beyond the glass in Aurélie's private room, as her father talks urgently into his phone. It's at that same moment that I feel my own phone ringing, and for a second I actually believe it is him calling me – until I see Jack's name on the screen. I don't immediately answer as a nurse glares at me for holding the phone and points at a sign on the wall. I should have turned the phone off as soon as I entered the hospital, but in my defence I was somewhat distracted by keeping my face away from the waiting cameras.

Heading out of the ward, I call Jack back the moment I step outside the hospital, deliberately steering myself away from the much larger pool of journalists and cameras only a few feet away.

'Thanks for phoning me back,' he begins, though he sounds distracted. I immediately sense this isn't a personal call.

'No problem. What's up?'

'Big news potentially for our investigation! Have you watched the news yet this morning? Missing French schoolgirl Aurélie Lebrun has been discovered some thirteen years after she was abducted from a beach in Worthing. Incredible, right?'

Oh, this is awkward. I can't tell him that this isn't news to me, and that I've already met her.

'Oh, really?' I say, trying to sound as blasé as possible, and failing miserably.

'From what I understand she walked into a hospital in Poole of all places a couple of nights ago, and has been receiving treatment ever since. Have you seriously not watched this morning's news? The story is trending on Twitter too; I'm surprised you haven't seen it yet.'

I can't tell if this is a slight dig, as Jack knows I'm not great with social media feeds. 'I've only just woken up,' I lie, and I don't really know why I don't come clean with him. He's bound to find out soon enough that I am already here, so I should just come out and say that I know she's here and have done since yesterday. It's because I know how much it will hurt him to think that I have kept this from him.

'What does it have to do with our investigation?' I ask instead. 'Hers wasn't one of the faces identified in the videos on the hard drive, was it?'

'We haven't checked until this point. Although her case was fairly high profile, it wasn't at the top of our list on account of how long she's been missing. I've prioritised it now though. It would really help if we can get a picture of her face now, so the tech guys can do their magic. I'm sure there'll be pictures in the press soon enough; or we can reach out to whoever is running the case and see if they'll share resources.'

'Sounds like a plan,' I say.

There is a pause on the line. 'I thought you'd be more excited?'

'I am, I mean it's potentially a big break, I guess, so it's great.'

'You're a terrible liar, Emma. What's going on?'

He's right, of course: I am a terrible liar!

'Okay, the thing is, Jack, I know about Aurélie Lebrun because… I'm already here, at the hospital, I mean. Her father reached out to my publishers and asked to meet me here this morning because he wants to hire me to write his daughter's story.'

I take a moment to allow the revelation to sink in, but I can't hear any kind of response. Peeling the phone from my ear, I check that we're still connected.

'Jack? Hello? Did you hear what I said?'

'You're already there…' he says, and I can hear the sadness in his tone.

'I'm sorry. That's why I had to rush away when I saw you yesterday. This was the lead I told you I had to chase up about Anna. You're right that her return could provide us with insight about the people who took and held her for so long, and potentially any other victims she met along the way.'

He doesn't answer, and again I find myself checking the screen to ensure I haven't lost signal. Still four strong bars though.

'Well it sounds like you've got it all figured out, and don't need me, so I'll let you get back to it.'

'Don't be like that, Jack. I was sworn to secrecy, and couldn't tell you where I was going. I didn't know that the story would get leaked to the national press this morning, otherwise I would have come clean sooner. I'm sorry.'

I can picture him now, with puppy dog eyes, wallowing in self-pity, and I wish I could give him a hug and show him how sorry I am.

'I'm sorry, Jack,' I repeat.

'Don't worry about it,' he says. 'It's fine.'

It clearly isn't, judging by his tone, but there's nothing else I can do.

'How is she?' he asks after a moment.

'Pretty banged up, I'd say. She is so skinny, and has this constant look of fear in her eyes, like she doesn't trust anything or anyone around her. I can't even imagine what she's been through, or how much strength it took to get away from whoever has kept her locked up all this time. They reckon she's been kept in some kind of dungeon for several years, with no sunlight or freedom.'

'Have you spoken to her yet? Has she said anything about who or where she was being held?'

'Not to me, but it's difficult as I don't think she speaks much English, and my French is limited. Plus, her parents arrived just after I'd met her, so I haven't really spent any time with her yet. Her dad certainly seemed keen on securing my writing skills though.'

'That's good for you; at least you know where your next royalty cheque will come from.'

I don't react to the snap, as I know he doesn't mean to be so snide.

'Actually, I turned him down.'

'What? Why?'

I squat down on a bench around the corner from the main entrance. 'Because there is far more at stake here than a story. This poor girl looks as though she's experienced agony for years, and I don't feel comfortable cashing in on that level of misery. What she needs is professional psychological evaluation and the brains of a valiant team of detectives to catch those responsible. I don't want to get in the way of her recovery.'

Jack is silent again, and I wish I could read his mood better. If we were face-to-face I'd be able to see whether he's still hurt about me keeping him in the dark, or whether there's something else on his mind.

'Why do you do that? Put yourself down all the time? When we first met I thought you were just self-deprecating, but I've noticed it more and more. Arrogance is an ugly trait, but your self-doubt is eating you alive, Emma.'

I'd argue but this is the theme of many conversations I've had with Rachel and Maddie these last few months.

'Besides,' he continues, 'if you're in with her parents, we could use that to our advantage. Even if you have no intention of writing about her story, your position on the inside gives us direct access to Aurélie as a victim. You need to speak to her as soon as you can and find out whether she was being held alone, or whether there were more victims like her. Also, find out whether she was ever forced to perform on video or for pictures.'

'It's not that easy, Jack. As I said, she doesn't seem to understand English, and my GCSE French isn't up to the task.'

'So, use her parents to translate for you. I'm sure they're as keen as anyone else to get to the bottom of what happened.'

I gasp at the audacity. 'I can't ask her parents to ask her whether she was forced to perform sexual acts in front of cameras!'

'Um, no, of course you can't,' Jack backtracks. 'Sorry, but

I'm sure you could use them to garner more information until we can sort out an alternative. I'm sure we could hire an interpreter or something.'

'She's pretty shaken up, Jack. I'll do what I can, but I can't promise anything.'

'How are they? Her parents, I mean.'

I think about the question for a moment. 'I haven't spoken to her mum yet, but she seems quite overwhelmed by it all from what I can see. Her dad – Remy – he seems a bit more pragmatic. Don't get me wrong, I'm sure he's over the moon to have her back, but the first thing he did upon arrival was take me for a chat to ask me to write a book about Aurélie. I would have expected him to at least greet her before pursuing publicity angles.'

'It's the world we live in now though, isn't it? Everyone's after their fifteen minutes of fame.'

'And there was something else... I don't know how to explain it, but when I watched him go to her, there was this look in her eyes... like she was absolutely terrified to be so close to him... I'm sure I didn't imagine it.'

'Really? Are you sure it wasn't just her way of dealing with the raw emotion? I mean, she won't have seen them in thirteen years, so they probably are virtual strangers to her.'

'Mmm... I don't know. It's probably nothing, but it just struck me as odd.'

'Well, did she say anything, or did he notice her reaction?'

'I was outside the room, so I couldn't hear what was said, but he was hugging her at the time, so couldn't have seen her face.'

'Well then, it's probably nothing. What's the alternative, that he's somehow involved in her going missing?'

I can't answer the question because somewhere in the back of my mind that's exactly what my brain is trying to process, and the thought disgusts me.

'Emma? Are you suggesting that Remy Lebrun was complicit in his ten-year-old daughter being abducted?'

'No... I don't know... I...'

'Don't let our experience with Lord Templeton Fitzhume cloud your judgement here. This is not the same as what happened to Cassie Hilliard. Okay?'

He's right, I know he is, but I have no other explanation for that look of pure terror I saw in Aurélie's eyes.

'Have you asked her about Anna yet?'

The question throws me. 'What?'

'Come on, it must have crossed your mind... Anna disappeared from a seaside town nearly twenty-one years ago now... Aurélie Lebrun disappeared from a seaside town thirteen years ago; you can't deny there's similarity there.'

I don't want to see the connection because to do so would mean to accept that Anna might have been held in similar conditions, and it breaks my heart to picture my sister in such a state.

'Not yet,' I reply.

'Do you have a picture of her you could show Aurélie? It wouldn't hurt, and you never know, it could be that big break you've been seeking all these years.'

I know he's right, and in my bag I have copies of the aged images I had mocked up of how Anna could look now. It wouldn't be difficult to show her them and ask if there's anything familiar, but I don't know if I could take it if she said yes.

'I'd better head back in there before her dad sends out a search party,' I say.

'Sure, okay. Will you keep me posted on anything you learn? I'll see if I can find out anything from this end; see if I can't reach out to the detective in charge and offer some support.'

'Thanks, Jack, and I really am sorry I didn't say anything sooner.'

'I know; given how things were yesterday, I don't blame you. Let's chat later.'

He doesn't wait for me to answer before hanging up. Switching the phone to airplane mode, I bury my face in the thin scarf again, and return to the ward, but when I reach Aurélie's door, the uniformed officer is gone, and there is a stern-faced woman in his place.

'Hi,' I say casually. 'My name's Emma Hunter, and I—'

'Oh, I know exactly who you are, Emma, and I'm here to tell you that you're not wanted. Not here, not now, and nowhere near my case. Is that clear?'

Chapter Fifteen

NOW

Poole, Dorset

I'm not used to being so publicly demeaned, and I instantly shy away from the door with no idea who the short, stern-faced woman before me is. Her hair is cut boy-short but shines with platinum peroxide under the ward's harsh lighting. The scowl she wears I can only hope isn't solely intended for me, and yet it is clear – although we have never met before – this woman has taken an instant dislike to me. It is a feeling that is almost a hundred per cent reciprocated.

'I'm sorry, who are you?' I try, suddenly conscious that she may have mistaken me for someone else.

'Detective Sergeant Zoe Cavendish,' she replies with a glower, holding her identification up so I can read it. The passport-sized photograph looks even sterner.

'Ah, I see,' I say quickly, 'you're the detective running the show here, aren't you? We haven't been properly introduced.'

I am putting on my most sincere and unoffended smile, even though her aggression has definitely put me out.

'Aurélie's father, Remy, asked me to be here,' I clarify.

She casually glances over her shoulder through the window, where I see Remy and Solange huddled close to Aurélie in the bed, before turning back to face me. 'In there.' She nods at the room next door, not waiting for me to respond before heading inside.

This is the room where, only an hour ago, Remy Lebrun begged me to help share Aurélie's story with the world, and yet I don't sense that Cavendish's response will be quite so generous, or delivered with anywhere near as much empathy.

'Sorry, have I offended you in some way?' I offer, determined to take the moral high ground, even though I'm not the one who should be apologising.

She grunts. 'What's your angle here, Emma? Hoping to stir another scandal? Has anyone ever told you that if you kick over enough hornets' nests, eventually you're going to get stung?'

I'm biting my tongue, but I'm not sure how much longer I can manage to keep my growing ire in check. 'With all due respect, Detective Cavendish, I was invited to be here today, and I haven't even decided whether to accede to Monsieur Lebrun's wishes and help.'

'Ha!' she scoffs. 'Do yourself a favour, and save the bullshit for your ever-growing fan base, will you? It doesn't wash with me. I know you couldn't wait to get here and sink your claws into yet another high-profile story; something your publishers are probably salivating over, and your readers will devour. Well, not on my watch, Missy.'

She straightens her shoulders, which are barely contained

by the tight black polo shirt she's wearing, and I have no doubt that her upper arms have been enhanced by a lot of gym work. There isn't an ounce of fat on her, and yet she's certainly no pushover; I feel intimidated just being in her shadow.

'I'm sorry, have I wronged you in a past life or something?' I try again. 'I don't understand where all this animosity is coming from.'

She wrinkles her nose in disgust. 'I know all about your type: outwardly claiming to champion justice, while looking for any angle that will help you sell more of your books. Oh yes, I read your bestseller *Monsters Under the Bed*, and despite everyone fawning all over it, I thought the writing was average at best, and the way in which you verbally attacked those who'd investigated those boys' allegations was tantamount to libel.'

Ah, finally the penny drops; you've got to love a critic!

'So you didn't like my book.'

'No, what I despised was the one-sided view you took, leading your readers to the only conclusion you wanted them to reach: that the police force failed those boys.'

'It did!' I snap before I can stop myself; the last thing I need is to rile her further.

She shakes her head dismissively. 'What you failed to acknowledge is the level of pressure those investigators would have been under. Do you think it's easy being in the police? Constantly being criticised for doing your best? There aren't nearly enough officers to handle the volume of crime that needs investigating. Yes, those officers who were tasked with investigating those boys' claims could have uncovered the web of lies being spun by that Arthur Turgood and his cronies, but only if they'd been given the resources to properly investigate. Tell me, Emma, if you were in that situation, thrown an allegation from an orphan in social care – a boy who'd been in trouble with the police several times before – and it is one allegation on top of a hundred other cases you're supposed to be investigating, would you give it the credence it deserved?'

Wow! I thought it was tough meeting fans of my work face-to-face but this attack is on another level. I want the ground to swallow me up, but it is clear we share some kind of common ground in that we acknowledge Arthur Turgood was a master manipulator.

'My book wasn't written to target those who failed to take Freddie Mitchell's claims seriously. It was an exposé of the poor controls around social care at a time when the world wasn't as aware of wicked and devious public figures.'

'Then why include reference to the police at all? If you were only after Turgood and his cronies, why name the officers who had looked into and dismissed those boys' claims?'

'I was trying to present an accurate account of what happened. I was telling Freddie, Mike and Steve's stories, and how they survived and overcame such a horrific upbringing. I wanted to bring their abusers to justice and that's what the book did. I'm not on some personal crusade against the police.'

She snorts again. 'You could have fooled me! In fact, I'd go so far to say that your motivation for writing that book and those that have followed is probably subconsciously driven by your anger towards the officers you believe failed your family in the disappearance of your sister; *my* colleagues.'

Tears are biting at the edges of my eyes, but I won't let her see how hurt I am. 'You're wrong. I have the utmost respect for the men and women who dedicate their lives to helping others.

I'm even working with one such officer to help identify other victims of similar abuses.'

'Anything to help you flog a few extra paperbacks, right? It must be tough having so many strangers singing your praises.'

She has no idea!

'I didn't ask for all the success that came with the publication of *Monsters Under the Bed*. That Freddie, Mike and Steve finally saw justice was all the reward I needed for dedicating three years of my life to investigating their claims. I appreciate that you took a different view of the book, and you're welcome to your opinion. In fact, I'm sorry that that's how you interpreted the story, but it wasn't meant to be an attack on anyone but Arthur Turgood and the other abusers at the St Francis Home for Wayward Boys.'

I'm suddenly conscious of my raised voice, and take a breath to compose myself.

'What's your angle here?' she asks, clearly not convinced by my argument. 'Hoping to pick apart the original investigation into Aurélie's abduction? Or maybe you're looking to get in there and solve the riddle before me and my team have the chance, so you can leverage some kind of one-upmanship.'

'I told you: I wouldn't even be here if it wasn't for Aurélie's father inviting me.'

'Oh yes, and of course I'm sure Remy Lebrun's only interest is in sharing his daughter's story with the world, and has nothing to do with his underlying political aspirations. Of course, it's so clear now,' she adds with more than a hint of sarcasm, 'if I was looking to cash in on my child's nightmare, you're exactly the person I'd hire to write the story.'

It is no use; DS Cavendish is clearly not open to listening to my version of the truth, and I suppose it was always inevitable

I would eventually meet someone who didn't agree with the conclusion of *Monsters*; I just hadn't realised she would be such a tiger.

The door to the room suddenly opens, and in walks Remy Lebrun, wearing a disapproving glare of his own. 'What is all this? We can hear your raised voices next door. Is there a problem?'

Cavendish offers him a bright and cheery smile as if butter wouldn't melt in her mouth. 'No problem here, Mr Lebrun; just straightening out one or two things. I came as soon as you called; you said Aurélie is remembering things? Can she tell me where she was being held all this time? Or perhaps who took her?'

He looks at me for confirmation that all is okay, and I don't have the heart to add to his troubles, so I offer a false smile of my own.

'I think, maybe, yes,' he replies, looking back at Cavendish. 'She said something about a forest; lots of trees surrounding the property. Do you know anywhere like that nearby?'

She ponders the question, images flocking past her eyes. 'Maybe. Can you give me and Miss Hunter a few minutes, and then I'll be in.'

He fires me another look of concern, but I'm still wearing the placatory smile, and he leaves without further comment.

'Believe me or not,' I concede when we're alone, 'the only reason I'm still here is because it's possible that Aurélie may be able to help me and my partner with our own investigation. This is about more than you and me, DS Cavendish. I'm as keen as you to see the men responsible for Aurélie's imprisonment brought to justice.'

Her eyes narrow, but she doesn't say anything more; for now we've reached an uneasy impasse.

She takes a large stride closer to me, so that our faces are less than a foot apart. 'In case I haven't made myself clear: I don't like you, and I don't like what you stand for, profiting from the victims of serious crimes. I will find the people responsible for Aurélie's incarceration, and those who took her originally. That is my duty and my responsibility. If Aurélie's father insists on you hanging around, there's very little I can do about it, but mark my words, Miss Hunter: if you get in my way – or if I get even a sense that you're not flying straight – I won't hesitate to have you arrested for interfering with an active investigation and wasting police time. Do you understand?'

Her breath is warm on my face, but I daren't nod, in case she sees it as some kind of attempt to head-butt her. 'I'm sorry if I've offended you, but I only have Aurélie's best interests at heart. I won't get in your way.'

She remains stock-still. 'Good, then you won't mind waiting outside while I conduct an official interview with the victim.'

I follow her out of the room, but she is determined not to let me enter, closing the door to Aurélie's room behind her, and even lowering the blind that hangs over the window. The last thing I see before the blind is drawn is Cavendish's cocksure grin.

Chapter Sixteen

THEN

Poole, Dorset

The detective returned, still dressed in the same tight black polo shirt Aurélie had seen her in yesterday. Aurélie welcomed the presence of anyone who might be able to cut through the tension rapidly rising as she tried to make sense of this new world dawning before her eyes. Her parents were virtual strangers to her, and whilst her mother had now made countless promises to make up for the last thirteen years, they meant nothing to Aurélie, and as each second passed, she longed for the routine and familiarity of the bolthole.

The detective spoke at length with her father, whose face looked as though he'd been forced to suck a bitter lemon.

'Aurélie, my darling,' he said, turning to her, 'Detective Cavendish would like to ask you some questions about where you were being held, and she has asked me to translate the questions for her. It does not matter if you cannot fully answer them, but please try to provide as much detail as you can. Okay?'

Aurélie considered the whole exercise pointless; what more could she tell them than she already had? She was underground, there were a lot of trees, and then that long road.

'Oui,' she nodded.

Her father turned to the detective and listened intently as she spoke. 'She wants to know how you escaped... Uh, did you climb stairs... or a ladder...? How far under the ground were you?'

It was all such a blur, those final moments in the darkness. Aurélie closed her eyes and tried to recall the exact moment she'd decided it was time to go; the adrenaline had been heavy in her veins, her heart racing like it never had before, and the constant feeling that it was all part of some test or game, and that he'd duped her again.

'There was a staircase,' she answered, remembering the rough and splintered wood tearing at the upper layer of skin on her palms. She'd been so fearful that it would creak or groan and alert him to her escape, but it didn't react to her slight frame. 'I climbed the stairs until I reached the outer door... I don't know how many steps, maybe twenty or thirty. I was on my hands and knees, and it was so, so dark.'

She kept her eyes closed as her father relayed the information in English. It amazed her how professional he sounded when speaking in English, and hearing his tone triggered a fresh recollection. That day on the beach when he'd taken that phone call, he'd spoken in the same professional voice then; spoken English. She'd giggled about it before making her way down to the beach's edge to collect water for the moat.

'This outer door,' her father now translated, 'what was it made of? Was it wooden, or metallic? Plastic?'

It had been cold to the touch, damp even. The stench of the bolthole had been less when she'd reached the door, as if the limited fresh air that draughted in beneath the bottom of the door had diluted it.

'Metal,' she answered forthrightly, though she had no idea what type.

It had been so difficult to push wider, and she'd had to lean her shoulder and use all her force to widen the gap sufficiently for her to slip through. Then there was the blinding light, seeping through the trees and into eyes so unused to it. Her eyes had watered instantly, and for those first few steps she'd stumbled blindly, her eyes clamped shut for relief. Had he grabbed her at that point and forced her back down the tunnel, she would have been grateful to escape the UV rays.

'Was this metal door inside another building? Or did you next find yourself outside?'

The fallen twigs and crackling leaves had stabbed at the soles of her feet, and as she'd crashed to the ground, she'd felt every one of the twigs and shards scratching at her hands and knees. It had been agony, but the fresh, clean air filling her lungs had offered renewed hope.

'Outside… with the trees.'

Her father received new instructions from the detective. 'What type of trees were they? Oak? Sycamore? Evergreen?'

She hadn't stopped to examine the dry leaves on the ground, and it had been too painful to look up into the branches, but even if she had, she wouldn't have known one type of leaf or tree from another. The barks were a dark brown, and the leaves on the ground a russet colour.

'I don't know,' she replied.

'Tall trees? Small trees? Wide trees? Thin trees?'

She had been too frightened to remain still for long enough. Keeping her eyes closed, she tried to recall any specific detail but all she could remember was the pain as she'd crashed from one trunk into the next.

'Tall,' she finally said, hoping it provided some kind of reward for them.

'How many trees were there? Was it like an orchard, or much larger, like a forest?'

Having never stepped into an orchard, it was difficult to contextualise the memory, but it had seemed to go on and on until she'd eventually reached the edge and located the road.

'A forest, I think. There were hundreds of trees.'

'And the ground? Was there grass?'

'No, no grass. Just twigs and branches, and mud.'

The detective seemed to consider her father's translation, before extracting a tablet from her bag, and tapping away at the screen.

The sound of the door being opened jolted Aurélie's eyes apart, and she saw her father had moved across and allowed the writer to enter, much to the apparent annoyance of the detective.

'No, no way,' Cavendish said churlishly, striding across to the door before remonstrating with Aurélie's father.

The writer ignored the disagreement, moving closer, her eyes permanently fixed on Aurélie's. 'Hello again, Aurélie,' she said in accented French. 'Your dad has asked me to stay in the room with you; are you happy if I am here to listen and observe?'

For a woman who'd seemed so uncertain of the language

earlier, it was as if somebody had coached Emma Hunter on what to say. The fact that she was clutching a phone in her hand didn't go unnoticed by Aurélie.

'You can stay,' she said, if only to alleviate more of the tension. Her father would behave better with more people in the room, of that she was certain, though unsure why.

Emma fixed Cavendish with a stare, before moving to the back of the room, allowing Cavendish to retake her place at the foot of the bed. The detective now proffered the screen towards Aurélie, revealing a map with a large area of green surrounded by squiggly lines in a variety of colours.

Cavendish asked her a question, which was subsequently translated: 'How far did you walk from this forest?'

Aurélie looked into her father's eyes, as they pleaded for her to respond, but it was an impossible question. It had felt like hours, but she'd been disoriented, barely able to see and in constant fear that *he* was following close behind and would find her at any moment. She'd stopped and started more times than she could remember, trying to avoid passing cars and pedestrians. With no watch and no idea of the time, she couldn't say whether she'd walked for twenty minutes, an hour, or even longer.

Suddenly, her father's face misted as tears threatened to spill. 'I – I – I don't know. I'm sorry, but I don't know where I was.'

'It is okay, my sweet,' her mother said, squeezing her hand. 'I know this is difficult for you, so take as much time as you need. The detective says there are a number of wooded areas near this hospital, and they want to narrow down their search. They will find the person who took you.'

Her father didn't look so forgiving, and beckoned for

Cavendish to leave the room with him so that they could speak in private. Aurélie didn't like to think that she had disappointed him, but there was so little in her memory that made sense. It was almost as if she was watching someone else controlling her every move, as if some puppeteer was pulling all the strings.

'Tissue?' Emma offered, now standing the other side of the bed, holding out a small packet.

Aurélie nodded and accepted one, wiping her eyes and blowing her nose, already feeling slightly calmer. She wasn't used to having people fussing at her beck and call. There had been others she had come into contact with down the years – those in a similar precarious position to her own – but she'd swiftly learned that they were all out for number one, and that the only way to stay safe was to prioritise her own well-being. She'd learned to be self-sufficient, and having nurses constantly checking her vital signs, and others choosing her food, was all alien to her.

And now here was this writer, only a few years older, who seemed to be totally in control of her life, and Aurélie couldn't help envying her. Emma Hunter was pretty in an unassuming way, empathetic, a good listener, and the only person she'd encountered today who didn't appear to be demanding anything of her. What it must be like to be so switched on and at peace with oneself. She probably had some handsome, rich boyfriend or husband at home, maybe a couple of children who would make the Von Trapp family seem unwieldy.

Aurélie's mother clearly approved of Emma being present in the room with them. In fact, Solange almost seemed to be glowing as she spoke in broken English to the writer, as if

Aurélie wasn't even in the room anymore. Maybe, in some sense, she wasn't.

As far as the detective was concerned, Aurélie was good for only one thing: helping identify the people responsible for her abduction and confinement, but she'd already proved ill-equipped for the task.

Clearly her father's intentions – the fact that he had hired a writer to document this period in their lives – were not totally focused on her well-being.

And that left Emma: probably only here to cash in on the revelation of this returned and broken woman, but at least she wasn't making demands. At least, not yet. The question for Aurélie was whether she could trust this woman. Her parents clearly did, but it appeared evident the detective didn't.

But Aurélie had to tell someone the truth about how and why she was taken. Her parents would refuse to believe; the detective would want evidence she simply couldn't provide; but would the writer stay loyal to the truth? Emma's intentions had yet to be revealed, but of the three of them she was the best bet. All of that would have to wait for now, until Aurélie could be certain that she would be listened to, away from the prying ears of those who would look to dismiss her claims.

Chapter Seventeen

NOW

Poole, Dorset

I can't explain why, but I'm certain there is more going on here than just this fragile victim coming to terms with seeing her parents for the first time in over a decade. She jumps and twitches every time her father Remy comes into the room, and whilst I'm sure she was doing her best to answer DS Cavendish's questions, I sense there is more she wants to say but can't. Maybe I'm just allowing my imagination to run wild.

Remy and Cavendish are still outside the room debating the case for my involvement in matters, and if it wasn't for this feeling that Aurélie needs me to hang around, I think I would have made my excuses and headed home. I haven't gleaned anything that I couldn't have extrapolated from the article Tessa Imbrock cobbled together overnight. Whilst I agree with my editor that there is a story to be told here, Aurélie is nowhere near ready to tell it, and I'm not going to be able to add anything more to Cavendish's investigation.

'Is there anything you'd like to ask my daughter, Mademoiselle Hunter?' Solange's voice catches me off-guard, and brings my attention back to the room.

There's only one question I want to ask, but I'm terrified what answer Aurélie will give. On the one hand, if she says she has no idea who Anna is, and in fact has never had contact with my sister, it will feel like yet another door has been slammed in my face. However, if she does recognise her, or tells me she did come into contact with Anna, I don't think I will handle the news well. The thought of poor Anna locked in a room several feet below the ground, answering every beck and whim of some nefarious monster, with no hope of freedom... It doesn't bear thinking about.

Yet with Cavendish and Remy out of the room, this is my best chance. Unlocking my phone, I flick to the image of Anna that was used in the newspaper stories twenty years ago, and lower the phone to Aurélie's lap.

'Can you ask her if she recognises the girl in this picture?'

Solange frowns as she studies the image on the screen, but then translates my question.

Aurélie's tearful stare meets mine, and then focuses on the image. She picks up the phone and looks at the screen for a long time, before lowering it back to her lap, and shaking her head.

I don't know if I'm disappointed or relieved. Flicking my finger across the screen, I know I have one of the mocked-up older pictures I had commissioned of Anna. I need to be certain, and when I reach it, I repeat my question to Solange who duly translates. Again, Aurélie stares at the image for at least a minute before shaking her head, but there is something new in her eyes; that fear again, I think. She flicks her finger on the screen and nods her head as she passes it back. Her voice is cracking under the strain as she says something in French.

'She says she knows *this* girl,' Solange tells me, and as I lift the phone and see what she has stopped on, the breath catches in my throat.

'This girl? You know *this* girl?'

Aurélie is still nodding, and fresh tears spill against the pale and dry skin of her cheeks. I'd forgotten that the picture I'd downloaded of Jemima Hooper would show in my phone's gallery, but that is now who I am staring at, and a hundred new questions hit my mind like a chaotic firework display.

'What can you tell me about this girl? Do you know her name? When did you meet her? Was she in the same cell as you? Do you know what happened to her?'

Solange duly translates, but Aurélie doesn't offer any response initially as she begins sobbing, unable to look at the image any longer.

'Please, Aurélie, I know this girl; she was abducted from outside a shop in Gateshead in the northeast of England. Please, how do *you* know her?'

Solange is now giving me a dirty stare, suddenly ready to defend her daughter from anything my question might be implying, but it isn't meant to imply anything, I just want to know how Aurélie could have come into contact with Jemima Hooper, and, if she did, whether she might have come into contact with any of the other victims on those videos.

Solange is suddenly on her feet, jabbing her thumb against the button to call a nurse. I don't understand why at first, but then I notice the small patch slowly spreading across the thin bed sheet covering Aurélie's legs.

'I think that is enough questions for now,' Solange warns

me, and I realise now that despite Remy's declarations to the contrary, my being here isn't necessarily a united decision.

A nurse enters and Solange indicates the small puddle, and the nurse doesn't bat an eyelid as she helps Aurélie to the small bathroom, before stripping the bed. I take my cue to leave the room, as I don't want to add to any embarrassment for Aurélie, or Solange. As I head downstairs and out of the hospital, the cool breeze blowing against my cheeks provides light relief, and serves as another reminder of what Aurélie has missed for the last thirteen years. We take freedom of movement for granted, but we all have it, and it really is a blessing; even if our only exercise is commuting to and from an office, at least we get to choose which route we take.

'Emma? Emma Hunter? Kirstie Greenacre, BBC News, can you spare five minutes for an interview?'

Oh no, I hadn't realised I left my scarf in Aurélie's room, and my face is totally exposed. I've also come out via the main entrance, rather than the back.

'Sorry, no, not today,' I reply, quickening my pace, but this woman is now following me.

'Please, Emma, just a few questions. You're here to see Aurélie Lebrun, right? Is she the focus of your next investigation? What can you tell me about the people responsible for keeping her locked up for so long? How is she doing?'

This is the last thing I need, and I can already picture the newspaper headlines that will follow. In the past, I would have just hurried away and phoned Maddie and begged her to sort it out, but this needs to be nipped in the bud before any other journalists see me and make the same connection.

Stopping, I lead Kirstie Greenacre away from the hospital

to an enclosed garden, shaking my head when she tries to make eye contact with her cameraman, who's too busy smoking and chatting to another cameraman. Her hair is the colour of fire, and her makeup so precisely applied that she wouldn't look lost on a catwalk. This is precisely the sort of person I once dreamed of being, before accepting that not every ugly duckling turned into a beautiful swan.

'Just us,' I quickly add, ducking behind a large, square, raised flower bed, so that we're out of sight. 'My being here has nothing to do with Aurélie Lebrun,' I declare matter-of-factly, as if the very suggestion is offensive. I'm not usually a great liar, but I'm determined to hold my own. 'I am here visiting a very sick friend, and the last thing either of us needs is you leaping to all the wrong conclusions.'

I've never met Kirstie Greenacre before and I can't say her face is overly familiar either, but from the way she is looking at me – scorn mixed with a hint of admiration – she doesn't look convinced by my story. I can't blame her; this is precisely why I brought the scarf with me today.

'So it's just a coincidence that a woman renowned for finding missing children happens to be at the same hospital as a woman who has returned after thirteen unaccounted years?'

'Yes,' I say, embracing my inner Maddie; God, I wish she was here with me right now. That woman could talk the hind legs off a donkey. This thought makes me chuckle, as that was the expression my mum used to use to describe Anna.

'What's wrong with your friend?'

What is her problem? Seriously, I hadn't thought I'd need to go into specific details, and I'm superstitious about making stuff up about friends in case it comes true; another throwback to my childhood.

'I'm not going to go into that with you; it's private.'

I know it's a weak response, but it's the best I can offer.

'So, on the record, you're telling me you have no involvement whatsoever with Aurélie Lebrun's sudden reappearance?'

It's an interesting way she's phrased the question, and I can only conclude that she must think I've helped bring Aurélie out of her nightmare, rather than being invited as an accessory after the fact.

I place my hand across my chest. 'I swear to you that I have absolutely nothing to do with Aurélie being found and brought to this hospital. I've had absolutely no involvement in what has occurred here. Okay? Can I go now? I have an important phone call to make to my friend's family.'

It's all I can do to keep the smile from my face when she nods wistfully, and heads back out of the ornamental garden. I use the alternative exit far from the gathered throng and quickly dial Jack's number. He answers on the third ring.

'Great minds think alike; I was just about to call you.'

'Aurélie recognised Jemima Hooper's photograph!'

I know I could have built the revelation up slowly, but I don't think we have the time; the possibility that our investigation into Jemima Hooper's abduction and murder could be directly linked to Aurélie's sudden reappearance means that Jack could potentially have her case switched to the Met, and oust the tiresome DS Cavendish.

'I'm listening,' Jack says, sensing there is more.

'I did as you suggested and showed her a picture of my sister to see if she recognised her. I guess, when I was scrolling between the images, she caught a glimpse of Jemima's face and said she'd met her.'

'Oh my God! This is incredible! Do you realise what this means? What else did she say? Did she say when and where she saw her?'

'I didn't get to ask. The picture of Jemima really shook her up, because she suddenly started sobbing, and then... then she wet herself.'

'Blimey! What did you say to trigger that kind of reaction?'

'Nothing! I merely asked how she knew her. Aurélie's reaction was odd, and I'm certain there's a lot more she hasn't told us yet. You need to get down here.'

'Already one step ahead of you; that's why I was going to phone. I spoke to DCS Rawani, and he thinks I could be of use to the team in Dorset and has arranged for me to come across for a few days. I'll be with you in the morning.'

'Rawani wants you to take control of Aurélie's case, right? Based on what I've told you, I think there are reasonable grounds to suspect that Aurélie's situation is relevant to the work we're doing.'

'It's not that easy. This isn't some American cop show where the FBI can claim jurisdiction of local cases. Aurélie identifying Jemima could be significant, or it could be nothing at all. I need to come down and do a little more investigating first.'

'Oh,' I say, unable to keep the despondency from my tone.

'Listen, it's a great discovery, and depending what else she's able to tell us, it might help shape how we direct our investigation into Jemima's time away, but we need to take this one step at a time.'

'I'm not sure the DS down here will appreciate you trampling on her investigation in your big size twelves.'

'I'm a size eight actually. *Tiny feet* is what some of our colleagues call me. Anyway, I'm sure it will be fine.'

'You haven't met her yet,' I warn under my breath.

'When you go back, see if she's able to tell you anything else. I'd come down straightaway, but I've got Mila tonight. Remember?'

I do recall him mentioning his daughter having been at a birthday party last night. 'Okay, what time will you be down?'

'I can pick you up from yours first thing? I really don't know the area well, and it would be good to make use of your local knowledge.'

'Sure, no problem. See you then.'

I hang up, pocket my phone and head back into the ornamental garden, sneaking a peek to see whether Kirstie Greenacre has bought my story. I can't see her anywhere nearby, but take a wide detour of the main entrance, heading around to the back of the hospital, and walking in undisturbed.

Chapter Eighteen

NOW

Poole, Dorset

Both Cavendish and Remy are back in Aurélie's room when I return, and although Cavendish glares at me as I enter, she makes no effort to speak to me or expel me from the room; presumably the quiet word she had with Remy ended with him victorious. Hardly surprising when he's forged a career in politics and diplomacy.

Cavendish is showing Aurélie the map on the tablet again, and asking if anything looks familiar. The tearful headshakes Aurélie is responding with are clearly not welcome, judging by the ever tenser tone of the questions.

'What can you tell me about the road you walked along? Any landmarks, shops or signs you can recall?'

At least Remy is treading more carefully with his translation of the questions, though it doesn't appear to be making any difference. Given everything Aurélie has been through, I'm surprised she's even able to communicate at all.

She looks exhausted, and the day is taking its toll as we reach lunchtime. The consultant whose care Aurélie finds herself under – a very tall man in a white coat called Mr Truffaut – insists everyone leave to allow Aurélie to eat, and whilst Cavendish excuses herself to go and make contact with her team, I'm left in the hospital's canteen with Remy and Solange.

'Why don't you two find us a table, and I'll get us some refreshments,' I offer sincerely. 'Tea and sandwiches okay?'

'Thank you but coffee will be fine,' Remy says dismissively, leading his wife into the throng of gathered visitors and hospital staff grabbing ten minutes to feed before returning to their purpose for being in the building.

There are other eating establishments in the hospital, upstairs, but The Dolphin Restaurant has the largest seating capacity, and being on the lower ground floor is out of sight of the journalists gathered outside. It's still possible that the three of us could be spotted, but less likely, given the volume of people already crammed around tables.

Satisfied that they have found somewhere for us to sit, I don't rush around the food counters, figuring the two of them could probably do with some alone time to process everything that has happened to them since they were first contacted by the British police yesterday. Locating tuna mayonnaise, chicken salad, and cheese sandwiches, I purchase crisps, fruit and hot drinks for the three of us, then tentatively carry the tray through the tables until I reach the two of them.

'I figured you must be hungry,' I say, placing the tray on the table, and showing Solange the selection. She accepts the tuna mayonnaise gratefully, before lifting one of the cups of tea from the tray.

142

Remy looks at the two remaining sandwiches, before picking up the chicken salad and thanking me with his eyes.

'How do you think Aurélie is coping with everything?' I ask innocently to break the awkward silence that has formed.

Solange nibbles at the crust of her sandwich. 'I just wish… I wish I could take away the last thirteen years and go back to that day… I never thought I would see my daughter again, and now that she is here, it doesn't feel real; she doesn't feel real.'

Remy's arm shoots across the table and squeezes her hand gently, and it is as if a silent message has passed between them: we must stay strong. She nods in acknowledgement.

'You have experience in reuniting parents with their children,' he says, turning to face me. 'Tell me, does it get easier?'

I don't doubt that every parent and child would react differently, and I'd certainly argue that the way Owen and Diane Curtis reacted to news that daughter Sally was in fact alive and well was quite different from how Richard and Elizabeth Hilliard did when I found Cassie. There is no manual on how to respond in the horrific circumstance that a child is abducted, let alone in how to do so when reunited. Not all parents are so fortunate, as I know only too well.

'You'll find a way,' I say eventually, opting for hope over reason. 'Is she how you imagined?'

'No,' Solange answers instinctively. 'She doesn't look like my little Aurélie, and I think that is the hardest part; it feels like we are reconnecting with a stranger.'

Remy is squeezing her hand tighter now, maybe because she isn't toeing the party line, but she pulls her hand from his grasp, chastising him in French I can't understand.

'Forgive my husband, Emma, it is not in his nature to show

emotion. What are your thoughts about our daughter? I just want to make her happy, but I don't think I know how.'

I lower my sandwich so she has my full attention. 'I don't think your daughter has been happy for some time, Solange. It's possible she's forgotten how to be happy.' I fall silent, allowing the proclamation to sink in. 'But the important thing is she is out of that person's clutches now, and although it is going to take time and patience, I can't think of two better people to help her remember how to find happiness again.'

Solange is now close to tears, but Remy remains unmoved. 'Aurélie seems to like you though, which is a good sign.'

I've barely said more than two words to her, so I'm not sure how he's reached such a conclusion, but I don't challenge it.

'Monsieur Lebrun, I know you were keen for me to tell Aurélie's story, but I still think it may be a bit soon. Her focus needs to be on recovery, and as she settles into her new life it may help her open up and share more details about what she's been through. The police – DS Cavendish – is keen to catch and prosecute the people responsible for her absence, and I sense she's not keen having me around.'

'I have spoken to Cavendish, and she understands that you are here at our request. She will not give you any more trouble.'

The glare she gave me upstairs would suggest the contrary. 'Even so,' I continue, 'I'd hate to be the reason her investigation doesn't run as quickly and smoothly as possible. Maybe it would be an idea for me to leave it for a few days, and come back when Aurélie is feeling more up to it?'

'No, please stay,' Solange interrupts. 'My husband is right: she responds better when you are in the room. I don't know why, but it's as if she trusts you more than anyone else. I know it sounds silly – maybe it's because you're of a similar age, I don't know – but I believe she is more likely to open up to you.'

'The language barrier makes it difficult,' I try to explain, ungrateful for the pressure I'm suddenly feeling. 'It's one thing to type my questions into a translation app, but I can't translate the answers back.'

'I don't mind asking the questions for you,' Solange offers eagerly.

'With all due respect, I'm not sure Aurélie will be able to answer my questions with either of you in the room. Believe me, there are plenty of things I wouldn't want my own mother to know about me.'

'That consultant Mr Truffaut perhaps could translate for you,' Remy now suggests.

'I'm sure he has more important things to do,' I smile. 'My agent did suggest we could hire an interpreter – a professional – and make them sign a non-disclosure document so that you would be satisfied the details wouldn't be leaked in the newspapers.' I take a bite of my sandwich. 'But that will all take time. Let me go and try and organise something, and then I can return after the weekend, giving the three of you time to just be there for each other. I'm certain it will do you *all* the world of good.'

Silence descends as we continue to eat, and when we are done, Remy thanks me for coming, and Solange hugs me. I pass them my business card, and promise that I will keep in touch. Watching them head back up the stairs, I can't help wondering whether the three of them will ever feel like a family again.

Finding my best friend eating an ice-cream on my porch is the best reward after what has been a challenging day.

'Hello, stranger,' she jokes, with a lick of the soft vanilla ice-cream. 'What can I say? Absence makes the heart grow fonder.' A small carry-on suitcase stands upright at her feet.

'Why didn't you tell me you were coming to visit?' I ask, reaching into my satchel to remove my house keys, and letting us in.

'I'm assuming you can probably guess why I'm here, and I'd put money on the likelihood that you're returning from Poole Hospital.'

'Your editor insisted you come down for the story about Aurélie then?'

She grimaces. 'He wasn't best pleased when I told him I'd outsourced it to Tessa Imbrock, but, in my defence, how was I supposed to know exactly who the strange woman at the hospital would be? Have you seen her then?'

The Lebruns haven't made me sign a confidentiality agreement, and although I was keen to avoid confirming anything to Kirstie Greenacre, I know Rachel won't share my secret.

'That obvious?'

'When you hurried home yesterday, I didn't connect the dots, but as soon as I saw the news this morning, I figured it had to be related. How is she? Tessa said she's in a pretty bad state.'

I nod, picturing Aurélie in that hospital bed and that look of pure terror she fired at me after my meeting with her dad.

'It's hard to imagine how she must be feeling. Kept in

captivity for most of her life, suddenly out in a world she doesn't recognise, and then to be reunited with parents she doesn't connect with. I feel so sorry for her. And that's not even considering what kind of mistreatment she's suffered at the hands of those who took her. The work I'm doing with Jack has already shown me how badly some of these abducted children will have been treated.'

Rachel's eyes widen in anticipation. 'So you're going to help me get an interview with the parents then?'

I'm dumbfounded at the question. 'What?'

She must sense my ire, and quickly tries to pacify me. 'Don't be mad! When my editor called me into his office this morning, he was livid that I'd passed the story to Tessa and given her the scoop. He threatened to sack me until I told him that I might still have an in that nobody else would get. I didn't mention you by name, but he knows we're friends so he'll probably figure it out soon enough.'

'And so that's why you're here? You want to use me to get to Aurélie and her parents, and to get yourself out of trouble?'

She opens her mouth to deny the charge, but then relents. 'I know that makes me a pretty shit friend, and I'm sorry to put you in this position, but I didn't know what else to do. He was this close to letting me go, and I was desperate. I'm sorry, I shouldn't have put you in this position, but in my defence, we are a great team. Just remember how well we worked together on the Sally Curtis case. You have to admit it was good being able to bounce ideas and theories off one another. This could be like that.'

I am silently seething because I am angry at her actions, but know deep down I am going to end up agreeing to help her because she is my oldest and dearest friend.

'This isn't fair, Rachel.'

She moves across the room and rests her hands on my arms. 'I know, and you're right to be cross with me. But there's something that might help sweeten the deal... I studied French at A-Level, and I'm still fairly fluent; could come in handy, no?'

She's got me there, and having her with me would mean not having to search for an interpreter. I'm not sure how DS Cavendish will feel about having another civilian in the room, but selfishly that feels like even more reason to have Rachel with me.

'Okay, okay, but we do this on my terms. I will introduce you to Aurélie's parents, but it is up to them whether they agree to allow you to be involved. I can't promise they'll agree to an interview either.'

Rachel's eyes glow as a huge smile breaks across her cheeks. 'Oh, thank you, thank you. You won't regret this, I promise!'

I hope she's right.

'Did you drive down?' I ask, as a fresh thought strikes.

'Of course. It's parked down the road. How come?'

I pull on my satchel, link my arm in hers. 'Because Aurélie told the detective in charge that she'd been held in a wooded area of some kind, probably within a five-to-ten-mile radius of the hospital. I thought we could go and take a look.'

Chapter Nineteen

THEN

Poole, Dorset

'What else can you tell us about the forest?' Cavendish asked again, unintentionally sighing as the frustration of the afternoon got to her.

What more could Aurélie tell her? No, she didn't remember any specific types of flowers that might help narrow down exactly which wooded area she was in. No, she couldn't recall any specific birdsong that might belong to a specific type of bird in a known location. No, there was nothing remotely memorable about the grey strip of road she'd trundled along. In truth, she couldn't remember much at all after that first breath of freedom filled her lungs. Vague flashes of memory were being bloated by whimsy and imagination. If she were to actually tell Cavendish what she remembered of the journey, Aurélie would say she'd sprouted wings and flown to the hospital. She knew it to be inaccurate, but right now it was difficult to tell the difference between the real and dream worlds.

In fact, she couldn't be certain all of this – the hospital, Cavendish, the wrinkled version of her parents, Emma Hunter – wasn't an elaborate dream from which *he* would forcibly wake her.

Cavendish showed her the device's screen again, this time a photographic view of dense foliage and bark. 'What about this one? This is from Canford Heath Nature Reserve; does this look like where you could have been? Does the name Canford Heath mean anything to you?'

Aurélie's father duly translated.

What was the point? *He'd* never told her where they were. It had come as quite a shock to find herself in such an open space surrounded by nature. For a long time she'd assumed she was being held on some kind of wasteland, where the passing public wouldn't hear her cries. She'd tried screaming for help – in the early days – but it had soon proved pointless; the only person who'd heard was the same monster keeping her in the darkness.

Aurélie nodded as her eyes wandered over the image. No, it didn't look like the forest she'd stumbled through, but then she could barely remember it, so who was she to say it wasn't right? If the forest was near the hospital, then it could very well have been where she'd stumbled from. If the police searched it, maybe they'd find the bolthole and his cabin.

'This looks familiar?' Cavendish said excitedly. 'You recognise Canford Heath?'

Aurélie waited for her father to repeat the words, anguish gripping his once warm eyes. She nodded again, relieved when it seemed to bring an end to all the questions.

Cavendish scrolled to a second image of the same forest but from a different angle. This time, a trail of grey concrete could be seen through the green leaves. It was possible it was the same road she'd found and staggered along, wasn't it? She nodded again, and watched as the detective's excitement grew.

'You've done brilliantly, Aurélie,' she praised. 'I'll have my team scour the forest now.'

'They're going to search the forest now,' her father translated.

Cavendish locked the screen of the device and placed it in a shoulder bag. 'I'll keep you updated,' she said to Aurélie's parents, before peeling out of the room, a noticeable spring in her step.

Remy slumped down in the chair to Aurélie's left. He looked exhausted, and as Aurélie tried to focus on his face, searching for the figure who'd been a superhero to her once upon a time, she suddenly felt overwhelmed by her own fatigue. She had no idea what time it was – the sun's rays still bright beneath the edge of the drawn blind – but she knew it was afternoon. All she wanted to do was sleep, but now her mother had started talking again; telling her all the wonderful things they would do together once Aurélie was discharged from the hospital: a ski trip to Val d'Isere, wine tasting in Bordeaux, sailing on the French Riviera, sightseeing in Paris. It wasn't that Aurélie wasn't grateful, but she couldn't look beyond the day. She couldn't escape the feeling that he was still out there, waiting to ruin this reunion.

A knock at the door was followed by the straight-shouldered, stern-looking Mr Truffaut. His thick salt and pepper eyebrows arched, practically meeting in the middle. Despite his advanced years – Aurélie estimated he was in his late fifties or early sixties – there was a rugged handsomeness too.

'Bonjour,' he greeted them all, before continuing in broken French, mixed with English. 'Monsieur and Madame Lebrun, I wish to speak to your daughter privately about... I need to ask her some personal questions about her time away... For her sake, I believe it might be better if you are not here when I speak to her.'

Aurélie's legs tensed beneath the bedsheet, but she kept a passive expression on her face.

'We're not going anywhere,' Solange answered for both of them, leaning over the bed as if somehow trying to form a protective shield.

'Please, Madame Lebrun, I understand you want to protect your daughter, but my questions are sensitive, and I must respect my patient's confidentiality.'

Aurélie didn't appreciate the serious nature of his tone, and remained very still, uncertain whether she should insist her parents leave, or hope they stayed to keep her safe.

'Absolutely not!' Remy responded forthrightly. 'We are her parents, and if you have anything to ask, you will ask in our presence.'

Frustrated, Mr Truffaut now looked directly at Aurélie, his grey eyes appealing for her accord. It was impossible to see what was going on inside that man's head, and what could possibly be so sensitive he felt the need to protect her privacy? Somewhere in the back of her mind, she continued to muffle the voice telling her exactly what Truffaut wanted to discuss.

Looking from Truffaut to her parents, she shook her head. 'I would prefer they stay.'

Truffaut's tongue probed the inside of his top lip, before he turned to the clipboard of notes in his hands. 'Very well, it is your decision, Aurélie, but if you change your mind after I begin, then you are only to say, and we can continue in private.'

The voice in her head was growing louder.

'When Aurélie arrived in the department,' Truffaut began, 'she was thoroughly examined by the team on duty, searching for injuries in need of priority treatment. We discovered evidence of bruising and healed bones courtesy of X-ray and MRI.' He looked down at his notes, as if making eye contact would be too painful. 'With Aurélie's consent we also carried out a sexual assault examination.' He looked directly at Aurélie again. 'Are you sure you wish me to continue?'

Her toes crossed and uncrossed beneath the sheet, barely perceptible to anyone in the room, as the voice in her head exploded. How could she justify asking her parents to leave? Instead, she nodded her agreement.

'Very well,' Truffaut said, again focusing on his notes. 'We identified lacerations of the hymen, followed by ecchymosis discolouration, and abrasions. Given the nature of the injuries, it is clear that Aurélie was exposed to sexual intercourse during her absence.'

Aurélie continued to look straight ahead, as she felt both sets of her parents' eyes turning on her.

'Furthermore, the nature of the scarring in that area is consistent with the intercourse being non-consensual.'

Solange burst into tears, the sound of her wail echoing off the low polystyrene ceiling tiles. Remy didn't seem to know where to look, his eyes darting over the walls as if trying to read some hidden meaning.

Why was it such a shock for them? What did they think

she'd been exposed to during all that time? She'd told them how horrific the situation had been – at least she'd given them the abridged version – but they must have suspected that *he* had assaulted her, surely? Had they naively convinced themselves that he'd kept her locked beneath the ground and kept his hands to himself?

'Photographic evidence of the injuries, along with a report written by one of our Sexual Abuse specialists, has been forwarded to the police, and, with your permission, Aurélie, I will communicate this message to Detective Sergeant Cavendish, who I expect will wish to discuss it with you too. I am very sorry.'

Truffaut remained where he was, waiting for her confirmation to continue.

Remy's tear-stained face lurched into view, blocking out Truffaut's arched eyebrows. 'I swear to you, my darling, we will find the man responsible and have him punished for what he has done to you. If it is the last thing I do, I will watch him hang.'

She appreciated the sentiment, even if it was thirteen years too late. Where was this anger and determination in the aftermath of her abduction? Why hadn't he kicked in every door to find her?

Aurélie bit down on the inside of her cheek for courage. 'Continue, Monsieur Truffaut. Ask your next question.'

The prospect that there was more horror to come had Solange and Remy turning back to face Truffaut once more.

'Are you sure you want me to say in front of your parents? I am sure they would understand if—'

'They need to hear,' she interrupted, 'and I would prefer it come from you.'

'Very well,' Truffaut said glumly. 'There was also evidence that Aurélie was pregnant in the last three years, and that she carried a baby full-term.'

Aurélie shut her eyes as the memory of the labour roared through her ears. She'd wanted the infant torn from her, not out of spite but because she could not forgive herself for bringing an innocent life into such a hellish environment. It had been his child, but she had vowed she would love him regardless, but she hadn't been given the chance.

'He was stillborn,' Aurélie told them, her eyes still closed so she wouldn't have to see their disappointed and pitying stares. 'He was taken from me, and buried where I could not see. It was a blessing for him, I think.'

The warmth of tears splashed against her cheeks, as she remembered cradling the baby in her arms, praying he would silently pass to a better place.

Solange's arms enveloped around her, lifting her from the mattress and holding her firm. 'My sweet, sweet child, I am so sorry.'

Aurélie felt the tidal wave of emotion crash over her, and then the tears fell. Burying her head in her mother's shoulder she wept for all the pain, the horror, the fear, and the tragedy of the last thirteen years. Though she did not recognise the face of the older woman, the embrace felt so real that for the first time she allowed herself to believe that she wasn't dreaming, and that the nightmare was finally over.

Chapter Twenty

NOW

Poole, Dorset

When I'd suggested Rachel and I drive to Poole in search of wooded areas where Aurélie could have been held, I hadn't taken into account the number of cars we would encounter as school-rush traffic dominated the road. We're now sitting in a traffic jam that I swear hasn't progressed in the last four changes of the lights ahead. The problem seems to be that this junction allows traffic to join from the left, and those cars are blocking the junction whenever our light is green, so it's impossible to move forwards.

Rachel's growling sigh is reflective of how we are both feeling. 'This is impossible,' she adds, though it isn't needed. 'Are we any closer to any of the locations on the map?'

I study my phone where the map app is open, focused on the area immediately surrounding the hospital at the southern point of Poole. 'If we abandoned the car here, the first location of interest is a five-minute walk,' I explain, knowing that abandoning the car is not an option, but looking to provide context. 'This is the wooded area furthest from the hospital, just under five miles away, so it would have probably taken Aurélie an hour or so to walk from here. Seems unlikely that she could have walked so far in her condition and *not* been spotted by passing traffic. This is the main road that leads eventually to the hospital, though, depending where she would have emerged from the trees, there might be alternative, quieter roads she could have followed.'

Rachel looks as though she is genuinely considering abandoning her hatchback, but then the brake lights on the car in front go off, and we shuffle forwards. This time, four cars actually progress, leaving us second at the lights and hopefully next to move through the junction.

'How far is Worthing from here, would you say?' Rachel says after a minute of comfortable silence.

I consider the question. 'Maybe ninety miles, give or take. A couple of hours in the car down the M27 and A27. Why?'

'I was just thinking, that's all… Aurélie was abducted from Worthing, and I would have assumed they'd have taken her somewhere further away where she wouldn't be recognised. It's almost as if the plan was to hide her in plain sight.'

'Underground is hardly plain sight,' I counter, though she makes a valid point.

I don't know why, but I've always assumed that when Anna was taken from us, she would have ended up somewhere far away from Weymouth, but is it possible that she's been much closer to home this entire time? That idea makes me shudder; that she could be so close and I haven't found her.

'Oh, we're *finally* moving again,' Rachel notes as the car in front lurches onwards again, and this time I'm relieved we make it through the lights.

Three minutes later we pull into the car park for Delph Woods in the suburb of Broadstone. A road sign indicates the nearby cricket club, but apart from a rust-covered campervan, we are alone in the car park. The trees lining the car park are tall, and cast an eerie shadow over the small concrete area we find ourselves in. I'm surprised there isn't a police presence here, but then I don't think this is the only car park for these woods, so it's possible we're just the wrong side. The last thing I want is to give DS Cavendish any more ammunition against me.

'You look pensive,' Rachel comments, as we exit the car.

I smile at her. 'Sorry, I was just thinking about the detective in charge of Aurélie's case; we didn't exactly hit it off.'

'Oh well, you can't expect *everyone* to fall in love with you, Emma, even if most of us do.'

She links her arm through mine, and drags me towards a gap in the low wooden barrier leading into the dense and dark forest. There is a sudden chill that bites at my bare arms, causing goosebumps to prickle my skin.

'You all right?' Rachel asks.

It must be the prospect that these very woods – though it is less likely – could have been Aurélie's prison for so many years. I get a similar feeling whenever I pass by an actual prison; it's like a thousand lost years call out their remorseful song.

'I'll be fine,' I tell her, tightening my grip on her arm as fallen twigs and leaves crackle beneath our feet.

It hasn't rained on the south coast for the best part of two weeks, and the early summer heat is showing no signs of dissipating, yet still the chill remains in the air. The trees are like bony arms stretching high above our heads, the branches interlocking like fingers to keep their treasure out of sight. Looking up, the sky is but a few snatches of light where the foliage allows the occasional gap. The ground is uneven, and although it feels like we are walking on some kind of path, in truth it is a route pocked with trees to the left, right and middle. The pathway isn't marked out, and so I would imagine the ground here has been worn by a deluge of dog walkers and bird-spotters down the years.

We move further into the forest's tight grip, and I'm now regretting ever suggesting we come on this search. Looking back over my shoulder, I can no longer see where we first entered, as if somehow the trees have moved to form a barrier around us, from which we will never escape. Rachel doesn't appear to be affected by the eeriness, striding onwards, tugging me with her. The woods didn't seem all that large on the map on my phone, but now that we're here there's no let-up in sight. No wonder Aurélie found it so difficult to describe where she'd come from. I've only been in these woods for five minutes, and I already feel lightheaded and disoriented.

The path is now gradually declining, and the loose twigs and branches beneath our feet slip against the dry earth, making it difficult for our shoes to grip. Again, maybe I was being naïve to assume that the area marked out in green on the app wouldn't be level, but I can see now that the belly of the forest is much lower ground than where we entered. Turning to look back over my shoulder again, it is only now I can see just how far we've already dipped.

'Can you hear that splashing sound?' Rachel asks now, and in truth I can't hear anything over my rapidly beating heart.

She doesn't wait for me to respond, instead pulling me in the direction of whatever she's heard, even as I try to plant my feet and slow our descent; I just want to head back to the car, and I can't explain why.

'Listen, do you hear it?' Rachel asks, pausing for a moment.

I stop and try to concentrate on any sound that isn't the drumming in my chest. She's right, there is the distant sound of splashing water, though it isn't obvious what is causing the disturbance.

'Come on,' Rachel declares excitedly, hauling me onwards once more.

I'm trying to keep my bearings so that we'll be able to find our way back to the car park when we're done, but we've now left the well-trodden path and have to duck beneath low branches, and avoid stinging nettles as we duck and dive. I wish I'd left a trail of breadcrumbs, and I can't ignore the feeling that we are Hansel and Gretel, about to encounter some horrible monster.

Rachel holds her arm out and stops me as the trees suddenly open before us, and I find we're standing on a manmade wooden pontoon that surrounds a large expanse of water. Beyond the lake the forest's tight grip prevents us from seeing what lies beyond the trees.

'Did you know there was a lake here too?' Rachel asks, scanning the horizon.

Unlocking my phone I check the map again, but I have lost mobile signal, and the map won't allow me to zoom in for further detail. 'No, I didn't,' I reply, grateful that the sun's rays are warming my skin here. 'Looks like it's a lake for fishing,' I add, nodding towards a placard to our left, which dictates the rules to be followed by those wishing to fish here.

'Well, you certainly wouldn't want to swim in it,' Rachel comments, turning her nose up at the grey-green colour of the water, and the noticeable pong now emanating from it.

It's no wonder there is nobody fishing here; I don't think I'd want to eat anything that emerged from such a bog. That said, it doesn't appear to have put off the local wildlife, as a seagull swoops down and scoops something into its mouth before soaring away. The same splashing noise we heard earlier accompanies it.

'Let's follow the pontoon around the lake for a bit,' Rachel suggests, setting off still heading away from where we parked her car.

The presence of the lake, and the probability that this place was once swarming with fishermen and fisherwomen, makes it even less likely to be the location of the underground prison, and my fear subsides as we continue along the pontoon. The trees to our left form an insurmountable fence, the network of branches intertwining in a deliberate way to keep unwanted guests out. But then we come to a break in the trees. There is evidence that this hole has been deliberately made, as there is evidence of sawn branches, though the cuts are years old.

Rachel doesn't think twice before driving us through the gap, and back into the woods. 'Sorry,' she tells me, 'I couldn't stand the smell any longer.'

The warmth instantly leaves us as we go in search of the well-trodden path once more, but it must have twisted off in a different direction, as we are now stuck ducking and diving again.

We both spot the roof of the shack at the same time, and we freeze.

'You can see that too, right?' Rachel asks, a small puff of condensation escaping her lips.

'Probably just a small hut for birdwatchers,' I suggest, not believing a single word.

'Only one way to find out,' Rachel says, pulling me closer, but this time I really plant my feet.

There was no mention of a nearby lake in the statement Aurélie gave to the police, or to her parents as far as I'm aware, so there is every reason this isn't what we were looking for. And yet…

'We should probably phone DS Cavendish,' I say cautiously. 'If this is—'

'We don't know *what* this is,' she interrupts. 'You said yourself that she isn't your biggest fan; how's she going to react if you drag her out on a wild goose chase? It's probably nothing, but if it turns out to be something more, she'll be our first call. Okay?'

She's such a bad influence, and that's why I like having her around, challenging me to be more than my neuroses. Nodding, I follow her through the trees, my clothes snagging on some pointier branches low down, until the trees part, at a clearing. There are ankle-high stumps protruding from the brown carpet of dried leaves and twigs, where trees have been felled to allow this single-storey cabin to be built. It looks long-abandoned; the perspex windows covered in mud and dust, and impossible to see through. It is much more of a lodge than a hideaway for bird-spotters, and a padlock hangs from the makeshift wooden door.

'Do you reckon anyone still lives there?' Rachel whispers.

'I doubt it; this is public land, so I wouldn't have thought anyone would have permission to build on it, let alone live here. I don't like it, Rachel.'

Memories of Hansel and Gretel illustrations flood my mind, and I'm relieved the roof of the shack doesn't appear to be made from gingerbread.

'I think we should phone Cavendish,' I say again, but Rachel isn't listening, moving closer to the shack, before circling around it towards the rear.

I remain rooted where I am, conscious that if this is a crime scene, we've already breached inspection procedures.

Rachel stops still, and calls for me to join her, her eyes not leaving whatever has caught her attention. 'I think you were right,' she says, as I arrive at her side. 'You should call that DS Cavendish.'

I can't disagree with her as my gaze falls on the two bolted wooden doors poking out of the ground.

Chapter Twenty-One

NOW

Poole, Dorset

'And what made you go to *those* particular woods?' Cavendish isn't happy when I deliver the news.

'No specific reason,' I say honestly. 'We were just out for a drive and this was the first place we checked.'

'And Aurélie didn't tell you to specifically go there when we weren't in the room. Just strikes me as particularly good luck that *you* are the person to discover the site.'

'We don't know that it is for sure,' I counter, biting my lip, hoping she won't hear the anxiety in my voice.

'Aurélie told me she was being held in Canford Heath Nature Reserve, so why would she do that if in fact it was Delph Woods in Broadstone? Why would she give me an alternative location unless... Wait, is this something you've cooked up with that father of hers? I'm sure book sales will be nicely boosted if it turns out the writer played an integral role in tracking down those responsible.'

'That isn't what happened,' I reply defensively.

'It all makes sense. I knew there had to be a reason he was so insistent you hang around. Is this how it worked in those other investigations? The victims' families gave you exclusive access and information that they kept from the police so that you could claim all the credit.'

What is her problem? I would never dream of doing something so underhand, but I don't know if there is any point in continuing to argue. Nothing I say or do will make a difference to Cavendish's opinion of me. Maybe Rachel was right, and it was inevitable that I'd eventually meet someone who wouldn't fall over their feet for me. If anything, I should be grateful for the refreshing change of a reader who doesn't want my autograph.

'You two had best not enter my potential crime scene,' she grizzles next.

'We wouldn't,' I reassure her. 'I understand the importance of preserving the scene.'

'Mark my words, Emma, if photographs of the shack that didn't come from my SOCOs end up appearing in your book, there'll be trouble. You and your friend wait in the car park for me and my team to arrive. Do you understand?'

I feel like a naughty child, chastised for not using common sense. 'We will wait in the car park for you.'

She cuts the line, leaving me alone in silence, and that's when panic sets in. I wasn't concentrating after we discovered those shutters in the ground, so when Rachel told me to find somewhere with a signal to make the call, I didn't question her decision to remain behind in case anyone emerged from the shack. Pocketing the phone, I rush back into the forest, though it isn't easy to maintain any kind of pace, such is the trail of twigs and branches.

By the time I reach the gap in the trees to the lake, I'm not even certain I'm on the right course. When I return to the woods, I can't see the shack, and panic begins to rise in my throat. The trees and foliage are so vast and nothing looks familiar. Trying to get any kind of bearings, I head right, believing the car park is to the left, but I'm soon returning to the car park, and have to double back. My chest is tight with anxiety at the prospect that not only can I not find my way back to the shack, but I may never find Rachel again.

It's a ridiculous thought, and I slap myself hard on the cheek to check my emotions and engage rationality. When I returned to the car park I didn't come via the lake, so all I need to do is follow the well-trodden path and keep my internal compass heading straight. After what feels like ten minutes – but is probably five or fewer – I still can't see the shack, and that's when I begin to call out Rachel's name. The forest swallows me deeper with my calling unreturned, and then as I'm straining to see anything I recognise, I catch a glimpse of the roofline, and plough through until I am once more outside the shack.

My relief is tempered, as Rachel is not where I left her. Calling out her name again, I'm conscious of getting closer to the outbuilding and shutters, but a part of me already knows Rachel reneged on her promise not to go investigating.

'Rachel!' I shout. 'Cavendish is on her way. We need to wait at the car park.'

There is no response, and no sound save for the roar of tension in my ears.

'Rachel!' I yell again, this time moving left and right trying to catch a glimpse of colour or movement.

What if whoever was holding Aurélie was still in the shack, and saw Rachel poking around and grabbed her? Or what if she was snooping around and fell into some kind of manmade trap, but is unconscious and that's why she's not responding?

I know I'm being irrational again, and that it's just as likely she got bored of waiting and headed back to the car park on a different route to mine.

'Rachel!' I try again, unsure how easy it will be to find my own way back to the car park unaided.

'Oh good, you're back,' she calls out, emerging from the rear of the shack.

'What the hell are you doing?' I reprimand to cover my relief. 'I told you to stay well back.'

She waves away my concern. 'It's fine, I didn't touch anything. Nobody will know I was poking about.' She pauses when she sees the anger in my glare. 'Relax, will you? I just wanted to make sure that the place is actually empty, and that the person responsible wasn't hiding inside. He isn't, as far as I can tell. I found another door at the back; this one was open, suggesting whoever was there last left in something of a hurry.'

I can picture Cavendish's face if she ever learns that Rachel went inside. 'We need to head back to the car park and wait for the police.'

'Hey, of course,' she says too easily.

I'd expected her to try and tempt me to snoop around inside too, or to suggest we take some pictures, and the fact that she hasn't must mean that she already has. We will cross that bridge later; right now I just want to get away from this creepy place.

We've only just made it back to the car when Cavendish comes screeching into the car park with unnecessary fuss. She parks directly behind Rachel's car, cutting off any chance of us leaving; not that we'd planned to.

'I want you to show me where this place is,' she demands when I've lowered the window to speak to her. 'The two of you will lead me and DC Dixon to the site, and then he will accompany you both back here to take your statements.'

It isn't a request, so I can neither agree nor disagree. Exiting the car, Rachel fires me a glance that suggests she gets my point about Cavendish strongly disliking me. This is further underlined as we dip into the forest, and Cavendish focuses her questions on Rachel, leaving me and DC Dixon to follow behind.

'Whose idea was it to come here today?' she asks Rachel.

'Um…' Rachel begins, trying to find a way not to drop me in it. 'It was a joint decision, I think.'

'A joint decision? How does that work?'

'Um, well, we looked at a map of the area, and this just happened to be the first one we came to from Weymouth, that's all.'

'I see, and so where were you due to go next?'

Rachel is visibly squirming directly in front of me, and I can't blame her, as we hadn't actually discussed where we would go next.

'I'm not sure,' she concedes. 'We hadn't got that far.'

'So when you left Weymouth today, it was your sole intention to come to these woods?'

'No, not exactly. We just wanted to have a drive around – get our bearings – and then return home. It was only by chance that this is the only place we got to.'

Even I can hear that it doesn't add up, and I can't blame Cavendish for jumping to the wrong conclusion about what we're doing here. DC Dixon smiles apologetically at me. He can't be much older than Aurélie; his cheeks are still plump with baby fat; and there are no thinning patches in his shaved head of hair. He is wearing a short-sleeved shirt and a tie that doesn't sit comfortably and looks as though it has already been tugged and straightened into submission. He remains silent as Cavendish continues to shoot holes in our story.

Rachel's internal compass is clearly better than mine, because we are soon approaching the low roof of the shack, at which point Cavendish tells Rachel and me to remain where we are, whilst she and Dixon survey the scene. They creep forward, separating so that she can follow around to the rear of the property, whilst Dixon heads straight for the front door, banging a fist against it to catch the attention of anyone who might be inside.

Cavendish stops as soon as she sees the shutter-type doors in the ground. They stick up at an acute angle, suggesting they lead to more than just a shallow hole beneath.

'There's no lock on those doors,' Rachel whispers. 'I wanted to open them and have a look, but there was a weird smell, so I thought it best to steer clear.'

Cavendish has no such reluctance, snapping on a pair of gloves and calling to Dixon to help open them. When his gloves are on, he heaves one of the doors open with little strain, though it takes Cavendish longer to lug hers free. They both take a noticeable step backwards as stale, warm air rushes up to greet them. It's difficult for us to see what they are staring at, but there does appear to be a narrow tunnel descending out of sight. It could simply be the entrance to some kind of coal cellar, but I know I'm trying to convince myself.

Cavendish and Dixon close the shutter-doors once more, and continue around to the back of the house. A moment later I see a flash of white beyond one of the murky plastic windows, and recognise Dixon's face as he stares out at us and waves. They continue to move about inside the property, before Dixon emerges and moves swiftly towards us.

'DS Cavendish has asked that I now escort you back to the car park and take those statements.'

'Wait,' Rachel challenges, 'just tell us one thing: is it the place? Is this where Aurélie was being held?'

He doesn't answer, but his eyes betray him; breakthrough.

Chapter Twenty-Two

THEN

Docklands, London

Ten years ago

The stale stench of urine hung in the air, and the walls in the tiny room she now found herself in were sticky to the touch. If this room could talk, she didn't want to listen to the tales of woe and horror it would tell. The area was all but pitch black, despite the only covering being a thin curtain that had been pulled shut after the man had shoved her inside.

She hadn't understood the command he'd barked at her, but the finger of warning and the glare in his dark eyes had told her that staying put was probably the safest step for her. She could hear muffled cries and screams coming from beyond the curtain, and she didn't want to be on the receiving end of whatever had befallen them. Crouching into a ball, she forced herself back into the corner, tucking her knees in, wrapping her arms around them, and then burying her head so they wouldn't hear the terrified tears as they fell.

Aurélie remained curled in that foetal-like position until the crying stopped, and when she did look up, she was no longer facing a thin curtain. Instead, there was a door. Thin indentations in the wooden panels drew her attention, and, shuffling forwards on her hands and knees, she traced her small fingers along the crevices, shuddering when she realised what they were: the scratches of other girls who'd been in the same position as her.

Sitting up on her knees, she now dragged her own fingers along the same crevices on the chance that she would be the one to finally break through into any life that was better than this one. The sequined dress they'd forced her to pull over her head was already dishevelled and had lost its sparkle the moment she'd been put in this room. It was now at least a year since she'd first found herself in such a small cell, awaiting the next stage of the evening's planned performance. The memory of that first time still sent panic through her mind, but she knew better now.

The smell of urine lingered; possibly she could smell her own in here now from that first time. She'd kept her head down, and when the night had ended, she'd done as she was told; compliance was the key to avoiding punishment. She'd learned all about following the rules since that night, and that is why she hadn't fought back when the dress had been crudely pulled over her recently dyed curls.

'They love blondes,' she'd overheard one of the other, older girls mutter, as they'd been told to sit and wait for hair and makeup to be done.

Before this life she'd always wanted to wear makeup and to

look as beautiful as Mummy, but she would have swapped the experience for that innocence now. The woman applying the makeup had looked like a zombie as she'd smeared the coloured brush over Aurélie's lips, telling her to press them into the hard and dry tissue. The woman's arms had tiny red spots all over them, and whenever she reached the end of her cigarette, she used it to light another. At one point she'd even asked Aurélie if she wanted one. Aurélie had said no because she knew smoking was bad, even though her dad did it; Mummy had always made her promise not to smoke.

'Smoking kills,' Mummy had told her once, and maybe that was why the woman with the makeup brush was doing it; maybe death was better than all this.

The Catholic priest who'd visited Aurélie's school had told the class that people who kill themselves go to Hell, and so Aurélie hadn't been able to understand why anyone would choose to kill themselves if Hell was the punishment. Crouched in this room though, her fingernails now broken and bloody as she scratched at the grazes in the door panel, she understood why some might consider Hell a better alternative. Maybe this was Hell, and she just didn't realise she was already dead.

The liquid they'd poured over her head to turn her brown locks a bright yellow still made her stomach turn. Is this what men really wanted? Women with smelly hair?

Footsteps tramped on the other side of the door, and she realised it was her time. Straightening, she pushed herself back against the wall, standing straight and tall, but keeping her gaze on her feet as she'd been told to do. Girls who dared to look up at those in charge always ended up with a hard slap across the cheek; again Aurélie had learned that rule before.

There were droplets of blood now shimmering on the white satin-heeled shoes they'd squeezed her feet into. She'd be in trouble if they noticed.

Keeping her hands tucked behind her back so that they wouldn't see the mess she'd made, she felt a large, warm hand fall onto her shoulder, beckoning her through the door and into the dark corridor. The hand moved up to the top of her head, keeping her vision on the floor but allowing her to see when the corridor inevitably bent and twisted. The walls left and right of her were dark and grimy, and looked wet as the man's torchlight washed over them.

Eventually they arrived at a large metal door with a firm wheel on it that he had to use two hands to turn before the door whined open. This led to a much brighter and more decadent room. The floor here was carpeted, a rich bronze colour; the walls lined with embossed, glossy paper. Higher up, small flickering light fittings gave the impression of Victorian streetlights. This was the waiting room, where prospective clients were invited in to peruse the stock ahead of the auction.

'Look but don't touch' was the message each potential client was given as they entered, though few seemed to adhere to the rule.

Most of the men – and they were *all* men – who entered were overweight, and with tanned skin. Most wore sunglasses despite the dim light in the room. Most were dressed in business suits, but rarely wore ties. These were men who wanted to show off their wealth, but weren't used to being told what they could and couldn't do; powerful men.

The one who approached her now was grossly overweight. His shiny black hair was scraped back over the top of his head, and his large, bulbous lips grimaced in a sickening smile when his eyes fell on her. His tongue poked out to wet those enormous lips, and his sausage-like fingers brushed through her coloured hair, grazing her earlobe, causing her to shudder. His sunglasses were too dark for her to see what his eyes were looking at, but she pictured them almost on stalks as they surveyed her thin and fragile frame. He reached into his jacket and removed a pad and pen, and scribbled her number on it, before moving on to the girl seated next to Aurélie.

She didn't see him write any other numbers on his pad, but he muttered something to the man guarding the door before he left, to which the man replied, 'Yes, we're expecting her to be a popular choice tonight.'

More men came and went, each of their faces merging into one, apart from the last one. He stood out as his skin was deathly pale, and he didn't carry the weight of any of the other men. He wasn't wearing a suit jacket either; just black trousers and a black shirt, the top two buttons unfastened. She didn't know why she noticed this particular detail; maybe it was because it showed just how skinny he looked beneath his clothes. He didn't come too close, didn't try and touch her; this was a man who knew what he was looking for, but also knew how to obey the rules.

She knew better than to look at his face, but she did notice the shiny gold bracelet around his wrist, and the grey skin that hung from his bony hands. He paid none of the other girls in the room any attention, just watched her. And then he turned and left.

No more punters were allowed in, and the man who'd led her into the room now barked for her to stand and follow him back through the door they'd come through, back into the grimy corridor, only this time, he led them away from the cells, and into a second waiting room. This one wasn't nearly as luxurious. No carpet or wallpaper in here. Just concrete walls and a concrete floor; a single light hung down from the concrete ceiling. No windows in any of these rooms; they didn't want people looking in.

Then, one by one, each girl would be called through to the next room. Aurélie felt sick to the stomach when her turn arrived. The guard pushed the dark hood over her head, and wrapped the gown around her, as if she was some kind of present waiting to be unwrapped. She didn't resist despite the absolute ice-cold fear coursing through her veins. The satin material of the gown was cool to the touch, and tickled her skin as she was pushed ahead. Beneath the hood she could no longer see her feet, and had to trust that there was nothing she would stumble over. The room here was so dark, but she knew it wouldn't remain that way for much longer.

The guard stepped away and then she felt the heat of the overhead bulbs burning through the gown. Although she couldn't see anyone, she could feel their eyes on her, and as soon as the guard ripped off the robe and hood, all she could see were reflections of herself. Mirrors lined the room, floor to ceiling, but beyond those mirrors the silent auction had begun.

The last time she'd stood in a similar room, she'd wet herself and the warm liquid trickling down both legs had made her collapse to the ground in floods of tears. Nobody had bid for her that day, which had felt like relief at the time, but she wasn't so certain now. Ten pairs of her reflected eyes stared back at her, willing her to be strong; willing her not to show her fear; willing her to learn from this experience. Her coloured hair looked so at odds with the rest of her appearance; so bright and golden, when the rest of her was tired and broken.

She remained in the room for minutes only before the hood and robe were pulled back over and around her, but this time the guard didn't push her back into the waiting room as he had last time. Instead, he steered her to another room behind one of the mirrors, and she heard words that made her blood run cold:

'We'll get her cleaned up for you.'

Suddenly her makeup had been reapplied and the sequined dress had been removed, replaced by something lacy and short. The heels were snatched back, and her feet pushed into more comfortable plimsolls; at least it would be easier to walk without the fear of collapsing.

The guard barked orders at her that she didn't understand, and eventually he pushed her forwards, out of another door with a firm wheel, and into the darkness. She didn't know where she was but the salt in the sea air streamed through her nostrils, reminding her of a home a million miles from here. It was too dark to decipher what any of the coloured buildings in the background were, though in her dream's vision she was sure she recognised Big Ben on the skyline.

The dock was lined with large, well-lit, expensive boats, but it wasn't to these that she was led. Instead, she was pushed along the dock, and then away from the water's edge, and towards a large van. Her last experience of a van hadn't been pleasant, and as she was pushed closer to the open rear doors, she desperately wanted to run away, but there was no strength in her legs, nor courage in her heart. The last thing she remembered was the gold bracelet on the grey, wrinkled skin as her new owner shook the hand of the guard, and thanked him for a smooth transaction.

Aurélie woke screaming, her bed sheets soaked through, and the room promptly filling with kind-faced nurses, alarmed at her sudden outburst and instantly checking her over, reassuring her that she was safe.

They didn't understand; they *couldn't* understand.

Something cool entered her arm, and when the darkness returned, she welcomed the relief of a dreamless obscurity.

Chapter Twenty-Three

NOW

Weymouth, Dorset

Is there anything more idyllic than the warmth and comfort of your own supple mattress, whilst the air fills with the smell of crisp bacon and fresh coffee? I'm certain I'm dreaming until I hear Rachel knock gently against the door.

'Peace offering,' she says, when I've rubbed my eyes, and straightened. 'It was a crappy thing for me to do, using your name and influence to pacify my editor, and I wanted to thank you for not slamming the door in my face and sending me packing yesterday.'

She's making unnecessary puppy dog eyes at me, though there really isn't any need; if she hadn't turned up yesterday, I wouldn't have driven to Poole and we wouldn't have discovered what may or may not be the site where Aurélie has been restrained for so many years. Besides, anyone who brings me tea and bacon in bed can't be all bad.

'I didn't realise I had any bacon in the fridge,' I say, beckoning her in.

'You didn't; I went out early and picked up a few bits and pieces. Do you realise how bare your kitchen was? When you suggested we get fish and chips on the way home, I just assumed it was because you couldn't be arsed to cook.'

I know she's right, and I instinctively look away to hide my shame. I'm not making excuses, but things have just been so manic these last couple of weeks, what with me spending so much time in London supporting Jack, and then the commitments of the Anna Hunter Foundation, that groceries have been the last thing on my mind.

'I'll transfer you some money for the food later,' I say apologetically.

'Oh no you won't! It's the least I can do, especially as you're letting me crash here. Anyway, I have expensive tastes when it comes to wine, and there's no reason you should have to foot the bill for that!' She grins and hands me the tray. 'Take this, will you, and I'll go grab mine.'

She returns a moment later carrying a mug and a small plate. I bite into the bread and salivate as my taste buds are tickled by the saltiness of the bacon.

'I think this needs to become a new tradition,' I say, swallowing the mouthful. 'You're free to crash here as often as you like but you must make me bacon sandwiches *every* morning!'

'Deal!' She nods. 'How are you feeling after yesterday? It took me ages to get to sleep; kept thinking about what it must have been like to live underground with no fresh air or natural light. I mean, can you imagine what something like that would do to someone?'

I know what she means. It might help explain some of the odd behaviour I've seen Aurélie display in the hospital. It also has me wondering how Anna would react to such conditions. When we were growing up, she hated being trapped indoors. She loved being outside, and on rainy days during school holidays she would be miserable as sin until it was dry enough to go out again. Nowadays they call it cabin fever, but back then it was considered insolence. Either way, I can't see that she would have been as compliant as I'm guessing Aurélie learned to be.

'Imagine how sick a person needs to be to inflict such cruelty on another human being,' I conclude.

'Whoever it was, he was long gone from that cabin when we turned up. Maybe he took off as soon as he knew she'd escaped, out of fear that she would lead police back to the location.'

Cavendish's voice echoes in my mind: *Aurélie told me she was being held in Canford Heath Nature Reserve, so why would she do that if in fact it was Delph Woods in Broadstone?*

'Not according to Cavendish; she mentioned something about a different location Aurélie gave them. Given what she's been through and how much of an emotional rollercoaster escape would cause, it's a wonder she's even able to speak. I remember when Jack and I finally located Cassie Hilliard, she barely said a word when we brought her back to her normal life. That Aurélie is alive and well is a miracle by modern standards.'

'Goes to show how strong the human spirit can be,' Rachel agrees.

I wash down my latest mouthful of bacon with a gulp of tea. 'Did your editor print what you sent him last night?'

Rachel nods. 'It made page five, but I think the tabloids printed their own versions on the front page. One of them quotes a mystery source confirming it's definitely the location, but that could just be conjecture. I take it you haven't heard anything from Cavendish or Dixon yet?'

I glance at my phone's display. 'No, but then I doubt I'd be the first person she'd share any news with.'

Rachel guffaws at this last statement. 'What is her problem? She was firing daggers at you when she turned up at those woods yesterday! You'd never have guessed we'd brought her such a potentially huge breakthrough in her case. A little gratitude wouldn't have been unwarranted.'

'Forget about it,' I reply. 'The most important thing is that they now use what we found to bring Aurélie's captor to justice, and stop anything like this occurring again.'

The doorbell sounds and we exchange frowns.

'Do you want me to go?' Rachel asks, nodding at my nightwear.

It's too late, I'm already out of bed, slotting on my slippers and wrapping a kimono around my shoulders. It's only when I open the door and see Jack on the doorstep that I even recall our last conversation. I'm not sure which of us looks more embarrassed.

'Sorry, did I wake you?' he asks, checking his watch. 'We did say before nine, didn't we?'

I close my eyes in frustration. 'No, it's my fault, I forgot you were coming here first. You'd better come in because I need to shower and dress first.'

I open the door wider, but he doesn't make any effort to step forward. 'I'm not alone as it happens... After you mentioned crossed wires with the DS overseeing the case, I thought I'd reach out to whoever it was and smooth any wrinkles. Turns out, I know her. In fact, Zoe and I go way back. We were in police training together at Hamble in Hampshire. I hadn't realised she'd moved to this neck of the woods.'

Cavendish's face pops out from behind his back to complete my humiliation. I can't now not allow them in, having been willing to invite Jack when I thought he was alone.

Remaining where I am, I attempt my most welcoming smile as the irritation bubbles below the surface. 'Please come in.'

Jack leads the way with Cavendish following slowly behind, her eyes darting from the fading wallpaper to the carpet I haven't hoovered in nearly a month, to the dust clinging to every surface. I can see she is adding it all to her bank of disapproval, but there's nothing I can do about it now. I show them into the living room, and meet Rachel in the kitchen. She's close to giggling at the ridiculousness of the situation, quickly composing herself when she sees the frustration in my eyes.

'Relax,' she whispers. 'I'll make them both a drink while you go and get ready.'

I squeeze her arm in thanks and hurry to the bathroom, closing and locking the door behind me, before opening my mouth wide to bellow out a muted scream.

I know Jack was trying to be helpful, and I don't blame him for trying to build bridges between me and her, and maybe he'll be successful, but I wish she wasn't here. And what's worse is, I am failing to ignore the voice in the back of my head that noticed how he called her Zoe. It shouldn't bother me; it's not like Jack and I have anything more than a professional relationship; and even if there was something more formal between them once, it doesn't mean that there still is.

Oh God, why does this bother me so much? I'm behaving like a teenager, when there are far more important things at stake. Showering in silence, I keep the temperature low as punishment for my immaturity, and hope it will make me more alert when I emerge. Stepping out of the shower, I brush my hair and teeth, select a figure-hugging cotton dress and a pair of slip-on sandals. I'm not usually so fussy about what I wear, but it's all I can do to shut up that niggling voice in my head.

'You look fabulous,' Rachel mouths, as I appear at the doorway to the living room.

Jack and Cavendish are both sitting on the small sofa, but their knees are pointed away from one another, suggesting an awkwardness in their body language. Jack stands as he sees me at the door, offering me the seat, but I politely decline, determined to keep distance between us.

'Zoe was just telling me that it was you two who discovered the dungeon in the woods,' he says, his voice pitched unnaturally higher than usual. 'I was saying to her that you seem to have a knack for those types of things: seeing connections where the rest of us might not.'

'I don't know about that,' I respond defensively, as my cheeks burn again. 'Yesterday was dumb luck, that's all.' I look directly at Cavendish, who is watching the exchange. 'According to one of the newspapers, you do believe it is the right place?'

She remains perched on the end of the sofa. 'I'm not at liberty to discuss an ongoing investigation. However, off the record, the team have been working through the night on collecting soil and blood samples from the cavern discovered in the ground. There is every reason to believe that this was the tunnel Aurélie described in her statement. We're still waiting for the lab to provide confirmation, but it's looking likely. As soon as they confirm we'll let the family know.'

She pauses. 'That's why I wanted to come here and see you today, as it goes.' She pauses again, looks away, before meeting my gaze again. 'I wanted... I wanted to thank you for your help.'

I blink several times; did I just dream that, or did she thank me? That can't have been easy for her to say, given the notable animosity between us. Maybe Jack has managed to persuade her that I'm not just some hack looking to profit from those in need. I'm certainly happy to bury the hatchet.

'I'm just relieved that we were able to help; hopefully it will bring Aurélie some much-needed comfort.'

She stands now, and takes a step closer to the three of us. 'That was the other thing I wanted to talk to you about. Jack?'

He starts at mention of his name. 'Oh yes.' He smiles awkwardly at me and Rachel. 'Zoe and I were talking on the way over here, and we both feel it might be better if you... postpone your planned interviews with Aurélie. Given everything she's been through and the local force's desire to progress the case, it makes sense to delay your project and allow Aurélie to focus on ways she can help them.'

The penny drops. The reason Cavendish was prepared to swallow her pride and thank us was to keep Jack sweet when he dropped this bombshell.

'Given Aurélie's recognition of Jemima Hooper's face,' Jack continues, 'it makes sense if you and I focus on that angle. I've told Zoe all about our little project, and how we're trying to uncover those responsible for producing the videos discovered on Arthur Turgood's hard drive. She's agreed to hand over all the case information she was passed about Aurélie's original abduction to see if it helps us find a link to Jemima Hooper. Meanwhile, Zoe and her team will work the case from this end, and maybe we'll all end up meeting somewhere in the middle.'

I can see the sense in what Jack is saying, and I wouldn't ordinarily argue, but I am annoyed that Cavendish appears to be using him to keep me out of her way; and I'm not sure how well Remy Lebrun will react to the news. There is no point in me voicing my concern while Cavendish is here, so I bite my tongue and nod.

'I'm going to drive Zoe to the hospital, and then I'll head back here,' Jack says, making his way to the front door. 'I've brought down the boxes of Jemima's paperwork that we can start to go through again when I'm back.'

With that the two of them leave, and Rachel's face reflects the anger simmering in my own mind.

Chapter Twenty-Four

NOW

Weymouth, Dorset

'What a jerk!' Rachel erupts, folding her arms, and breathing heavily. 'Can you believe that guy? Who is he to rock up here and dictate who you can and can't speak to? What has it got to do with him anyway?'

I share her sentiment, even if my ire isn't directed at Jack.

'I don't think it's his fault,' I say defensively, my eyes still glued to the door he just closed. 'If you ask me, Cavendish is the one behind this sudden change of heart. She's been trying to squeeze me out of the picture since day one, and now she's found her perfect marionette in former flame Jack.'

The spit is bubbling on my lips when I finish, and when I look at Rachel, her eyes have widened.

'Oh, were those two… Were they an item?'

I detest the images running through my mind right now: the two of them cavorting, tearing at each other's clothes.

'I honestly don't know,' I say to repel the images. 'Do *you* think they were? What did their body language say?'

I desperately want her to tell me I'm being ridiculous; that I imagined the intimacy between them. And that's when the realisation finally hits me. I've denied it over and over, but what other reason is there for me to be so jealous of the spark between him and Cavendish?

His goofy smile; his lame 'dad' jokes; his ability to get under my skin; the patchy beard where hair simply won't grow; the lid is off Pandora's box, and suddenly I can see what's been there since the first moment we met at Uxbridge police station.

I can feel the bacon sandwich waiting to be regurgitated.

'They seemed close,' Rachel eventually offers, 'so I suppose it's possible. But it could just be that they were friends.'

'You think?' I can't keep the hopeful desperation from my lips.

'Either way, I still don't think it's right that he should be dictating what you do. If he wants to work on that side project, then let him. You came back here to do a story on Aurélie's experiences in captivity, and that's exactly what you should do!'

I'm not surprised that Rachel's reaction is to do the opposite of what she's been told; this has been her greatest flaw and most noble quality for as long as I've known her. It's why she can rub people up the wrong way, but what makes her such a brilliant journalist, and loyal friend.

'You said it was her father who pitched the idea to your publishers, so he clearly wants you to stick around,' she continues. 'There's no reason why you can't still speak to Aurélie too. So, maybe you step out of the room when

Cavendish is asking her questions, but she won't be interviewing Aurélie nonstop, will she? There will be loads of downtime when Aurélie is just lying in that hospital bed thinking about all the shit she's had to put up with; that's when she could be speaking to us instead. If you want this story, you're going to have to fight for it!'

These are all valid points, and if it was just about Cavendish, I'd already be bolting for the door, but it isn't.

'I don't want to go against Jack's wishes.'

'You don't owe him anything. It is *his* job to solve crime; you're just giving him some of your skill and experience. Besides, what better place to start on figuring out who abducted Aurélie than hearing it from the horse's mouth?'

'You're right,' I concede.

'You're damn right I'm right! It's what the likes of Emmeline Pankhurst, Mary Wollstonecraft and Simone de Beauvoir fought for; you have just as much right to determine your future actions – more so – than any man.'

She is eyeing the door.

'You mean we should go *now*?' I clarify.

'There's no time like the present; plus, if we wait around here any longer you'll probably change your mind, so come on.'

With that she hooks her arm through mine and drags me out of the front door, down the porch steps and to her car. We're in Poole within the hour, though traffic hasn't helped. It's a gloriously hot day, and I would bet half the cars we've met are headed to the beach and coastline. If it weren't for Aurélie's sudden re-emergence, I think I probably would have spent the day reading on the sand across the road from my flat.

Rachel was right; now that my mind has had time to

process what she suggested, I'm starting to get second thoughts. It isn't that I feel the need to overlook what feminists spent their lives fighting for, but I'm worried that Jack will see my disobedience as a personal affront, and that isn't what this is about. I'm not making a stand because it was a man who said I shouldn't speak to Aurélie, it's because I think it's the wrong call, and I don't want Cavendish to continue to intimidate me; despite what she thinks of me – and my own self-doubt – I *am* a good writer, and my motivation for helping others has never been about anything but truth and justice.

Despite reciting this final statement over and over in my head as we catch the lift up to the ward, my nerves are all over the place as we arrive at the door to Aurélie's room, and I nod at the familiar face stationed there.

'Sorry,' he says, 'DS Cavendish said I wasn't to let you in.'

Standing on my haunches, I look over his shoulder and through the tiny vertical window in the door. I can just about make out Aurélie's face beneath the white bed sheets. Solange is in her usual chair, wearing a confused look. Remy is standing beside her, his attention shared between his daughter and someone off to the left whom I can't quite see, but would imagine is Cavendish. I can't see if Jack is still with her, or whether he just dropped her off and is fighting his way back through traffic to my place.

The officer slides across to block my view, and I lower my heels again. 'It's nothing personal,' he concedes, 'but she'd have my guts for garters, you know.'

I know that if I could just get Remy's attention, he'd beckon us in, but clearly Cavendish has considered Rachel and I would ignore her wish and try to make contact.

'But she's the one who phoned and asked us to come here,' Rachel says from over my shoulder.

The officer's forehead wrinkles with doubt, as Rachel nudges my lower back.

'That's right,' I echo, realising what she's doing. 'Ask her if you don't believe us. We'll wait here.'

It is clear from his uncertain reaction that he fears the repercussions of disobeying Cavendish's command, but equally fears her wrath because he had misinterpreted what she'd said.

'Hold on,' he relents, turning and knocking gently on the door, before opening it a crack and peering in. Because of his bulk, I have to jump up and down to see over his shoulder, but Remy's stare is fixed on Aurélie, and he can't see me.

Cavendish spots me though, and judging by the venom in her glare, she isn't pleased at the interruption.

'Remy?' I eventually call out, before Cavendish blocks my bouncing.

He waves in recognition, and just as Cavendish closes the door, he reopens it fully and invites me in. Rachel grabs hold of my wrist and pushes past the officer to follow me through.

'Emma, what are you doing here?' Jack asks from behind the door. 'I thought we agreed that you'd delay your book work until we've finished the investigation.'

So he did stick around; at least I don't need to worry about him arriving at my empty flat.

All of Rachel's pertinent arguments as to why we've come have emptied from my mind, and I can feel the eyes of the room all staring at me in an equal blend of anger and confusion.

'She needs to be here,' Remy says after a beat. 'She is

writing the book about Aurélie's experiences, so she needs to hear *everything*.'

'We'll sit quietly in a corner, and won't interrupt your questions,' I say quickly in an effort to appease Cavendish's glowering expression.

The fight has gone from her, and she turns away dismissively, retaking her place beside Aurélie's bed. 'Let's get on with this; I have an investigation to continue.'

The officer returns to his post outside, closing the door behind him, while Rachel and I hover in the corner, as I promised. Jack is sitting in the only chair in this part of the room, and he doesn't stand to offer it to either Rachel or me. I keep glancing down at him, but he is refusing to make eye contact. The frustration is reverberating off him in waves, which is precisely what I wanted to avoid.

'I need a description of the man who was holding you there,' Cavendish is barking at Aurélie as if she is some disobedient pet. 'Was he tall, was he short, what colour was his hair, was he young, was he old?'

Remy relays the question, and listens for his daughter's response, before translating. 'He was average height, but taller than her by at least thirty to forty centimetres; he had long grey hair; he was thin; she thinks he was probably in his seventies at the end.'

'Was he English? Did she ever hear a name? Did anybody ever call him by a name?'

Remy asks the questions, and listens for the responses. 'She does not recall a name, but thinks he was English.'

'If I ask an artist to come here, will she be able to describe him so we can draw a picture?'

Remy translates. 'Yes.'

'Does she have any idea where he might have gone? The place we found was empty. Did he have a car? Does she know what type of car he drove? Make, model?'

'She says he had a car, but she never saw what type of car. She doesn't know where he would be. Can't you use his DNA from the house to identify and track him that way?'

'We are processing the scene and trying to locate as many DNA profiles as we can; it isn't a quick process. We have found Aurélie's DNA all over the cell beneath the ground, so we are confident she was there, but we need to find this person – or persons – as quickly as we can.' She pauses, breathing deeply to relax her shoulders. 'I will have a sketch artist over here in the next hour.'

She spins on her heel, and leaves the room; she doesn't look at me, Rachel or Jack as she departs. I sense any favour he managed to curry has just dissipated.

'Can I have a word with you outside?' Rachel whispers into my ear.

'Sure.'

We leave the room, nodding apologetically at the officer, who is several feet away down the corridor receiving his public admonishment.

'What's up?' I ask, when Rachel has closed the door.

'Did any of that routine strike you as odd?'

I frown. 'What routine?'

She is quiet, choosing her words carefully. 'So, I was listening to what Cavendish was asking, and trying to translate it in my head – kind of like practice – and more or less Remy asked what I would have expected... But he was less direct, almost like he was trying to soften the blow.'

'Well, that's understandable, given he was addressing those questions to his fragile daughter.'

'Yeah, but the thing is, her answers to the questions were as direct as Cavendish's.'

It's my turn to frown. 'I'm not following.'

'I don't know – maybe I'm reading too much into it – but it was almost as if Aurélie was answering Cavendish's questions, rather than her father's – as if she could understand exactly what Cavendish was asking.'

'Maybe she can. In fairness I could probably understand more than I could say in French, so it's possible that she suffers the same affliction.'

Rachel shakes her head firmly. 'It's more than that. I think she understands a lot more than she's letting on. The only questions are why, and what else is she lying about?'

Chapter Twenty-Five

THEN

Poole, Dorset

She was relieved when the angry detective left, and pleased to find the writer had returned despite what her father had relayed from Cavendish. This time she'd brought a friend with her that reminded Aurélie of someone, but she couldn't be sure whom. There was tenderness between them, so at the very least they were two women who knew most of each other's secrets. Aurélie wasn't sure she'd ever be able to trust anyone enough again to share the intimacy of her own secrets.

Having been brought a cup of tea and a small packet of biscuits by one of the nurses, Aurélie was now feeling more alert as the writer and her close friend returned to the room, minus the detective and her own overbearing parents. Having not seen either of them for thirteen years, the twenty-four-seven attention was all a little too much to take. It felt as if her mother was trying to make up for the missing years by cramming them into every available second for the foreseeable future.

'Bonjour, Aurélie,' Emma said as she came closer to the bed, sliding the bag from over her shoulder, and depositing it on the ground. 'This is my friend Rachel, and she's going to translate for me.'

Emma paused and waited for her friend to chime in. They needn't have bothered, as Aurélie could now understand virtually every word Emma was saying, but the pretence had gone on so long that it wouldn't be easy to admit the truth.

'Bonjour, Aurélie,' the friend said. 'Je m'appelle Rachel, et je vais traduire ce que dit Emma. D'accord?'

Aurélie nodded, impressed by Rachel's accent and attention to detail; time would tell whether she'd be able to maintain such high standards.

'We'd like to ask you some questions about your abduction,' Emma said, 'but before we begin, is there anything we can get for you? Food, drink?'

Aurélie watched her speak, then looked at Rachel for the translation, before nodding her head to indicate she was ready.

Rachel lowered herself into Solange's vacant chair, while Emma perched on the far end of the bed.

'I know this won't be easy for you, and I urge you just to do your best; nobody here will judge you for crying, or for any pain the experience of recall will cause. All I ask is that you take your time, and tell us what you can. Is that okay? Are you happy to begin?'

Aurélie found it odd that Emma would have such an interest in what had happened thirteen years before – the detective certainly hadn't seemed all that interested – and it wasn't like they would likely catch up with the people responsible for Aurélie's abduction. Even if they were still alive, Aurélie's memory of them and that time was so foggy, she couldn't picture their faces, certainly not well enough to describe in any detail. All of her memories prior to the night when she was purchased at that auction were a blur, but she could still recall *that* night and the days that followed in crystal-clear Technicolor.

It was so dark in that van, but the gentle roll of the vehicle's tyres, and the exhaustion brought on by the paralysing fear, had been enough to rock her to sleep. When she heard the door slam, jolting her out of sleep, she had no idea how long she had been out for. It could have been minutes or hours. The journey had started in London, but she now had no idea where she was, and as he opened the lid of the boot, she wanted to kick out, knocking him off his feet, and bolting for an escape, but all thoughts of escape disappeared as soon as the boot's internal light reflected off the blade's shimmering steel.

The bracelet jangled on his wrist as he raised the hunting knife up and down, indicating for her to climb out. He didn't speak a word, and there was no sense of panic in how he held himself. She didn't dare look up into his eyes, certainly not on that first night. She didn't know if this would be their first or only night in each other's company.

The short, lacy dress was damp at the bottom where she must have wet herself without realising it, and she immediately covered it with her hands, but he pulled them away, taking one in his, walking her casually towards what resembled a gîte, though it was difficult to see anything properly with only the car's dimmed lights to guide their path. The ground stabbed at her feet, and at one point she wanted to scream out, but repressed it, her eyes never leaving the blade in his left hand. It would have taken no effort for him to swing that arm around and gut her like one of the fish her mother used to prepare for dinner.

They didn't enter the gîte, instead moving past it, further into the darkness, where she couldn't see a thing, but he clearly knew where he was going. He stopped suddenly, and she heard what sounded like an old wardrobe creaking open, but before she could process the thought he had her hand again and they were moving again, only this time it seemed as though they'd entered some kind of corridor. The ceiling and walls were close; close enough that she could smell the damp, and feel the cool against her skin. He sparked a cigarette lighter and used it as a makeshift torch, and as the faint orange light danced around the tunnel, she gained the sense that they were slowly descending. Onwards they went, with neither speaking, until they arrived at a round door, like something she had seen on a submarine during a school trip to a naval museum. He battled with the large bar securing it, before pushing it open and nodding for her to enter.

As soon as they were inside, he used the knife to cut the straps of her dress, and it slid down her legs into a crumpled heap on the floor. She half-expected to feel his cold, dead hands on her immediately, but he let her be, searching somewhere in the darkness, before passing her a small bundle. Another wave of the knife and she knew he wanted her to dress; she eagerly obliged, pulling the cotton top over her head, and sliding the bottoms over her still damp underwear.

He used the lighter on two candles, before pocketing it. The room was small and round; compact. The candlelight provided little illumination, but she could now see he was sitting on the only chair beside a small square table. The candles reflected off the small plastic bottle of water beside them. Her mouth suddenly felt so dry, and there wasn't enough spittle to wet her lips. He didn't speak, gauging her reaction to the liquid. Did he know how thirsty she was? He hadn't offered her the drink, but it was there on the table.

She was about to ask if she could have it, when he lifted the bottle and placed it on his lap. She opened her mouth to speak again, but he simply shook his head, maintaining eye contact the whole time.

'I will give you a drink soon,' he croaked hoarsely, 'but first you will listen to me.'

She could barely understand a word, but knew enough to keep quiet. She was so desperate for the water that she'd do anything he asked.

She eyed the bottle, imagining the cool, refreshing liquid as it slid down her throat. She started as he banged his hand against the table and her eyes shot up to his face. Before she could react his hand shot out of the darkness and grabbed at her chin, holding it so firm she wondered whether he might break her jaw there and then.

'Pay attention; I don't like repeating myself.'

Her heart felt as though it would explode from her chest, but she remained quiet, keeping her eyes on his, and not on the bottle she craved.

'Good. This is your new home. It isn't much, but it is safe. There is no way you can escape from here so don't waste your time trying. I own you now, and you are here to serve at my pleasure. If you do as I say, you will be fine; if you disobey me, the punishment will be severe. Do you understand?'

She nodded despite the resistance of his hand.

He loosened his grip on her chin, opened the bottle and

poured some of the water over her lips. She choked as she tried to swallow as much of it as she could, but as much washed down her neck as went in her mouth.

He replaced the lid on the bottle and stood it back on the table. 'That is all the water there is until the morning. I will bring you food and drink once a day, and you will need to make it last.'

'Where are we?' she dared to ask, instantly regretting it as his hand lashed out and slapped her hard across the cheek.

Her eyes welled instantly, and it took all her strength not to scream in agony.

'You will only speak when spoken to. Is that clear?'

She hadn't known whether to respond, and had opted for a nod to show her compliance.

'Good. From now on your name is Four; do you understand? When I say Four, I am referring to you.'

Aurélie couldn't be sure she'd understood what he'd said, and simply nodded.

'I want you to do something for me, Four, to show that you understand that you are mine now. If you refuse, I will be forced to hurt you. You don't want me to slap you again, do you, Four?'

She shook her head, averting her eyes in case he lashed out again.

'There is a mattress on the floor behind you, Four. This is your new bed where you will sleep. I want you to go over to that mattress now and lie down on your front. Do you understand?'

The nausea rose in her throat; even though she could not begin to imagine what he had planned, deep down she sensed that it would not end well.

Emma coughed, drawing Aurélie's attention back to the hospital room. 'Are you ready, Aurélie?'

She nodded, blinking away the urge to cry over the memory of that first night; determined to provide the answers the writer wanted.

Chapter Twenty-Six

NOW

Poole, Dorset

The hospital room feels stuffy and confined, and even after only five minutes in here, I feel like I want to pull open the door and just run in search of freedom and fresh air. I can't help wondering what Aurélie is making of all of it; has cabin fever struck her, or is it just more of what she's used to?

She looks close to tears, and I regret forcing our way into her room to make these demands of her, yet I sense Cavendish will do all she can to prevent further encounters, and the information Aurélie is holding could be critical to our investigation both into how Jemima Hooper ended up discarded like waste at a park in Tamworth, and also my own sister's whereabouts.

'I'd like to ask you some questions about Jemima Hooper,' I say, nodding for Rachel to translate for me. I unlock my phone and flick to the image Aurélie saw yesterday. Angling the screen towards her, I pinch the screen to zoom in on the face. 'Do you remember? You told me you recognised her.'

Aurélie looks from Rachel to the screen, and back to me, her eyes misting up. But I can see that look of recognition again, and I need to apply just the right amount of pressure to unlock the information.

'Can you tell us how you met her?'

When Aurélie opens her mouth to speak, the last thing I'm expecting to hear is English. 'She was there… At my prison.'

Rachel fires me a look of caution, but I don't know how to explain this development. Was it just an assumption on my part that she couldn't speak English, or is that what I'd been led to believe? Either way, it suddenly makes me question everything that has transpired since I first arrived in this room yesterday morning.

'Sometimes, we would have a visitor,' she continues, staring away at the ceiling as if the memory is playing out on the tiles. 'People passing through; friends of my captor. Girls would come and go, forced beneath the ground with me… It was my responsibility to watch them.'

'Watch them how?' Rachel asks.

'He… he would make me explain the rules to them, so that they would know not to cause trouble. So long as we did as we were told, he would not punish us.'

'To be clear,' I interrupt, moving closer, and forcing her to look at Jemima's photo, 'you're saying the girl in this picture was in the underground room with you?'

As she nods, a single tear escapes and rides her cheek.

'When was this? Recently? Years ago? When?'

I know that Jemima was abducted in 2015, and her abused body was discovered a little under a year and a half later, but I feel the need to fact-check Aurélie's claim, and I can't explain why.

'I don't know… It is hard to say. Time is a blur. I didn't have a clock, or calendar; I could not tell when it was day or night. It was some time ago… maybe two years? I am sorry, I cannot be more certain.'

'What can you tell us about her? Did she speak with an accent? Did she tell you her name, or where she was from?'

Aurélie shrugs again. 'We didn't really speak… When she arrived in the hole, she was – how do you say? – not awake… um, she was passed out?'

'You mean she was unconscious?' Rachel offers.

'Oui, yes.'

'Had they given her something? Had they drugged her?'

Aurélie nods rapidly. 'Yes, often when these girls would arrive, they would have been drugged, to make them easier to control.'

'Do you know what they were drugged with?' I ask.

'I am sorry, I do not know. I did not see, but I think maybe there were needles, as some of the girls would have scars on their arms.'

'Were you ever drugged?'

She shakes her head. 'I don't think so.'

'Would your…' I pause, considering the best way to describe the man who held her. 'Would your guardian tell you when someone was coming to stay, or would they just turn up?'

There is a half-smile, reflecting a bitter memory. 'He never told me anything. One day it would be just me and him, and then another time, he would arrive with this girl or that girl, and he would tell me to make sure she understood the rules.'

'He would bring the girls in himself?' I ask. 'Did anyone ever help him? Did you see any other people with him?'

'No, it was only ever him there. I think maybe these girls would belong to someone else, but I never saw who.'

I don't know why but I'm picturing the old human railroad used by enslaved people to escape in the nineteenth century; moving from one hideout to another, slowly making their way across country to safety. Only in this situation I'm seeing perverts and paedophiles moving their prey from one location to another, under the radar of the authorities hunting them. That would suggest a network of likeminded individuals, and – worst of all – more underground prisons like we discovered yesterday, and more victims just like Aurélie. It's enough to make this morning's bacon sandwich temporarily resurface.

'And Jemima – the girl in this picture – she was one of the girls he brought into your prison?'

She nods. 'He called her Seven. She was there for one night, and then gone.'

Rachel looks over to me, as if seeking my permission to ask a question; I've no idea what she wants to ask, but nod my consent.

'You said earlier that you were forced to tell them the rules... to avoid punishment... Can you explain what you mean? What would happen to someone who didn't follow the rules?'

Aurélie is suddenly overcome with sadness. 'He didn't like it when we disobeyed. I learned quickly that it was easier and safer to do as he asked.'

'Did he ever punish you?'

More tears escape as she nods again. 'Yes, when I first arrived, he would hit me if I looked at him or refused his requests. I tried once to escape, and he beat and kicked me until I could taste blood, and I thought I would die; one time he used a – what is it called? – a device with electricity?'

Rachel gulps audibly. 'A Taser?'

'Oui, that is it. He wanted me to... but I refused, and he fired the device into my belly. It was the most painful experience of my life. Again, I thought it would kill me, but I wasn't so lucky.'

Anna's face fills my mind again, and as much as I just want to hug the woman before me, I won't be able to rest until I find out whether Anna could have been smuggled along this underground pipeline.

'Can you remember how many girls came and went over the years?'

She wipes her eyes with the bed sheet. 'It is difficult to remember. I know that the girl in your picture was Seven, and I was Four... I think maybe I remember there being an Eleven and Twelve possibly, but we did not have anyone stay for some time now. For the last few years I think maybe it was just me and him.'

Jack coughs, and I start, having forgotten he was still in the room. He's been quietly observing the scene playing out. 'Do you think if we showed you other faces of missing girls, you might be able to identify those that stayed with you?'

Aurélie looks equally surprised by the question, but nods. 'I could try. You must remember that it was very dark where I was. There was no electricity in the hole, so the only light was from candles he would bring when the food and water arrived. Sometimes I would spend the entire day in the dark.'

I flick back to the photograph of Anna, and show it to her again. 'Can you look carefully at this picture, and tell me if you ever saw her? She might have been older than this, and her name was Anna.'

She accepts the phone, and studies the image carefully, occasionally looking back into my desperate eyes, and then back on the image. 'This girl, she is important to you?'

I fight against the sting at the edge of my eyes. 'Yes, yes, she is. She is my sister, and she was abducted – like you – many years ago. She is still out there somewhere, and I'm desperately hoping to find out what happened to her.'

She finally hands the phone back. 'I think maybe it is possible she was there, but I cannot say for certain. It is difficult to remember what happened in those early years. There are a lot of black spots in my memory, but there is something maybe familiar about her face. Yes, it is possible that she was there too.'

My heart skips a beat, and I lurch, almost toppling from the edge of the bed. This is the news I've been waiting to hear for years, and I wasn't expecting it to come today. Again, I'm torn as to whether I should be happy to hear that she lived past the day she disappeared, or should be horrified at the prospect that she has been forced to endure something as gruesome as Aurélie has.

Jack has stood and moved closer to the bed. 'Wait, you're saying you think maybe this girl Anna Hunter spent time in the same prison as you?'

Aurélie looks so desperate to please, but there is sadness there too. 'I can't say for certain that she was in the hole, but there is something about her face… It is possible I saw her at one of the auctions. Maybe.'

'Auctions? What auctions?' Jack stutters.

'That is how I ended up with that man: he bought me at an

auction and took me to that place. I don't know if I am using the right word. There was a room, and there were rich men who would offer money to buy the girls there. They would sell to the highest bidder. You understand?'

My stomach is turning again, but I choke down the urge to vomit. 'You were at one of these auctions?'

She nods. 'It was soon after I was taken. Nobody bought me at the first one, but then after that, there was another room and my captor, he was there and he paid money to buy me.'

The blood has drained from Jack's face. 'Can you tell me anything more about these auctions? Do you know where they were? How often? Who organised them? Anything?'

Her eyes are tearing up again. 'I am sorry, it was so many years ago. I think I was in London when I was bought… I think I saw Big Ben the clock in the distance, but I can't be certain that isn't my imagination filling a blank spot.'

'Do you realise what this means?' Jack mutters under his breath to me.

I know only too well; it is what we have been fearing since DCS Rawani first paired us and we started reading Missing Person files: the prospect that children are being abducted to order, bought and sold at will, and then disposed of when they've served their purpose or no longer fill a need.

The world has never felt as dark as it does right now.

Chapter Twenty-Seven

NOW

Weymouth, Dorset

An hour later and we are back at my flat in Weymouth with more questions than answers. Aurélie's lack of time awareness hasn't helped determine exactly when her path would have crossed with Jemima Hooper's, but at least we know it was somewhere in the last six years. If we could somehow narrow that window further – get it to within a week, say – it might be possible to monitor local CCTV or traffic cameras and somehow pick out persons or vehicles of interest. I realise this would be a mammoth – and potentially fruitless – task, but there has to be a reason that fate has sent us this connection.

Rachel heads into the kitchen, offering to make us all a much-needed cup of tea, while Jack carries in the three large box files containing the details about Jemima's case. In this day and age it seems silly for him to have transported the paper files when he could probably have brought a digital version, but I find it easier looking at physical things than at screens. With paper copies of reports and glossy photographs, I can build a picture – like putting together a jigsaw – in front of me, and that then helps cement details in my mind's eye.

Jack teases that such an approach wouldn't do for modern detective work, but it's my process, and if it isn't broken, why fix it?

He lowers the first box to the living room carpet and then leaves without saying a word. Maybe I'm reading too much into it – after all we travelled back in separate cars – but I sense he is giving me the silent treatment. He is usually so bright and bubbly, but the expression on his face is that of a wounded animal. I'd like to think it's just the impact of what Aurélie told us, but it's more than that.

When he returns with the second box, I step in front of him, blocking his way out of the room. 'I'm sorry we went to the hospital when you asked us not to.'

He lets out a heavy sigh. 'Forget about it.'

He looks so defeated that I just want to wrap my arms around him and tell him everything will be okay, but we're not there yet.

'I don't want to forget about it,' I say instead. 'I didn't appreciate you making decisions about my work without consulting me, and *that* is why I ignored your request. It felt like an ambush when you and Cavendish turned up here with your little plan all agreed. I warned you yesterday that she had something against me, and it just felt like… It felt like she was using you to squeeze me out.'

'That's ridiculous, Emma,' he says, sighing again. 'Zoe is a genuinely nice person, and a brilliant detective at that. She only wants what's best for Aurélie, and you saw what your questions did to her today; she looked exhausted when we left and it isn't even lunchtime yet. Can you imagine how hard it must be for her, adjusting to a strange new world, and being forced to relive such dark and terrifying memories? It's a wonder they haven't had to sedate her yet! It must be such a mind-screw for her. Zoe knows it will be hard enough for Aurélie to concentrate on trying to help catch her captor, let alone tackling memories that have been repressed for thirteen years. It isn't personal.'

I hadn't quite looked at it that way, and now it's me who is embarrassed at our behaviour. 'Well, as I said, I'm sorry that we chose to ignore the request, but you must admit there was some benefit to it; you've heard for yourself that she recognises Jemima, and that gives us a chink of light in our investigation, doesn't it?'

He looks back at the two boxes behind him. 'Does it? We still don't know exactly when the two of them met, or for how long. Jemima was taken from Gateshead and wound up in Tamworth; it isn't unreasonable to assume she remained in either of the locations, so is it really a breakthrough that she was possibly in Poole as well? I'm not so sure it's worth shouting about. Excuse me.'

I step aside and allow him to go and fetch the remaining box.

Rachel appears in the kitchen doorway. 'I don't think you should be the one apologising.'

'No? Did you hear what he said? What if our pursuing this causes her to end up having some kind of nervous breakdown?'

She raises her eyebrows. 'Are you for real? Believe me, if

that woman was due a nervous breakdown, I think it would have happened already! I don't doubt that she's already been through more stress than the average adult can handle, but she is the key to finding out what really happened all those years ago, and who is responsible. It would be reckless *not* to pursue it. Think about the people responsible for your sister's disappearance. Had they been caught before that day, you wouldn't have lost her. You owe it to these people's future victims to do whatever it takes – and I mean *whatever it takes* – to put a stop to their nefarious activities *now!*'

She turns away as the kettle reaches a crescendo, and I move further into the living room, awaiting Jack and the final box.

His head is bent low when he does return. He stands the box next to the two others and then removes his jacket and tie and lays them on the sofa cushion beside me. He then crouches down at my knee, and for the tiniest of moments I imagine him proposing, but quickly shake the image from my head.

'Listen, I don't want there to be any animosity between us,' he says quietly. 'I'm sorry if it felt like an ambush this morning; I certainly didn't mean for it to come across that way. When I called down yesterday and heard that it was my old training buddy running things, I reached out and suggested we meet for breakfast; I figured it was my opportunity to tell her what an amazing individual you are without it coming across as some fanboy. I explained how you are the only reason Cassie Hilliard was discovered, and that your work in *Monsters Under the Bed* exposed historical abuses that would have otherwise gone unheard.'

My face is on fire, and my eyes dart around the room searching for anything to focus the tension on.

'I should have let you know that I was bringing Zoe here with me, and I could have asked you about staying away, rather than dictating it. I accept your apology, and I hope you will accept mine.'

This is unexpected, but really shouldn't be; Jack's a good guy, and I don't want there to be any awkwardness between us either.

'Then that's settled,' I say, blowing my fringe up, suddenly aware that the entire room feels like an oven. 'I'm going to open some windows,' I add, standing and kneeling on the sofa so I can open the windows in the bay behind me. The relief that comes from the breeze blowing in is palpable.

Jack moves from his crouch to a sitting position beside the boxes. 'Where do you want to begin?'

I slouch back on the sofa again. 'Well, we know she was standing outside Greggs in Gateshead six years ago. We have the limited-angle security camera footage confirming that. We also know that her blue and broken body, covered in fresh welts and left tangled in nettle was discovered inside the gates of a park in Tamworth eighteen months later. So, what we now believe is that during that eighteen-month window she was forced to appear in the video found on Arthur Turgood's hard drive, *and* briefly stayed in Aurélie's hole in the woods in Poole.'

Jack reaches into the first box and removes the picture of eleven-year-old Jemima Hooper that was used on all the Missing posters at the time. The freckled face and ginger plaits look as innocent now as they did when I first looked at the picture on Tuesday morning.

'Gateshead to Tamworth is nearly two hundred miles,' Jack estimates, sucking air through his teeth, 'and then it's almost the same distance from Tamworth to Poole. Six hours' worth of driving in all, assuming no traffic or rest stops, but what I don't understand is why. Why would she be in Poole at all? It's not like it's close to either of the other destinations.'

I can already see what he's suggesting but there's no evidence to support the theory yet. 'Maybe Poole is closer to something else; maybe where she was held, or where the filming occurred, is down this way somewhere.'

'Either that or the auction site was somewhere closer. Aurélie reckoned she was auctioned in London, but I'd be surprised if they used the same location every time. There definitely does seem to be something tying all of this to this part of the country though. But it feels like we're looking for the tiniest needle in the biggest haystack.'

I close my eyes, trying to piece together the picture-less jigsaw. 'We know that Jemima Hooper, Freddie Mitchell and my sister all appeared in videos that wound up on Arthur Turgood's hard drive, but we also know that given his age and feeble body, he probably wasn't responsible for recording Jemima's video, and so far there is nothing connecting him directly with the video of my sister. Freddie has told us that Turgood would offer rewards if any of the boys would agree to perform certain acts on video, but where were those videos recorded? Maybe that's what links all of this: the location of the filming site.'

Jack is pulling a face. 'That's some leap in logic. The films could all have been made independently of one another; different crew and locations.'

It's a fair challenge, and it is possible that I'm getting a bit ahead of myself. 'What do James Bond, Harry Potter and *Santa Claus the Movie* have in common?'

He frowns at the question.

'They were all filmed in part at Pinewood Studios on the outskirts of Slough,' Rachel replies, entering the room, and handing us both a mug of tea.

'Exactly!' I say. 'Different concepts, different crews, different years, but all share a common filming location.'

Jack's frown deepens. 'You're suggesting Jemima Hooper and Freddie Mitchell were filmed at Pinewood too?'

'No, don't be absurd! I mean, we don't know that there isn't a makeshift recording studio somewhere that lots of different crews use to produce their smutty movies. I haven't seen the footage, but you tell me, Jack: did it look like they'd been recorded in someone's basement, or was there more of a professional feel to them?'

He grimaces at the memory of what he has seen. 'Okay, yes, there is a certain *professional* look to them.'

'Do you think it would be possible for your tech wizards to have the facial recognition programme search for commonalities between the videos? I'm thinking bed shapes, lampshades, curtains, bed sheets, that kind of thing. If there is a location – or several locations – used, it would help to narrow down which videos share certain props.'

Jack shrugs. 'I can ask them the question.'

'Can you also find out if all the footage is inside a building, or whether there's any external shots that might help narrow down the location?'

'Sure, but unless we have an idea of where that location might be, I'm not sure it would help.'

I take a sip of my tea. 'Yes, well, I might have a potential lead on that.'

It's Rachel's turn to frown. 'What lead?'

'Freddie Mitchell told us that he would be driven somewhere when videoing was required; I'm going to ask him if he remembers where.'

Chapter Twenty-Eight

THEN

Poole, Dorset

She'd been pretending to doze since her parents had returned to the room, but in truth, Aurélie wished they would all just leave her alone. This room was too bright, despite the permanently drawn drapes, and she resented the fact that strangers could come and go as they pleased; she wasn't used to such an invasion of privacy; at least she would hear *him* coming before he entered her room. She longed for somewhere she could barricade and remain at peace until *she* was ready to allow people in. She missed the trips to the exercise room where he would allow her a few minutes to burn energy once he realised life underground was causing her to put on weight.

'Do you want something to drink?' Solange asked from the seat beside the bed, but Aurélie remained silent, hoping her mother would take the hint and just leave.

Solange tugged on the bed sheet. 'Aurélie, my darling, do you want something to eat or drink?'

Aurélie wanted to remain quiet, but Solange would only continue disturbing her.

'Non, merci,' Aurélie finally answered.

Her father had been in and out of the room on his phone, and was out there now, pretending nobody knew what he was really doing. Aurélie had seen the way his eyes had widened the moment he'd seen her. Was she merely a pay cheque to him now?

Solange stood and left the room, muttering something about getting herself a drink, and promising she'd return with a drink for Aurélie too, despite her protestations to the contrary.

And now that she was alone, she wanted nothing more than to get out of bed and push a chair or table against the door to stop anyone else coming in, yet she remained where she was, still not able to walk more than the few yards to the private bathroom. Her muscles still ached from the treacherous journey from the forest, and ironically it was being trapped in this bed that was preventing her body from truly recovering.

If she were to yank the needle and tube from her arm, she wondered how far she'd manage to get before someone caught up with her and dragged her back. Would she make it off the ward? Maybe as far as the elevator; maybe down to the ground floor; would she make it to the taste of fresh air? Or would she be manhandled back to bed as soon as she opened the door? They couldn't keep her here forever, and if she could just build up her strength – emotional and physical – they'd have to let her go, and life could restart once again.

She closed her eyes, and willed dreamless sleep to take her, but there was that face again: Seven's wet eyes, whimpering as she realised the pain that was about to befall her.

'It was your own fault,' Aurélie whispered beneath the bedsheets that began to blot her own tears. 'You shouldn't have disobeyed the rules.'

Aurélie hadn't lied to Emma and the police officer when they'd asked her what she remembered of the girl – Jemima Hooper, they called her: they had only met that one night, but it was a memory that would never allow Aurélie to escape; it held her in its clutches and would forever more.

'I need you to help me escape,' Seven had said within ten minutes of being in the hole. Her voice had been high-pitched and she didn't enunciate English words in the same way as Aurélie had learned to hear them.

She'd been no more than a whippet of a child, and who was she to question Aurélie's choice to remain in such squalor? It wasn't like Aurélie hadn't considered every angle and possible escape plan. She'd spent months of her life formulating plans for escape, but what had held her back was the knowledge of what would happen when she inevitably failed. She had seen – had felt for herself – how cruel her captor could be; it didn't bear thinking about. And what if he was right all along? What if she was safer with him than out there in the real world? She could only cling to the moments when he was warm and affectionate, even if they weren't as frequent as she wished.

'They'll come for me again, and we need to be ready,' the girl had continued, so confident and self-assured for one who couldn't have been much older than thirteen or fourteen at most; though it was difficult to truly judge age and appearance in the darkness.

He'd left them a larger candle than usual when she'd been

brought down here. He'd told Aurélie to explain *the rules*; to tell her there was no benefit in causing trouble. She knew what he expected of her, and she knew what he would do if she failed.

'No, I'm sorry,' Aurélie told Seven.

'What's your name?' Seven asked.

The question had thrown her. 'Je m'appelle Quatre. I am Four.'

'No, your *real* name. Do you even remember it? Before all this? You're French, right? Did they snatch you from France?'

The questions were intrusive, and each one was a blow that threatened to strike at the thin structure Aurélie had built to protect herself. She'd turned away; crawled to the darker corner of the hole, covering her ears, so she wouldn't have to hear any more. But Seven hadn't been prepared to roll over so easily. Picking up the candle, she'd carefully carried it away from the table, surveying the small perimeter, before joining Aurélie in the corner.

'I know you're scared,' Seven had said, casting light over the shadow, 'but if we work together – like a team – we can get away.'

Aurélie would have knocked the candle from her hand, but she didn't want to create a mess; he would be furious if he suspected the candle had been moved from its spot on the table.

'How long have you been down here?' Seven continued.

Aurélie hadn't known the answer, nor had she wanted to think about it. This had always been her home, and would be for evermore.

'Out there is a real world; a world where they won't beat and hurt us; a world where my mam and dad are waiting for me to come home; a world full of sausage rolls and éclairs. What do you miss the most? I miss Curly Wurlys. Do you know that chocolate bar? It's caramel twisted into a web of sorts, and then covered in chocolate. Me and my grandpa stick them in the freezer until they're solid, and then we have a mug of warm milk that we dip them into to soften them. It's a canny snack.'

What was wrong with the girl; did she really think a trip down memory lane would bend Aurélie to her will?

'So, go on, what do you miss the most?'

How could you miss what you couldn't remember?

'Or, if not a thing, *who* do you miss the most? I miss me mam; she can be such a nightmare at times, but she gives the best hugs. That's the first thing I'm gonna do when I get back home: give her the biggest hug, and tell her how sorry I am about everything I ever did wrong. If *this* – all of this – is a punishment, I wouldn't wish it on my worst enemy.'

At the time, Aurélie couldn't remember what her mum and dad looked like; in fact it had taken their walking into her hospital room to fire any kind of recognition.

'It doesn't have to be like this, you know,' Seven had kept on. 'I know it's scary, but I've heard about others who've escaped. They want us to live in fear, so we'll be more compliant; that's why they threaten and hurt us, but it isn't in their best interests to leave any lasting damage. Think about it, we won't be able to… *perform* if we're in too much pain, right? So they threaten violence – inflicting only a little to show they mean business – and have our own imaginations act as prison guards.'

Aurélie hadn't wanted to listen, but was there some truth in this child's words? How could one so young be so smart already? It was impossible that she could have been in their clutches for as long as Aurélie, and yet she was so much more clued up; how was that possible?

'What time does he bring you breakfast, like? That's probably when they'll come and collect me, and that's why we need to be ready. Is there anything in here we can use as a weapon?'

The girl was talking so quickly, it had been difficult for Aurélie to understand her, despite the language tapes she'd studied to stave off boredom.

'No, it is impossible,' she had tried to reason. 'There are rules; if you try to escape, he will punish me; *they* will punish us.'

'They'd have to catch us first.'

Aurélie had grabbed the girl's arms at that point, had implored her to see reason, but she had refused.

'My name is Jemima – Jem for short – and I plan to get out of here, even if you don't. Tell me your name and I'll get a message to your parents and let them know you're still alive, and where they can find you. How about that? You help me escape, and I'll lead the police to save you.'

No, no, no, she'd wanted to scream, but it had been like talking to a broken record; she'd had more sensible conversations with the muddy wall of her inherited home. Seven would not listen, despite Aurélie's best efforts.

'All you need to do is tell them I'm not well; tell them I slipped and banged my head. I'll be lying on the floor so they will think I'm unconscious, and as soon as they come close, that is when I'll attack them. Your only job will be to tell them I'm hurt, and then try and block them from chasing after me. Please? I can't do this without you.'

The plan was full of holes, and no matter how many times Aurélie pictured the attempt, it *always* ended with the two of them being caught and punished.

'I am sorry, but I cannot help you. It will not work, and we will both be punished. Please do not do anything stupid.'

It was shortly after this point that Seven had agreed she wouldn't cause Aurélie any trouble, and had suggested they both go to sleep, leaving the candle burning. Aurélie had climbed onto the mattress, leaving a space for Seven to lie in, but she had refused, opting for the cold floor instead. Aurélie must have drifted off, only to be woken an hour or so later. Keeping her eyes closed save for a fraction, she watched the candlelight dancing over the walls as Seven snuck about, obviously looking for something she could use as a weapon in her crazed plan. That was why she hadn't wanted to sleep on the mattress, to avoid disturbing Aurélie when she started her search.

Aurélie remained silent, trying to ignore the less than subtle movement, and when she heard *him* coming, her senses were instantly on high alert. Sitting upright, it had been impossible to see as the candle had been extinguished. She wanted to scrabble around on the floor, to pull Seven close, and hold her there, but if he opened the door and found her not on the mattress, he wouldn't be happy; that was one of the rules.

'Psst, Seven, come to the bed,' she whispered into the darkness. 'We must be in bed when he arrives or he will be angry. Please?'

She'd strained to hear the sound of any movement, but the room had been deathly silent. She'd gasped when he'd opened the door wide, shining his torch over at the mattress to check she was in place. He immediately saw that Aurélie was alone, and as he shone the torch around the rest of the room, he didn't see Seven step out from behind the door and crack the chair over the back of his head. To the sound of splintering wood, he crashed to the floor, the torch spinning on the ground.

'Come with me.' Seven beckoned from the open door. 'Please? This is *our* chance to escape.'

Aurélie had looked at him, prone, and probably bleeding. He wasn't moving, but she couldn't tell if he was dead, not without getting closer. She had wondered for a moment whether they could actually get away, but something held her back, and she remained where she was, shaking her head firmly.

'Oh well, your loss,' Seven called, disappearing through the door and beginning the ascent to the surface.

In that moment, Aurélie had prayed that Seven would be rewarded; that she would find her way out and avoid capture, returning to her life of warm milk and Curly Wurlys, but the dream had lasted fewer than sixty seconds. That was how long it had taken for him to come to his senses and charge up the tunnel after her.

Aurélie heard the kicking and screaming long before she saw Seven dragged back in through the door, and mercilessly flung to the ground like an old cloth. Then he'd made Aurélie watch as Seven's body had writhed with the jolts of electricity.

'You did well,' he said when it was over, pressing a hand to Aurélie's cheek, passing her back the small piece of paper she'd managed to push under the door when Seven's back had been turned. 'Thank you for warning me. You'll be rewarded.'

Chapter Twenty-Nine

NOW

Weymouth, Dorset

The summer dress is clinging to my lower back by the time I arrive at the former church hall, now homeless kitchen, where I first interviewed Freddie Mitchell. It's shortly after two, the lunchtime queue has dwindled, and there are only three people waiting inside at the table for a fresh batch of rolls to be brought out and the fruit platter to be topped up. I'm given wary looks as I move past the queue and head to the front of the table. I look apologetic as I try to offer reassurance that I'm not pushing in.

The three of them seem tired and famished, their clothes hanging from gaunt frames, hair too out of control to be styled. Each carries a rolled-up coat presumably holding the precious belongings they daren't allow out of their sight.

'Have any of you seen Freddie?' I enquire, but it's as if they don't hear me, because their attention has been diverted by a basket with arms and legs moving from the makeshift kitchen area.

The basket is lowered, and I instantly recognise the shaved head and vibrant eyes of my close friend Freddie, the man who dared to let me into his world, turning mine upside down in the process. I will never forget meeting Freddie, and I feel truly blessed that he was able to open up to me about his troubled past. I owe him for all the success and rewards that writing *Monsters Under the Bed* has brought with it.

'Hello, stranger!' he coos when he spots me waiting at the side of the table. 'Don't tell me sales have dropped so much that you've come here for your supper.'

Freddie has a gift for extracting potential tension from any situation. He is incredibly self-deprecating, and doesn't display any illusions of grandeur about himself or anyone he meets. The Queen herself could step through the rickety old doors of the shelter, and he'd offer her the same deference, humility and hospitality as any other person in this room right now.

'We've got tuna and mayo, ham salad, and cheese and pickle,' he says now to the woman at the front of the queue, whose expression has changed from weariness to glee upon seeing him. 'Help yourself, and make sure to take two different pieces of fruit this time, Dawn; we don't want a banana-belching issue like yesterday, do we?'

He smiles at her and she beams back, rifling through the basket of wrapped rolls until she finds one with a 'C & P' scrawled on it. She places it on the brown tray before her, along with an apple and a satsuma, before shuffling down the line to where the tea urn awaits. It was Freddie's idea to offer visitors a tray on which to carry their menu choices, so it would feel more like they had stepped into a café like any normal person, rather than that they'd reached rock bottom. It's those little touches that make Freddie who he is; all the more reason why I wish I'd come here with a less selfish motive.

With the three diners stocked and seated, he now turns back to me, and wraps his arms around my shoulders. 'I wish you'd said you were coming; I'd have hoovered and dusted and rolled out the red carpet.'

He's only teasing, as he always does, because he knows I prefer to shy away from my new-found celebrity status.

'I like what you've done with the place,' I say back to him, 'though you didn't need to put on this buffet just for me.'

He chuckles. 'I hope you've brought your Marigolds with you, as there's a stack of cups and plates need washing up through there.'

'Actually, it's more of a social visit,' I say reluctantly.

'Oh yeah?' He's eyeing me suspiciously, almost as if he can already read my mind, and is raising his defences in anticipation. 'Well, you know me: I charge by the hour, and unless you've brought a chest full of gold and diamonds, you're going to have to do something else to earn my time.'

'If you wash, I'll dry,' I say, sliding the bag from my shoulder and making my way to the kitchen doorway.

In truth, I'd rather speak to him out of earshot, and hopefully, with his hands wet with suds, he'll be more of a captive audience.

'Is this about the summer fête?' he asks when we are alone, and the sink is beginning to fill.

He wasn't joking about the stack of cups; it's like four towers of a makeshift castle, with battlements built from crockery plates and bowls. I know he won't admit he's struggling to keep the operation running, but it wouldn't surprise me if he's been the only one working here today, preparing the food as well as serving it. Most evening shifts at the shelter are operated on a rota basis, but it's harder to find staff during the day; all are volunteers and most have day jobs.

'Summer fête?' I question.

'To raise funds to fix the leaky roof,' he says, looking towards the ceiling. 'It's not a problem whilst it's so warm and dry, but as soon as autumn arrives you won't be able to move about without fear of tripping over one bucket or another. So, your Uncle Freddie here thought we could use the shelter to host an afternoon fête for locals to promote their businesses, and to harness the cash of the well-off tourist trade that flocks to the beach every weekend. I've been doing the rounds at all the local churches asking parishioners to bake cookies and cakes, donate unwanted clothes and, if nothing else, just come along and see if there are any bargains to be had.'

Whilst I am in awe of this wonderful man who has every right to hate the world for the hand he was dealt, it doesn't surprise me that this is what he has been ploughing his energy into since finishing work as a consultant on the televised version of *Monsters*.

'You're amazing, Freddie. When is it? I'll be sure to come down and serve tea or whatever you need me to do.'

'I was hoping you might be able to do a little more than that.'

'Name it. Do you want a signed book? No, wait, I can do better than that; how about signed copies of all my books? Maybe you could auction them off or something? No, wait, that's a rubbish idea, who's going to want to buy books I've scribbled in when they can go up the road to Waterstones and get a clean copy? Sorry, that was a silly idea.'

I'm getting flustered, and he immediately comes to me and places bubbly hands on mine. 'That would be incredibly generous, and we would really appreciate the signed books for an auction or raffle. Thank you.'

I wish the burning in my cheeks would dampen.

'I was actually going to ask if you would mind being our celebrity guest at the fête; it would be great if you could officially open the event, and pose for some selfies with those who want them. I reckon if we could put your name on the flyers that will be going up around town, we'll draw a much larger audience. Would that be okay?'

Whilst I don't believe my presence will draw more than a few book-club members, I'll never be able to refuse Freddie. 'Whatever you need, I'm here for you.'

'Then good, it's settled. There's a dry towel hanging in the cupboard that you can use now.'

I head over to the cupboard, remove a pressed towel, unfold it and reach for the first cup on the draining board.

'So, how have you been, Freddie? Clearly keeping busy.'

'Yes, well, you know I don't like to be without a purpose; that's a dark and slippery slope I hope never to find myself on again.'

Given the trauma Freddie experienced at the hands of Arthur Turgood and the other abusers at the St Francis Home for Wayward Boys, it was almost inevitable that he would seek solace in substances that would help temporarily numb the pain and suffering, and with that came petty crime and eventually a life on the streets. When I met Freddie he was still using, but wanted to get himself cleaned up, and had already started volunteering at the shelter a few days a week. It is incredible to see how much he has changed his life in the last four years. The man before me now stands proud in his sleeveless flannel shirt and denim jeans cut short at the knees. He has a way of brightening any room.

I dry cups and saucers in silence for several minutes, uncertain where to start, wishing I hadn't come to ask him about his traumatic past, but knowing I can't leave here until I have.

'What's on your mind?' he asks, pausing in the middle of scraping something dried and red from the edge of a soap-covered plate. 'You're not usually this quiet.'

Here goes.

Lowering the towel, I lean closer to him, my voice barely louder than a whisper. 'There's something I need to ask you about, and I don't know how.'

I feel his shoulders tauten beside me. 'I think I know what you're going to ask.'

'You do?'

I feel him nodding. 'It's been months since I told you your PC Jack had found videos of me in compromising positions on Turgood's computer, and we haven't talked about it since. I figured a day would come when you'd want to know more, but I secretly hoped it wouldn't.'

I can't bring myself to look at him, and I don't know if I'm doing that for his benefit or my own. 'I'm sorry, Freddie, I know it's probably the last thing you want to have to relive, but I have to ask you about it. Did you hear that Aurélie Lebrun has been found thirteen years after her abduction?'

'I've got eyes and ears, so I don't know how I could have missed it. Even though I try to avoid reading newspapers and watching television, local gossip like that filters through even to homeless shelters. It's not often towns like Poole make the national news.'

'I'm working with the local police to try and make sense of what happened to her and identify who took her all those years ago. I can't go into all the detail, but it's clear this goes much wider than just one girl. Aurélie has been able to confirm she met one of the victims who also appeared in videos on Turgood's hard drive, and now *I* believe there may be a link to yours and Anna's situations. I'm not sure exactly what, but I wanted to ask what you remember of where they took you when they made those films.'

He returns to scratching at the remnants on the plate. 'I'm not too sure what I can tell you. I said they would offer rewards if we agreed to appear on film, right?'

I nod, because I know if I try to speak, the bubbling sob will escape.

'They would drive us to the place, we'd be taken into a darkened room, and… well, you know the rest.'

I take a deep breath, swallowing my trepidation. 'Did you ever see anyone else there?'

'I really don't remember; I think I blotted it from my memory, repressed it. As I said in December, I'd totally forgotten about the videos until your PC Jack reached out to me.'

If I was a real friend, I would leave it there. I can see how painful this conversation is for him, and I desperately want to stay quiet and allow silence to return. But I can't; Jemima Hooper and my sister deserve more, and it's a cost I'll have to pay.

'Do you remember if there was any kind of film crew? Presumably it wasn't Turgood operating the camera?'

'I'm sorry, but I don't remember who was there. Yeah, probably there was someone holding the camera, but I don't remember who. I mean, you've got to be pretty messed up in the head to be able to film things like that.'

'What about other children? Do you remember seeing any other victims being forced to perform there?'

'What's this all about, Emma? Do you think this Aurélie appeared in films too?'

'No, not her – at least I don't think *her* – but someone she met where she was being held.'

He places the cleaned plate on the draining board. 'No, I'm sorry, I don't remember seeing anyone else there at all. My only memory is being put in the back of Turgood's car and driven somewhere, and then returning to the home with some kind of chocolate bar.'

I just want to hug him and assure him that I won't keep pressing, but the voice in my head won't stop.

'Can you remember what the place looked like? I'm working on a theory that some kind of film studio might have been used. Does that ring any bells? Did the place they took you look like that, or am I totally on the wrong track?'

He pulls the plug and empties the sink, before refilling it with fresh water and soap. 'I'm sorry; I wish there was more I could tell you, but my mind isn't what it once was, and I don't think it wants to remember any of that.'

I sigh with regret. 'Okay, Freddie, I understand, and I'm sorry to ask you all these sordid questions. I know how difficult this is for you. Just one last question: do you recall any distinguishing features about your journey to the place? Did you pass through any towns, or familiar landmarks?'

He turns to face me, the bright eyes sterner now. 'No, I told you, I don't. I think I slept most of the way there and back.'

I know better than to press any more; I may already have done irreparable damage to my friendship with Freddie, so I put a lid on my questions, and allow the awkward silence to descend as I finish wiping the crockery.

Chapter Thirty

NOW

Weymouth, Dorset

The walk back to my flat is stifling, yet sobering. I promised Freddie I would drop off the signed hardbacks for the raffle or auction, and he said he would keep me posted about the date of the event, though he's hopeful it will be before the end of the month. Freddie is a smart man, and I know he won't see my visit today as anything more than me following my journalistic instincts, and yet the guilt sweeping through my mind right now is overwhelming. At what point does the desire to find justice for victims cross into making their lives unbearable?

When I first met Freddie and he told me about his time at the St Francis Home, he *wanted* me to find the evidence – to finally prove once and for all – that he was telling the truth. He (as well as Mike and Steve) had tried to tell the authorities countless times before but their claims had been dismissed,

239

belittled and ignored. My desire to find justice for them was in their best interests and they welcomed the support.

All the same – and this applies to Aurélie as well – is it not unkind to force them to recall such horrific trauma when there is no guarantee of finding the people responsible? In Freddie's situation, even if he did recall the precise location of the studio where Turgood made his film, what good would it do? It's not like there will be much evidence to prove who is running such a place and how these various nefarious groups are tied together. It won't bring Jemima Hooper back; it won't allow Aurélie to bury her past and move on with her life.

I suppose maybe catching the man who held Aurélie below the ground for so many years would bring her some closure, but is that worth the emotional cost she will have to bear? It was Remy's idea for me to be introduced to Aurélie and tell her story through her words, but did anyone consult her? If I was in her position and had been subjected to such horrors, would I really want them displayed for the world to see? I'm not convinced I would.

There's no sign of Jack's car when I arrive home. Opening the door, I can see Rachel in the kitchen, sitting on the floor, her back against the freezer, an open tub of ice-cream beside her.

She extends the tub towards me. 'You want some?'

Nothing would be as welcome right now as bathing in a tub filled with ice-cream, but until that's an option, eating it will have to suffice. Grabbing a spoon from the drainer, I slide down the cupboard, plopping onto the floor beside my best friend.

'You look like you need this more than me,' she says, passing me the tub. 'Rough day?'

'Yeah, pretty sour, to be honest; what's your excuse?'

'I asked first. You look like you're carrying the weight of the world on your shoulders.'

Putting the spoon in my mouth I savour the cool texture and saltiness of the caramel, and for a fleeting moment I'm transported to a flightless world where there is nothing more troubling than choosing which cloud to float on.

'Things didn't go great with Freddie. He couldn't recall anything of where he was taken, nor whether it was some kind of bespoke film studio. And now I feel like it was a stupid idea going there to ask him at all. He was doing so well – organising a summer fête to raise funds to fix the roof of the shelter – but was crestfallen by the time I left. Who needs a wrecking ball when they've got me in their life?'

She puts her arm around me. 'I do. My excuse for devouring half a tub of ice-cream is that Daniella messaged me, saying she thinks we need to talk.'

I drop my spoon in the tub and sit bolt upright. 'That's brilliant news! Why didn't you tell me sooner?'

She pulls a face. 'I'm not so sure it *is* such good news. She didn't say she wants us to get back together.'

'No, but she hasn't told you she doesn't. Remember, it was *her* idea that the two of you split up, so maybe her request to talk is so that she can apologise and start making it up to you.'

Her frown deepens. 'I doubt it's that…' She scrunches her eyes closed to hide her embarrassment. 'Last night after you'd gone to sleep, I stayed awake online,' she sighs, 'cyber stalking her as I do most nights when I'm feeling lonely. I think I might have commented on a few of her Instagram posts, and not in a good way. The horror of what I'd done hit me like a thunderbolt first thing, and I deleted them straightaway, but if she saw any of them, it would explain why she would want to talk. She's probably looking to file some kind of restraining order against me.'

'Oh.' It's hard to argue with her logic.

'Yeah, which is why this salted caramel whirl is my new love; you can say a lot about how bad ice-cream is for your health, but it never fails to call when it's promised it will, and it never breaks your heart.'

I have another spoonful and savour the ice on my tongue before swallowing. 'You know we can do one of two things right now: we can either spend the rest of the day wallowing in self-pity and eating things we will regret in the morning—'

'Sounds like a fine idea to me,' she interrupts, plunging her own spoon into the tub.

'Or we can put the ice-cream away and have another go at trying to figure out who was responsible for Aurélie's abduction thirteen years ago.'

'I vote self-pity and ice-cream,' she says, raising her hand, but I've already taken the tub from her and replaced the lid.

Dropping the tub back into the freezer, I drag Rachel up off the floor. 'Sorry, but you lost all your democratic privileges when you cyber stalked your ex.'

She groans playfully, but doesn't resist when I tug her by the arm into the living room.

'Where's Jack anyway?' I ask, searching for the box of materials relating to Aurélie's abduction.

'He got called up by Cavendish and apparently his presence at the hospital was required.'

I raise my eyebrows at her snooty voice.

'I asked him what it was about or whether either of us should be there too, but he said she'd only asked for him.'

'I'm sure he'll keep us posted if it has any relevance to this,'

I say passively. 'Let's begin with this,' I add, reaching into the box and extracting a DVD with indecipherable writing scrawled on it. 'This is a copy of the public appeal Remy and Solange made a couple of days after the abduction.'

Placing the disc in the player, I switch on the television and settle back into the sofa beside Rachel. The picture quality isn't great and looks as though the original recording was made on tape and then transferred to DVD; it lacks any of the sharpness of modern filmmaking. The scene opens with the picture of Aurélie – freckles either side of her nose, her fair hair plaited in pigtails, the red and white ruffled dress – hanging from the wall behind a long table. A moment later, two suited men lead in the grief-stricken parents, a younger Solange bawling, Remy beside her trying to remain resolute.

The lead detective reads out the carefully worded brief confirming the date and time of the abduction, describing Aurélie and pointing out that she speaks little or no English. He explains that the parents have asked that he read out a prepared statement on their behalf. I could almost recite the words without hearing them, having heard the same words tumble from my own father's mouth. They ask for the kidnappers to return their precious angel to them, and call on anyone with information that can lead to Aurélie's return to come forward and help the investigative team. Maybe it's the passage of time, or the fact that I know their wish won't be realised for another thirteen years, but the words sound so flat.

But no, it's more than that, there's something very wrong with the scene before us.

'Don't you just wish you could go back in time to the day before and warn them what is going to happen?' Rachel says rhetorically.

I skip back to the beginning of the footage, and watch again, this time ignoring the image hanging from the wall and the bobbing shoulders of Solange. Instead, I'm carefully watching Remy's body language.

There's no doubt that he is shaken by the events as described by the lead detective's wooden voice, but there is more. Maybe it's the poor quality of the footage, or the old-fashioned 4:3 image ratio, but I would swear there is a lot more to Remy Lebrun's reactions on the screen. He isn't just a terrified and grieving father; he wears a look I'm more than familiar with: guilt.

Chapter Thirty-One

THEN

Poole, Dorset

The nurse had just advised that dinner would be delivered to Aurélie's rom in the next fifteen to twenty minutes, signalling the end of another day stuck in the bed, her anxiety growing as the prospect of facing the real world grew in the pit of her stomach. At least her mother's crying had finally subsided.

'You should go for a walk, get some fresh air,' her father had suggested an hour ago.

Aurélie had been reluctant, her eyes still not accustomed to the hospital's artificial light, let alone natural sunlight, but Remy had offered her his sunglasses, and that had left little reason to refuse. He'd helped her out of bed, arranged for the nurse to transfer her pouches to a mobile stand, and bought her a coat from a shop inside the hospital so she'd have more than just the hospital gown to protect her dignity.

He'd taken her hand in his, supported her arm as they slowly moved out of the room, along the corridor and towards the elevator. It had felt like everyone's eyes followed every step of the journey, but she kept her gaze glued to the floor, unable to seek confirmation that she was right; why would anyone be interested in her?

The calling of her name as they'd emerged through the sliding doors had been more than a shock; she'd suffered what felt like her heart attempting to explode in her chest, and she'd begged her father to take her back inside. He'd listened and comforted her; told her he would support her in whatever decisions she made, before helping her back inside, offering a solitary wave in the direction of the gathered journalists and cameramen. It had been a huge relief that none of them had attempted to follow them back in.

'What do they want of me?' she'd asked as she'd clambered back into the bed, discarding the coat on her mother's lap.

'You are big news, my darling,' Remy had said, unable to keep the excitement from his voice. 'Everybody wants to know that you are safe and well.'

Why would any of them care about her? She was nobody; a girl who had allowed herself to be taken when she should have known better; a girl who had been forced to do things she didn't want just to survive. She was nothing special.

Dinner's arrival would signal her parents' temporary disappearance while they went to replenish their energy levels; at least that would bring the silence and solitude she had been craving since her arrival. A knock at the door signalled the moment she'd been waiting for, and seconds later, a young man entered, carrying a tray, which he deposited on the sliding table at the foot of the bed.

'Can I get you a cup of tea or coffee to go with that?' he enquired.

'Tea, please,' she replied. 'No milk, no sugar.'

He nodded, offering a friendly smile, and disappeared back through the door. He returned with a steaming mug as her parents departed.

'There you go,' he said, before turning back when he realised they were now alone. 'Can I just say how brave I think you are? After everything you must have been through… To find the strength to get away and come back… You're such an inspiration.'

He was beaming, and it felt as though he was talking about someone else.

'I'm Carl, by the way. If there's anything else you need, or you just want a friendly face to chat to, just ask the nurses to call Carl; they all know me around here.'

She nodded, watching him leave, grateful he hadn't asked for a picture or autograph. What had happened to the world she'd left? Was it normal now that unimportant people such as herself were treated as celebrities? Or was all the attention just her father's ploy? Would she ever be able to just slip away and find some level of normality and simplicity once more?

A second knock at the door wasn't welcome, even less so when Detective Cavendish and the other policeman entered the room, carrying a folder, approaching the bed without hesitation.

'Good evening, Aurélie,' Cavendish said without a trace of a smile. 'Are your parents around?'

Aurélie shook her head, staring at the tray of food, the plastic lid over the plate filled with condensation. 'They have gone for dinner.'

'Good,' Cavendish said, nodding at the man, 'that's probably for the best. How are you feeling?'

Aurélie shrugged.

The policeman was shuffling from one foot to another, clearly uncomfortable about being here.

'This is my colleague PC Jack Serrovitz,' Cavendish said when she spotted Aurélie staring at him. 'I've asked him to be here with me, as I have some further questions I'd like to ask you about your time away. I appreciate you're waiting to eat, but it is really important we ask you these questions. Okay?'

It was less of a question, and more of a statement; would she even have listened had Aurélie refused and said she wanted to wait for her parents? She doubted it.

'We have finished processing the scene in the woods,' Cavendish began. 'We have taken a number of samples from both the cabin and your cell, and will be reviewing those against a database of similar samples, looking for any matches. We will also compare them to the sample of your DNA that was taken upon your arrival at the hospital for cross-examination purposes.'

She paused and took a step closer, tightening her grip on the folder. 'The thing is, Aurélie, we also found something else at the site that we'd like to discuss.' She opened the folder and extracted three large photographs. 'The white markings you can see on the ground here are graves. Examination of the ground in and around where you were being held revealed the shallow nature of these holes, in which we discovered a number of bones; *human* bones.' She looked up at her colleague again. 'One of the graves contained the remains of a baby.'

Aurélie's heart skipped as she thought back to that night of agony when he had ripped the lifeless child from her womb.

Yet if the detective was right, then what he'd told her the last time she'd seen him was a lie. She stared down at her hands.

'We will perform a DNA test on the bones to confirm the baby was yours,' Cavendish continued, 'but what I'd like to ask you about is the other remains we found. One set of bones belong to an adult male. A thorough examination of the skeleton is now under way, and it is believed the victim was aged between eighteen and thirty on account of the size and shape. Do you recall any other men being at the site?'

Aurélie shook her head immediately. There hadn't been any other men in her life for many years, and yet something stirred somewhere in the embers. There had been a man there once, hadn't there? The memory was just out of her grasp.

'Exhumation of the bones revealed markings consistent with an axe of some kind. We believe this victim may have been murdered, the body burned on a fire to remove the flesh, and then the bones buried in the shallow grave. Whilst it is feasible that this man's grave has nothing to do with the man who was holding you prisoner, he is our prime suspect at this time. You could really help us out if you can tell us anything about this victim. Did your captor ever bring other men to see you?'

The sound of her captor arguing with another man filled her head in an instant, but it had been when he was transporting her back to the hole from the exercise hall. They'd been arguing about her, hadn't they? He'd shoved her into the hole, and then returned to continue the argument. She hadn't heard any more after that.

Aurélie shook her head. 'No, he would not share me with anybody… He would say I was his, and nobody else's.'

'Can you recall your captor mentioning an argument with

another man? Or do you recall ever hearing an argument, raised voices, shouting?'

Aurélie avoided looking at her, shaking her head. What if they thought she'd caused the argument that had led to the younger man's death?

'Or were there any times when your captor seemed… I don't know, seemed angrier, or worried about anything?'

Again she shook her head.

'Did he ever speak of a partner, or someone he worked with?'

'He never spoke of himself so I knew little about him.'

Cavendish flashed a glance at her colleague. 'What about family? Did he ever tell you about his family? Do you know if he was married, or had any children?'

She wanted to cry, thinking that trapped in her prison she could have been so close to a burial ground. 'No, I'm sorry.'

Cavendish pointed at the second image of the three grave sites. 'We believe this grave contained the remains of two victims; probably not much older than ten when they died. You've previously spoken of other girls staying in the hole with you; can you recall whether any harm may have come to them?'

The ball of anxiety that had been building in the pit of her stomach suddenly moved north, and she couldn't breathe. Aurélie began to gasp, trying to inhale oxygen into her body, but her lungs refused to inflate.

'Are you okay, Aurélie?' Serrovitz asked, stepping forward, and placing a warm hand on her back.

'I – I – I can't breathe,' she stammered.

He looked around for an oxygen mask and, not finding one,

suggested Cavendish call for a nurse to come and help. She fumbled for the call button, while Serrovitz located a latex glove.

'You need to steady your breathing,' he said, passing her the glove. 'Put this over your mouth and nose, and just breathe in and out. Count slowly to twenty as you do, breathing in on the odd numbers and exhaling on the evens.'

She did as instructed, forcing the memories into the ether of her mind where she hoped they would remain for eternity.

A nurse arrived in the room a moment later, and helped swing Aurélie's legs over the edge of the bed, talking calmly and telling her just to focus on her breathing as the PC had.

'It may be best if you two wait outside,' the nurse said firmly.

'Did he kill any of those girls, Aurélie?' Cavendish continued, as if there had been no disturbance to the interview.

Eleven, twelve, thirteen, Aurélie counted silently in her head as she breathed in and out, feeling her pulse slowing at last.

'Please, Aurélie, we want to get the man who did this to you, and you are the key to finding him,' Cavendish persisted, even as her colleague dragged her away and out of the room.

He closed the door, leaving the nurse to check on Aurélie and ensure her anxiety attack was subsiding. 'You were a bit hard on her in there, you know.'

She sighed with frustration. 'I didn't mean to be, it's just… You know that feeling when you're sure there's more going on than you can see? I feel like we've barely seen the tip of the iceberg here, but I don't know how to get beneath the surface to see the rest. I wish I could see inside her head and piece it all together.'

He smiled, and placed a hand on her arm. 'I understand, but you have to remember what she must have been through. Sometimes taking it slowly is the most effective method of uncovering information. Emma taught me that; it's one of the things she's really good at.'

She rolled her eyes. 'Please don't give me another glowing reference of your girlfriend, Jack.'

'That's not what I'm doing; all I was going to say is that this kind of thing is her speciality. I've never met anyone better at coaxing answers out of a person than her. I know you have concerns about divulging too much, but you could do far worse than ask for her support with Aurélie. Just tell me you'll think about it.'

She returned his smile. 'Okay, I'll think about it. Happy now?'

'Much.'

'Good. Listen, I don't know what your plans are for this evening or whether you're heading back to London, but I intend to sit up and wait for the results of the post mortem, and the forensic pathologist's report.'

'Actually, I need to find a hotel or something. My DCS has given me a few days' grace down here, and I think I want to stick around to see how things unfold.'

'You can always crash at mine if you want?'

He narrowed his eyes. 'At yours?'

She batted away his concern with a churlish grin. 'Relax! I have a couch you can crash on. It's been years since... well, you know, and I'm not about to jump on you the moment I get you through the door. I wouldn't want to upset your girlfriend.'

'Emma's not my girlfriend; we're just... we're just friends, that's all.'

Cavendish raised her eyebrows. 'If you say so. Are you up for curry while I wait for a call from the lab?'

Chapter Thirty-Two

NOW

Weymouth, Dorset

The road outside my flat is already tail-light-to-tail-light, as cars scour for spaces as close to the beach and seafront as they can find. Weekends in Weymouth when June is as warm as this are always the same. It's great for the local tradespeople, but a nightmare for the residents. When Rachel suggested we drive to the home to see Mum, I warned her that we'd be better off catching a bus or walking, as her parking space would be long gone by the time we returned.

We spent the rest of yesterday afternoon poring over the interviews and investigative notes formed in the wake of Aurélie's abduction, but I can't say we turned over anything we didn't already know. Neither Remy nor Solange came under any serious scrutiny, given that witnesses placed them on the beach and in the hotel respectively at the time of the abduction. Whilst no beach visitors had seen the moment she was taken, several had seen her playing at the sea's edge and building the fortress out of sand, so there was no doubt that she had been on the beach with both her parents that morning. Apart from the phone call Remy had received, there had been no hint of a chink in their story.

The call had been placed from a withheld number, and when questioned Remy had claimed it was one of his aides calling from his offices in Paris regarding some paper he was due to deliver as part of his overseas tour. Within a day, the aide had been found and made a statement confirming the nature of the conversation. Maybe that was all the guilty look I'd seen on his face at the press conference had been: guilt at putting work before his child's safety. How many of us are guilty of making similar reckless choices? A sin rather than a crime. That said, it didn't explain the fear I'd seen on Aurélie's face at the hospital on that first day. Maybe a lifetime of abuse had made her wary of any physical contact with a man.

I know I'm clutching at straws, and trying to find links that simply might not be there.

'You need a break from all this,' Rachel had said over breakfast (alas, no bacon sandwiches today). 'Why don't we go and see your mum? It's been years since I saw her, and it might help take your mind off all this; you've spent every waking hour this week thinking about Jemima Hooper and Aurélie Lebrun. A break should clear your head, and I'm sure she'd love visitors. Maybe we could buy some scones and clotted cream on the way there and sit outside and enjoy a spot of high tea.'

She always knows how to put a smile on my face. Deep down I'm sure she's hoping that the visit to Mum will also help keep her mind off her impending meeting with Daniella. They've agreed to meet for dinner in London tomorrow evening, and I wish I could go there with her for moral support, but whatever needs to be said needs privacy.

The town centre is packed as we walk through, and even though it's not even ten, the temperature must be in the high twenties. Anyone planning on spending their day on the beach needs their head examined. Having bought the scones, cream and jam, we cross the bridge to Portland and continue the climb until we arrive at the home some forty minutes later. The walk has certainly helped stimulate my appetite if nothing else.

The wrought-iron gates are wide open as they usually are, and, heading through, I stroke the overweight ginger cat on the stone steps as I always do. She arches her back as my fingers brush gently over her fur.

'Cute cat,' Rachel comments.

'She's called Ginger, and she greets me every time I come here.'

Pressing the buzzer on the door, we head in and sign the guestbook at the front desk.

'A word of warning,' the nurse behind the desk says as she catches my eye, 'today isn't a great day for your mum. She woke screaming and when we went in to attend to her she started accusing us of keeping her here against her will. We've managed to settle her down now, but I just thought I should let you know she's not keen on visitors to her room today.'

I nod my understanding. 'Listen, if you want to head back to my place, I won't be offended,' I tell Rachel quietly; nobody deserves Mum on one of her bad days.'

'In case you hadn't realised,' she whispers back, 'I'm not actually here for your mum, but for you. Let's go up and see her; I'm famished.'

Part of me wants to tell her she'll regret that decision, but I resist, and instead lead her along the corridor to Mum's room. She used to be upstairs but was moved down for additional care after a nasty fall in the shower over Christmas. Down here, she still has independence, but the carers make sure she washes regularly and offer any support required. I know we're all watching the sand slowly dissipate, but it feels more real when I'm here. It's only natural to wonder whether I'll one day end up in a place like this watching the world go by as death slowly approaches.

Knocking twice, I head in, and have a mild panic when I find the room empty. If she is having a bad day (by which I mean she still sees herself as a woman in her thirties, before I was born) and she's wandered off then she could be anywhere by now. The sound of the toilet flushing eases the tension immediately, and a moment later she emerges from the small bathroom in the corner.

'Yes? Can I help you?' she demands sternly.

'Mum, it's Emma,' I say coming further into the room, 'and I've brought my friend Rachel with me. Do you remember? We were at university together.'

Mum stares at me blankly, and there's no recognition as her eyes fall on Rachel.

'Hello, Mrs Hunter, it's lovely to see you again,' Rachel choruses breezily, closing the door behind her. 'We brought some scones and clotted cream; would you like some?'

Mum looks at the brown paper bag Rachel is holding out. 'You must be one of the new nurses here, are you? I don't think we've met before.'

Rachel moves forward with no concern. 'It's a lovely day outside, would you join us for a cuppa and a scone?'

Mum blinks three times. 'Only so long as it's served in the proper way: jam first and *then* cream. To do it any other way is preposterous.'

This last statement makes me smile at past memories of the age-old debate as to whether the Cornish or Devonshire method of preparing scones is correct. Mum firmly believes that it should be jam and then cream (the Cornish way), whilst my dad preferred cream and then jam (the Devonshire way). I'm happy with either so long as the cream is thick and cold.

Rachel opens the double doors into the enclosed garden space. Another benefit of Mum now being on the ground floor is access to the lawn and garden. A small wooden table and two chairs stand on a small patio immediately beyond the doors. Across the lawn there are other residents sitting at their tables, some reading books, another knitting, while one man is playing a game of patience. He smiles as he looks up, before offering me his spare chair so that I can join Rachel and Mum at the table.

Once we're seated, I remove the scones from the paper bag, and cut them in half with a plastic knife that came with the pack we bought. In hindsight I probably could have brought tea with us, or should have asked for some to be brought to the room, but Mum doesn't seem too bothered as she slathers cream on top of the jam.

'Has Emma told you about the big case she's now working on?' Rachel asks her to break the silence.

Mum stares absently into the garden.

'This girl who went missing nearly two decades ago has turned up alive and well, and your Emma's been asked to help solve the mystery surrounding her disappearance, and to help catch the men responsible for it.'

Mum drops the knife suddenly, smearing jam and cream on the woodwork, and her hand shoots up to her mouth.

'Whoopsie,' Rachel offers, picking up the knife and wiping the mess with a paper napkin from the bag. 'Is everything all right, Mrs Hunter?'

The blood has drained from Mum's face, and she suddenly looks so much older than her sixty-five years.

'What's wrong, Mum? Are you okay?'

She doesn't respond, her gaze fixed on a bare wall across the way.

'Mum? Are you in pain?' I ask, dropping to my knees beside her, taking her free hand in mine to check her pulse. 'Mum? Talk to me. It's Emma, Mum. Can you tell me what's wrong?'

She's not reaching for her chest or crying out in pain, but all I can think is that she's having a heart attack or stroke.

She looks down at me, and for a second there is something in the way she looks at my face, but then it goes and she frowns. 'Stop fussing with me, young girl.'

'Are you okay, Mum?'

'I'm perfectly fine, dear, and I'd prefer it if you didn't refer to me as "Mum". I'm nowhere near old enough to have a daughter your age. I do wish you nurses would call me Bronwyn or Winnie.' She spots the scone, promptly picks it up and takes a delicate bite. 'At least you got the jam and cream the right way around.'

I look over to Rachel, who simply shrugs. Returning to my chair, I've lost any appetite for a scone, and instead return it to the bag. Alzheimer's is such a cruel illness, and it pains me that there is nothing I can do to help her. Days like this break my heart a little more every time.

Chapter Thirty-Three

NOW

Weymouth, Dorset

Exiting Mum's small bathroom, I pause and pick up the only picture in here of the four of us. The frame is weathered, and the glass bears a lifetime of dust and grime that only industrial cleaner will get off. But it's an insight into a happier time. The words 'Brighton 1998' are scrawled in pencil on the back of the image – I know this as I recall Mum telling me all about this trip when she was having one of her good days just before Christmas. We are all beaming, and in the background I can see what looks like a seafront, pier and some amusement arcades.

She told me Dad had won us a weekend break away at a fancy hotel along the seafront, and how Anna and I had been so excited to stay in a hotel that had a never-ending supply of Coco Pops. I have no memory of the trip, but in May 1998 I would have been five – Anna seven – and maybe all the mournful memories since she was taken haven't left room for the good ones.

I must have looked at this photograph dozens of times over the years, and I've never really thought about *how* Dad won this holiday. He wasn't one for entering competitions as far as I recall. He'd put money on the Grand National once a year, but he wasn't one for gambling. He'd had a destitute upbringing, and so every spare pound was saved 'for a rainy day'. Of course most of the family savings were soon wiped out after that day in 2000 when Anna simply vanished. With Mum unable to work, we couldn't survive on one salary without dipping into the limited pot, and I can remember overhearing arguments between them, always fuelled by the subject of money.

Carrying the frame out to the garden, I hand it to Mum. 'Do you remember this holiday, Mum?'

She takes the frame and squints at the glass. 'Is this you and your family, is it?'

'No, Mum, that's *you* there,' I say, and point at each figure. 'That's me there, that's Dad and that's Anna. Do you remember Anna?'

She glares frostily at me. 'Of course I remember my own daughter! What do you take me for? I do wish you nurses would accept what I say when I tell you there is nothing wrong with my memory; sharp as a tack it is.'

'It looks like you were all having a good time,' Rachel chimes in, looking down at the frame now in Mum's lap.

'Do you remember where the picture was taken, Mum?'

Her glare softens to a frown. 'How would *I* know where you had this picture taken?'

My eyes narrow. 'It was taken in Brighton in 1998, Mum.

Dad won us a weekend at a posh hotel; do you remember? You told me Anna and I were mad about playing on all the arcade machines. Remember?'

She suddenly pushes the table away, sending the contents flying as it topples over.

'Mum, what is it?' I ask, trying and failing to stop the table hitting the floor.

She doesn't answer, instead disappearing through the door and out of sight behind the net curtain.

'Don't worry, I'll go,' Rachel offers, standing and heading in too, leaving me to pick up the now empty pots of jam and cream, the remnants leaving a bloodlike stain on the trimmed grass. Picking up the bag with my scone, I carry the jam and cream pots into Mum's room, and deposit them in the wicker wastebin in the bathroom.

Mum is perched on the end of her bed, fiddling with the television remote while Rachel fires unanswered questions at her.

'I'm sorry, I can't get any sense out of her,' Rachel comes over and whispers.

Crouching at her feet, I look up and force eye contact with her. 'Is everything okay, Mum? Was it something I said?'

She shushes me, staring down at the remote like it is some alien contraption she doesn't know how to work, even though it is the thing she relies on most in the room.

'Are you looking for a particular programme, Mum? It's Saturday morning so *Countdown* won't be on today.'

She shushes me again.

'Why don't you let me find whatever it is you're after?' I offer when she's typed incorrect numbers and failed to change the channel. Resting my hand on the remote, I keep it there until she loosens her grip.

'I just want to watch the news; I need to know if they've found her yet.'

The breath catches in my throat, and I have to cough to clear it. 'Found who, Mum?'

She rolls her eyes dismissively. 'Who do you think? My daughter, of course! She's been missing for days, and they still haven't found out where they took her.'

I can't ignore the icy shadow creeping over my skin as I remain perched at her feet. 'You're talking about Anna's abduction.'

'Yes, obviously. Put the news on; I need to know if they've found her yet.'

I don't have the heart to tell her that the police stopped actively looking for Anna over fifteen years ago, and instead turn on BBC News 24, even though I know she won't find what she's looking for. Something else is bothering me though: *haven't found out where they took her.*

The screen fills with red as the ending report cuts back to the newscaster in the studio. She has the most ginger hair I've ever seen and a lurid pea-soup-green suit jacket that makes her resemble a leprechaun. Someone in the wardrobe department needs shooting, as it clashes with the bright background behind her. There's no doubt I'm watching Kirstie Greenacre, who cornered me at the hospital on Thursday.

'There you go,' I say calmly. 'No news about Anna.' I allow her eyes to dance over the screen to confirm what I've said, before continuing. 'What did you mean, the police don't know where *they* took her, Mum? Who are *they*?'

Her eyes are darting as she reads the ticker tape headlines

scrolling at the bottom of the screen, but she is lost in the programme. Rachel and I could explode in a puff of smoke and she wouldn't notice.

'We should probably just go,' I say to Rachel, whose face is looking more and more concerned as she watches the screen.

'No, wait, you need to see this; can you turn it up?'

Frowning, I increase the volume, turning my attention back to the leprechaun, but the screen splits, leaving her on the left, and a grey-haired man with a navy shirt and salmon-coloured cravat on the right. My eyes widen as I realise who I am looking at.

'Thank you for joining us this morning, Monsieur Lebrun,' the news presenter says, and he smiles in acknowledgement.

'Avec plaisir.'

'It's four days since you received the news that your daughter Aurélie had been found in Poole; what have the last four days been like? How is your daughter now?'

Remy's smile widens a fraction more. 'She is still in some pain, and recovering from her injuries, but I am pleased to say she should make a full recovery. We feel blessed that she has been returned to us, and I am just so thankful that we have her back.'

'It's a story that really has captured the public's attention. Missing for thirteen years – you must have all but given up hope that you'd ever see her again?'

He shakes his head gently, but the smile remains. 'Non, I think we always knew that she was still alive; my wife and I would talk about her every day, hoping that the power of our longing would travel across the airwaves to her. She must have heard our voices and come running. It truly is a miracle!'

My eyes haven't left the screen. I cannot believe what I am

watching, and yet there is a part of me not totally shocked to see Remy being interviewed via a video call on the British news. I'm trying to work out where he is, as the mirror on the wall behind him doesn't look like the hospital.

'Has Aurélie been able to tell the police much about where she's been for all this time?'

'Unfortunately, I am not allowed to discuss the police investigation, but suffice to say, she is helping them with their enquiries. I am hopeful that the police will find the people responsible for keeping her from us for so long. We have missed so many of her formative years, and we are keen to make up for lost time as quickly as possible.'

'I'm sure, I'm sure. And you told me before we came on air that your daughter has been released from the hospital now too, which is a sure sign that she is making good progress.'

This is news to me. I can only wonder if that was what Jack was called to the hospital for. I did message him last night to see whether he was staying down here somewhere or had headed back to London, but according to my phone he hasn't seen the message yet. I don't want to think about where he stayed, or with whom.

'We are glad that she is here with us in this beautiful hotel, and we intend to treat her as a princess until such time as we are allowed to return home to Paris.'

'And you have an announcement to make as well, I understand?'

'Ah, oui, that is right. For many years I have had a dream of returning to public office, but my heart has been broken, and I did not feel I could commit the rest of it to what the role requires. However, with my heart now mended, I have unfinished business with diplomatic matters, and so, as of today, I would like to tell the French people that I intend to run for President at the elections in 2022.'

There is more than a glint of excitement in his eyes, and I can't help the nausea rising in my throat at watching him cash in on his daughter's miraculous return. I'm just grateful he hasn't thrust Aurélie in front of the camera too.

'And there are plans afoot to share the details of Aurélie's horrifying experience too, is that correct?'

'Yes, of course, we think it is important for the world to know that there are some truly horrific monsters out there, which is why the bestselling writer Emma Hunter has been interviewing Aurélie for her next book.'

My heart sinks, and I can feel Rachel's gaze on me. 'Did you know he was going to—'

'No,' I say dismissively. 'I had no idea, and I'm not happy having my name dropped like that. I haven't even officially agreed to write any such book.'

My neck is clammy as the heat rises to my face.

Remy's smile stiffens to that of concerned diplomat. 'Parents should know that they cannot be complacent when caring for their children. Did you know that there are approximately 210,000 reported incidents of missing children each year in the UK alone? That is a frightening statistic, and whilst most are found and returned safely, there are many who are not. We are lucky to have our daughter back in our lives, and we want to use her tragedy to benefit others.'

Spoken like a true politician, even if the sentiment is true. I switch off the television, as I can't bear to watch any more of it.

'Have they found her then?' Mum questions. 'Is Anna safe? When can I see her?

I drop onto the bedspread beside her, and take her hands in

mine. 'No, Mum, I'm sorry, they haven't found Anna. Not yet, but I'm doing everything I can to find her for us. Okay? I won't rest until I know exactly who took Anna and why.'

Her eyes remain fixed on the television's black screen, but I can't be certain she heard a word of what I said. Pulling her into a hug I repeat the words in a whisper into her ear, praying that they will find a way through the fog of confusion permanently swirling around her brain.

'I will find her, Mum, I promise.'

Chapter Thirty-Four

THEN

Poole, Dorset

Pulling the duvet up and over her chin, Aurélie only allowed her eyes to peek out at her father's stern face on the television screen in the corner of the room. It wasn't much bigger than the room at the hospital, but at least the bed was larger; not that she'd managed to get much sleep, as the mattress wasn't as firm as she was used to. Eventually she'd given up and had pushed the duvet onto the carpet and curled up on top of that instead.

She'd been quick to get back up onto the mattress when she'd heard her mum's voice telling her father that she would check if Aurélie was awake yet. She'd pretended to be fast asleep, and had been grateful that Solange had made no effort to wake her. Despite the door to the room being closed, she'd heard them moving about out there since before seven. She hadn't understood what all the fussing was about until she'd heard her mum criticising him for arranging a television interview so soon.

At least he hadn't asked her to appear beside him; it wouldn't have surprised her if he'd bundled into the room, squashed up beside her and filled the screen with the pair of them. She had her mother to thank for avoiding such an atrocity.

Solange hadn't managed to save herself, however, and now joined her husband to the right of the news presenter's window. For a woman in her mid-fifties, Solange looked good. She'd often said she'd been blessed with youthful-looking skin, and she wasn't wrong. Whilst it looked less taut than it once had, there would be women half her age out there green with envy right now. Wearing a dull-blue crêpe dress, she had lost none of her model's poise, pointing her chin up to stretch the skin from her neck and jawline.

'We are joined now by Solange Lebrun, Aurélie's mother and still a style icon years after retiring from the catwalk. Solange, tell us how you felt the moment you walked into that hospital room and were reunited with your only child.'

Remy would have instructed her on how to reply to such questions: speak factually, avoid too much emotion, only lower your guard a fraction.

'I thought it was a dream at first,' Solange replied. 'Then there were many tears, some of sadness for our lost time, but most of pure joy and love. She is the part of my life that has been missing for too long.'

Aurélie didn't doubt a word of it, recalling snippets of what life had been like before that day. Whilst she had spent many years desperately trying to cling to happier memories, there had been bad times too: the days her mum wouldn't rise from bed, the tumbler of pastis and bottle of pills not far from her on the dressing table. The image of her parents so close together on the screen was not in keeping with how Aurélie recalled the days before she was taken.

The sound of someone frantically knocking at the door fired in her mind at that moment. Her mother wasn't home – away on some modelling jaunt perhaps? – so it was just Remy and Aurélie at the apartment in Paris. The rain was hammering against the window while Aurélie had read a book at the dining room table, but that had stopped when the knocking began. Her father had told her to continue, but she'd snuck to the doorway to see who had disturbed their evening.

A woman in a drenched overcoat had been waiting, her face panda-like where her eye makeup had run down her cheeks, but it wasn't obvious if that was a result of the rain or of some other accident.

'You cannot be here; my daughter is home.' He'd spoken rapidly, the anger not far from the edge of his tone.

'But I had to see you, my love. I missed you.'

He'd looked back towards the doorway, and Aurélie had stayed out of sight, but she'd still heard his response.

'You know I love you too, but now isn't a good time.'

'But you said you were going to tell your wife the truth about us... You said we could be together.'

'And I meant what I said, but you have to understand it isn't easy for me. It isn't just about telling my wife... I have a daughter too.'

'And what about me and *our* baby?'

Aurélie hadn't understood at first; it certainly wasn't her mother at the door, and she wasn't aware of any other brothers or sisters.

'I will tell them before he or she arrives; okay? I promise, we will be together soon.'

Aurélie shook her head at the memory – repressed for God knew how many years – but now causing her to feel light-headed. All their talk of her going to a boarding school and her not wanting to go, had that been because her father was planning to divorce Solange? But if that had been the intention, how was it they were acting so affectionately for the televised interview?

'You both stepped away from the public eye after she was taken,' the newsreader continued. 'Remy, you have already spoken about a desire to return to politics; Solange, do you have any similar plans to return to the world of fashion?'

What sort of a question was that to ask?

Solange maintained her poise. 'I gave up that life a long time ago, and it is too late for me to return. Besides, my daughter needs me, and she is all I need to bring joy into my life.'

Was that barb aimed at Remy, following his announcement? Was she not on board with his proposal to run for election? Had she ever been on board with his chosen profession? Had she pushed him to step away after the abduction?

'Given your years of experience and a growing trend towards changing the shape and face of modelling, are you not tempted to run the catwalk again?'

'Aurélie is my only priority.'

'And are there any plans to take Aurélie back to the beach in Worthing to see if she can recall anything about that day?' the newscaster pressed.

'We haven't made any decisions about that yet,' Remy replied cautiously. 'Right now, we just want her to recover physically and then emotionally. We will arrange some counselling for her as soon as we return to Paris.'

Another memory stirred at the back of Aurélie's mind; Pandora's Box had been opened, and suddenly fresh light was being cast upon the far recesses of her mind.

She was no longer in the hotel room, but back on that beach, the warm sand slipping between her toes as she ran from the pavement towards the crashing waves at the water's edge.

'Stay where we can see you,' her mother called after her, but Aurélie was too excited to listen and only stopped when the sea's froth instantly cooled her toes. This wasn't like the seas she'd become accustomed to in Marseille, Sicily and Corfu. This water was colder, harsher on her skin, and she quickly hurried back onto the dry sand, welcoming the warmth on her soles.

Her parents had set up base about halfway back up the beach: two flowery-coloured fold-out chairs, a beach towel secured by a handful of rocks found nearby, a windbreaker, a large plastic cooling box containing bottled water and fresh fruit. Mum had said they would be here until at least early afternoon, though Dad had said he might need to head back inside to check emails at lunchtime.

They'd bought her castle-shaped buckets and a plastic spade, and once they were seated she began to attempt to build castles, but they failed miserably. Then her dad had spoken to her about the wet sand required for such structures and she hadn't looked back. Hours must have passed, now all blurred, until the beach was much fuller, and it was almost impossible to see a patch of sand undisturbed.

Her mum had stood and said something about going to

fetch a book, but Aurélie had only been half listening, and then Dad's phone had started to ring. Now she could remember him looking at the dial, but not answering it. But then it had rung again, and his face had looked concerned as he'd stared back at the number, before glancing down to check she wasn't paying any attention.

'You should not have called me,' she now heard his voice say in the memory.

He turned away from her, trying to keep the conversation quiet while she clawed and dug out the moat.

'No I have not told her yet… Yes, I do understand what is required…'

She sensed he was speaking to that lady with the panda-like eyes again, only now his voice was crisper in the memory.

'Don't threaten me… Do you know who you are speaking to? I am not some brainless junkie. I am… You will get your money…'

Had Aurélie really witnessed this phone conversation, or was her imagination plugging the gaps? It felt as real now as if she was physically on that beach thirteen years ago.

'I swear to God, if you hurt her…'

Aurélie sat bolt upright in bed. Had her father been on the phone to the kidnappers when she'd wandered down to the sea's edge to collect the water for the moat? Had they been watching the whole time, and were threatening him for some reason? Had she really lost the last thirteen years because of something he had done?

Pushing back the covers, she stormed to the door and pulled it open, but they weren't in the main body of the suite; clearly they were undertaking the interview from the confines of the room they'd shared last night. She was about to push open their door and accuse him to his face when she spotted his mobile phone on the large round table in the middle of the room. It had a blue light flashing in the corner, and as she picked it up, and typed his date of birth into the passcode reader, she saw the notification that he'd missed a call from Emma Hunter.

Pressing redial, she put the phone to her ear. 'Miss Hunter? It is Aurélie Lebrun. I need to speak to you about my father. I think he is the reason I was taken.'

Chapter Thirty-Five

NOW

New Forest, Hampshire

I wasn't expecting to hear Aurélie's voice down the phone, and certainly not as frantic and anxious as it sounded. My instinct is to go to the hotel and listen to what she has to say. Rachel told me not to bother reaching out to Jack and Cavendish, but I've had enough of feeling like I'm treading on eggshells. Aurélie reached out to *me*, not them, and yet I still send Jack a message to tell him where we've been called to.

The hotel is on a former country estate in the middle of Hampshire's New Forest, and several miles north of Poole and Weymouth; certainly not somewhere you would find unless you went looking for it, and maybe that's why the Lebruns chose it. In fact, as we come up the long gravel drive towards the building, I'm reminded of the trip I made with Lord Fitzhume when we attended the Priory Hospital to visit his recovering daughter; this place has a similar feel of wealth and prosperity that I'm not accustomed to.

'What do you think she's going to tell us?' Rachel asks as we hunt for a parking space as close to the entrance as she can find.

'I've no idea,' I answer honestly, though as soon as Aurélie mentioned her father's possible involvement I couldn't help thinking about that guilty look in his eyes when he'd attended the public appeal for information all those years ago. I'd all but dismissed the possibility that he could somehow be involved – what kind of father could allow his daughter to be taken? – but now my mind keeps asking questions that I can't answer: why was he on the phone, and not watching Aurélie? Why didn't he offer a reward for information about her or to encourage her safe return? Why didn't he raise the alarm as soon as he saw she was missing?

'It would certainly make for a sensational opening to your next book: Presidential candidate embroiled in own daughter's abduction and abuse.' Her eyes are wide, imagining the headline and her name on the byline. 'Sorry,' she eventually says, when she spots me staring. 'Force of habit. I promise I won't report on anything without your agreement.'

In her defence, she's allowed me to review both of the articles she's written so far, and I doubt her broadsheet would opt for such a tabloid-like headline. We exit the car without another word, just as Jack's car reaches the top of the driveway, and I subconsciously force myself to look away when I see who is in the front of the car with Jack. Yes, I know I said I wasn't interested in him in that way, but I can't deny the feelings of jealousy *every* time I see the two of them together.

Strangely, this time, Cavendish actually smiles at me as she comes over, and it's quite disarming. 'Thanks for the message; can you tell me exactly what Aurélie told you on the phone?'

'I wasn't really concentrating, but she said her father was involved in her abduction somehow. I don't think he knew she was using his phone to ring me, and she just gave me the address of this place and told me to hurry.'

I now have a sinking feeling about what we're about to walk into. What if Remy did overhear the call and has gone ballistic up there? Rachel and I couldn't find a history of violence when we were looking into his background yesterday afternoon, but even the calmest person can snap when pushed to extreme limits.

'You did the right thing messaging us,' she says with a nod, leading the way to the hotel.

I keep a calm exterior, walking beside her, but inside I'm cringing; were they already together when Jack received the message? That's the only explanation for how they got here so quickly. Is that why he didn't message me back? Oh God, has she already got him in her clutches again?

I turn to look behind me, and smile in his direction. He half smiles back, but there is something awkward about the exchange. I try not to think about it, and focus on the task at hand.

The hotel lobby is sprawling decadence: ruby red carpets, skirting boards lined with gold leaf, the chandelier overhead sparkling like crystal. Cavendish shows her identification to the tall man behind the desk, and he provides the Lebruns' room number. They are on the first floor, and so we follow the winding staircase up, past large framed portraits of the Lords who once presided over the property.

There is no sound of shouting or violence coming from beyond the doors as Cavendish knocks. And Remy Lebrun looks surprised to see the four of us there as he opens the door.

'Pardonnez-moi, detective, but do we have a meeting I have forgotten about?'

'I phoned them,' Aurélie's voice calls out from somewhere behind him.

Remy steps back and ushers us inside, taking a discreet look outside the door before closing it, as if checking there isn't an army of uniformed officers waiting to storm the place.

Aurélie is sitting on the chaise-longue, dressed in a silvery-white kimono, her hair tied in a scruffy top knot. She doesn't stand as we move through to the largest room in the suite, but nods in my direction. I feel obliged to apologise for also dragging Jack, Rachel and Cavendish with me, but she doesn't look bothered by their presence here.

'Comment ça va, Aurélie?' I ask, recalling what little French still resides in the dusty corners of my memory banks.

She doesn't look well; her eyes are buried deep, and there is obvious perspiration at the edges of her hairline. She looks like she's just completed circuits at the gym, but I know it isn't physical fatigue that is leaving her this way.

'I…' she begins. 'I – I – I've been having dreams – memories – about what happened, and you need to know. You need to know what it is like; what they do.'

I instinctively switch on the voice recorder app on my mobile and place it on the large round coffee table between us, before joining Rachel and Jack on the long sofa across from Aurélie. Cavendish remains on her feet through choice. I'm half-expecting her to interrupt and demand any statement regarding Aurélie's incarceration be undertaken in a more formal location, but she remains tight-lipped, allowing me to take the lead.

'Are you referring to the people who took you, Aurélie, or the man who held you prisoner?'

She looks down at her feet. 'When girls reach a certain age… When they are no longer as alluring to prospective clients… they are forced to work instead. The woman who took me from the beach was very young. At the time I couldn't understand why she would take me to such brutes who would slap and push, but later I learned the truth… If you want to live, you help them… If you refuse, they kill you.'

This isn't the confession I was expecting to hear, but she clearly needs to get this off her chest, and so I – like the others – remain silent, and just listen to her story.

'You showed me a picture of your sister, yes? I told you that I did not recognise her, but the truth is that I did… I am sorry that I lied, but I did not think you would believe me if I told you where I saw her, and what she was doing.'

An icy shiver runs the length of my body, and it is all I can do to sit still.

'The traffickers use older girls to keep the younger children in line at the auction events. These are run every few months, and it is where wealthy men get to choose their next victims in exchange for a large fee. That is how I ended up with my captor. Sometimes, rings of men will pool their resources and buy several children at a time, but every now and again it is one man per child, as in my case. I believe your sister was the one who looked after me at the first auction I attended.'

She's clearly confusing memory with imagination, but I can't ignore the ball of tension tightening in my gut.

'They also use these girls to help find new younger children to be taken. The woman who took me from the beach was one of them. When she handed me over, I could see how frightened she was, and grateful when they did not hit her. She travelled in the back of the van with me, and she told me it was easier just to do what they wanted. She showed me bruises on her back where she had been kicked, and there was a scar around her neck, where a wire had cut into her flesh. She was submissive towards them only because it was what she needed to do to survive.

'Your sister was one of those too. Years of abuse at the hands of such monsters changes you. Your moral compass shifts, and obedience and coercion become second nature. Those girls know no different. Those monsters break their will and spirit, until there is nothing left.'

I've read about the Stockholm Syndrome she's referring to, where victims of kidnappers end up falling in love with their captors despite the emotional and physical abuse. It is the same psychology that entwines cult followers.

'Your sister... I believe she was being used to help snare new victims... When Seven – sorry, *Jemima* – stayed in the hole, she spoke of the woman who took her, and the way she described her... It could have been your sister who took her.'

It is all I can do to get to the bathroom before throwing up what remains of my breakfast into the marble-engraved toilet seat. It can't be true; my sister wouldn't have agreed to help the monsters who took her from us; I refuse to believe it. For all these years I've wondered whether she was still alive – certain in my bones that she is – but to think that she could be putting others through what she has suffered is beyond any reasonable belief.

A gentle knock on the door is followed by Rachel poking her head around it. 'Are you okay?'

I wipe my mouth on some tissue and flush it down the toilet, before washing my hands and face. 'I've been better.'

'She can't say for certain that your sister had anything to do with the abduction of Jemima Hooper. And it's possible that she saw someone who *looked* like Anna, but wasn't actually her. Don't let your overactive imagination get the better of you.'

I'm not sure Rachel even believes what she's saying, but I appreciate the sentiment. 'What must they all think of me? Throwing up at the mere mention of my sister.'

'I don't think anybody out there is judging you, and you know better than to think I would think any less of you.'

Staring at the pale reflection in the mirror, I barely recognise the woman staring back at me. I've been on the crusade to find my sister for so long, and right now I'm not sure I'd want to find her so deformed by all the misery she's had to endure. And I hate myself for even daring to think that I could choose *not* to find her. Regardless of what she has done – what she has become – I still owe it to her to bring her home; I owe it to all the children yet to fall under her spell.

'You feeling any better?' Rachel asks. 'If you want, I can tell them you're ill and we can just get out of here; we can go and find a bar within walking distance of your place and spend the rest of the afternoon getting trolleyed.'

I shake my head. 'No. We came here because Aurélie said she suspected her father was involved in her abduction, and she hasn't told us why yet. I don't know about you, but I for one want to know why.'

Chapter Thirty-Six

NOW

New Forest, Hampshire

The mood has changed in the main room when Rachel and I emerge from the bathroom. Despite the overwhelming humidity, it's as if the Lebruns and Jack have been struck by an icy blast of air that has them frozen to the spot. There's no sign of Cavendish but I hear the rumble of her voice off in one of the bedrooms, presumably talking to someone on her phone; maybe she's checking to see whether there's any way to bring charges against me on behalf of my sister.

'Are you all right?' Jack asks as I retake my seat beside him, and I don't like the bitter thoughts cascading through my mind; I hate that I feel I can't be honest with him anymore. I want my friend Jack back.

'I'm fine,' I reply curtly, when I'm anything but.

'Zoe is talking to the lab; they phoned and might have found a DNA match from inside the cabin.'

I suddenly realise exactly why moods have tempered in the room; if the SOCOs and CSIs *have* managed to secure a DNA match, it puts Cavendish a significant step closer to finding out who is responsible. At best it will pinpoint the name of Aurélie's captor; at worst it will identify someone who may be able to throw light on who was holding her; either way, it's a potentially huge step.

There is something not quite right about the Lebruns; given the monumental nature of such a breakthrough, I would have expected them to be affectionately supporting one another as they await the news, yet nothing could be further from the truth. Aurélie is perched on the end of the chaise-longue, hunched forwards as if she might bolt at any minute. Remy is on the opposite end of the seat, legs crossed, staring off into the distance; his body is turned away from his family. And then there is Solange trapped in the middle, neither gesturing to or looking at either of the loves of her life. Aurélie looks shell-shocked. If I didn't know better, I would think the three of them are pretending that they are not concerned about Cavendish's conversation, when in fact they are all straining to hear anything that will shed light on what has been found.

It reminds me of all the huddled meetings my parents would have with police in the days following Anna's disappearance, on tenterhooks for any positive sign that they were nearing finding her, and then the disappointment when the news was exactly the same as the day before. Maybe I shouldn't be so surprised by a family that has experienced such frustration every day for thirteen years. It also makes me question where they go from here: will they ever get back to any sense of normality? Is that perhaps why Remy now wants to use this to relaunch his political career; better to be out fighting the good fight than trapped at home in a vacuum of awkwardness and stilted conversations?

For all this time I've been fighting to find Anna, but what would I say to her if ever she did return? We've missed out on a lifetime of stories and shared events, and will be virtual strangers; can anyone recover from such a trauma? I'm not sure I'll ever get to find out.

Cavendish appears at the door and hovers for a moment, taking us all in, before returning to the room, and standing at the centre point between both sets of eager ears. For a moment I'm reminded of those old episodes of *Poirot* my grandma would watch when Anna and I were supposed to be playing together; the Belgian detective with his waxed moustache would gather the suspects together and slowly rule each one in or out of his conclusion. I'd say as much, to relieve the tension in the room, but I'm as keen as the rest of them to know what the lab has found.

'That was the lab,' she says, as if any of us didn't know. 'A single source of male DNA was recovered from inside the cabin when we examined the scene, found in multiple locations throughout the cabin. The sample has been run through the UK National DNA Database, which holds the DNA profiles and samples from convicted UK-based criminals. They have found a match and I've asked that my team send me a picture of this individual, and I'd like you all to look and see if you recognise him; especially you, Aurélie.'

She shudders at the mention of her name, but nods without looking up. I can't imagine how terrified she must be of seeing the face of her abuser again.

'Who is this man?' Remy sneers. 'What crime did he previously commit?'

Cavendish slowly shakes her head, looking to play her cards close to her chest. 'I'm not at liberty to say at this time, Mr Lebrun, as all the DNA evidence establishes is that he has been inside the cabin; it does not necessarily mean that he had any involvement in your daughter's abduction or incarceration.'

Remy glares at her. 'Of course it does! Please do not hide behind technicalities and false modesty. I think we all know there is *every* chance you have identified this bastard, and I want to know who he is.'

'I will confirm his name to you in good time, Mr Lebrun, but I would like my team to locate and secure the suspect first. In this country, individuals are innocent until *proven* guilty.'

I'm not sure if this is a direct dig at Remy, or the French judicial system where suspects are generally considered guilty until they prove their innocence.

'We've also identified the remains of the man discovered at the site yesterday. He was a local Poole man who has been missing since 2016. He lived alone but was known for rambling, and it was assumed he'd fallen from a cliff not far from his home. We have no reason not to connect his death with the man we are actively searching for. At the very least, your daughter's captor may have witnessed what happened to him.'

She takes a deep breath, ready to move on. 'Anyway, there was a reason we came here this morning,' Cavendish continues. 'Aurélie, you telephoned Emma here, and said you had information pertaining to your abduction that you wished to share; perhaps we can move to one of the bedrooms and discuss that in private?'

Remy and Solange both look at their daughter, surprised to

learn it was she who instigated this intrusion on their lives. Solange looks disappointed, and Remy looks nervous.

Aurélie slowly looks up, but rather than making eye contact with Cavendish, she stares daggers at me. 'No, I wish to speak here. I think everyone needs to hear.'

'What is this all about, darling?' Remy asks next, squirming slightly on his end of the chaise-longue.

Solange remains resolute, now forming a protective force field around her daughter, almost as if she senses what is to follow. 'Let her speak.'

In her hurried call to me this morning, all she said was that she suspected he was the reason she was taken, but I can't help thinking there is more to follow, and I am grateful I set my phone's voice recorder running when we arrived. Nobody seems aware of its presence on the table; we're all entranced by the waif in white with the scruffy top knot.

'Tell them, Papa,' Aurélie begins, without breaking eye contact with me. 'Tell them who you were really on the phone to that day on the beach.'

Remy shuffles uncomfortably – a politician slowly realising he is trapped, and looking for any means of escape – and offers a confused face. 'I don't understand; what are you saying?'

Her voice this time is less timid; she is growing in confidence. 'Who was on the phone, Papa?'

'I – I – I don't know what you want me to say. I was speaking with one of my staff; we were discussing a speech.' He looks pleadingly at Cavendish. 'You must have a record of all this; I was interviewed for hours, and then one of my staff made a statement corroborating my story.'

I recall reading this in the case file yesterday, but Cavendish's expression remains blank.

Aurélie now turns and fires her own glare at Remy, who instantly recoils. 'You said, "I swear to God, if you hurt her…" – who were you speaking to, Papa? Why did you think they would hurt me?'

Remy looks as though he's found a way out, as he straightens now, and his face becomes passive; more relaxed. 'Oh, my darling, I think you are misremembering what you heard. You were busy building your sand fortress; I don't think you could have overheard what we were discussing.'

'*I heard every word*,' Aurélie growls. 'You were angry with whoever you were speaking to; they were threatening you, I think. Your face was as pale as it is now. I want the truth! Why was I taken?'

Whilst it wasn't Cavendish's choice to remain in the room, I can see she is revelling in the outburst, and in her defence, there's nothing like a domestic row to reveal all the dirty secrets.

Solange has placed an arm around her daughter's shoulders, but remains resolute and silent, though her eyes are welling up, like a child waiting for a plaster to be yanked from the skin.

'My darling, I don't know why you were abducted that day; it has nothing to do with me, I swear!'

'Who was on the phone, Papa?'

'I told you, one of my office workers, that is all.'

Aurélie leaps to her feet, brushing off her mother's compassion, and towering over the rapidly shrinking Remy. 'Don't lie to me!'

Even I lean back slightly, anticipating the wake of her outburst. This is not the Aurélie I have seen before, and yet for some reason, her sudden defiance isn't as shocking as maybe it should be.

'Aurélie, please, you are making a scene in front of these people. You are embarrassing your mother and I. Please, sit down, and we can speak when they are gone.'

Aurélie remains where she is, spitting out the next words. 'You were the one who invited them into our lives! If you don't want them to hear your sordid secrets, perhaps I should phone the television company and tell that orange news presenter all about the real Remy Lebrun; the nights when half-naked women would arrive at our apartment when Mama was not home; the underwear I would find in the back of our car; the drawer in your office where you kept bags of white powder—'

Remy is on his feet now, and for a second I'm convinced he is going to raise a hand to Aurélie, but he catches himself, aware of his surroundings. He turns to face Cavendish. 'I wish to apologise for my daughter; she is stressed, and in need of a rest. I hope you understand that it may be best if you all left so that she can continue her recovery.'

Cavendish very carefully folds her arms, but makes no effort to acknowledge his request.

'Tell them the truth, Papa. Tell Mama that you were planning to divorce her; tell her about the baby you were having with that whore on our doorstep!'

This time Remy's hand does fly up, but before he can advance it, Solange is up and restrains it in mid-air, shaking her head. 'No, not like this. Not anymore. You tell the truth, Remy. I am sick of all the lies. I know about your infidelity.'

The fight leaves him instantly; a dejected man who now sees the consequences of his mistakes, and deeply regrets breaking the heart of the woman he once swore to love and protect until death. He is crestfallen.

'Very well,' Remy says eventually, dropping back onto the chaise-longue and burying his face in his hands. He remains that way until both wife and daughter sit. 'It is true that I was not talking with a member of my staff that day on the beach.' He sighs. 'I cannot tell you the name of who called me, as he did not give it; however, he did tell me that he was calling to collect my debt, and that if I did not pay what I owed, he would pay a visit to my mistress Giselle.'

Solange's shoulders sink a little. For years she must have suspected her husband of betraying their vows, but it doesn't soften the blow when the truth hits. To learn that their ten-year-old daughter had also borne witness to his philandering can't be easy to hear either.

'They had pictures of me,' Remy continues, 'with women, doing lines of coke. They were blackmailing me; my career would have gone up in smoke. I was in too deep, and I didn't know how to escape. When they threatened Giselle, I knew I would have to come clean, and find the money, but then Aurélie was taken, and all of that was the last thing on my mind.'

I think back to that image of his guilty face in the press conference.

'I did wonder whether it was *them* who had taken her, but they did not phone to threaten me about Aurélie. I thought maybe they would demand a ransom, but when they next phoned, maybe a week later, they did not mention her. I did not think it likely that they would have followed me to England to act in this way either; these are Parisian gangsters;

they use violence and blackmail to keep order, but they would not harm children.

'I needed time to sort out the mess, so I did not mention it to the police, and I forced one of our interns to make the statement that he'd phoned, in return for a permanent contract. Ironically, he only worked for me for six months before leaving to join the opposition. C'est la vie!

'They killed her; Giselle, I mean. Weeks passed and I had not managed to find the money they wanted, and I was less concerned about my career, and only wanted to get Aurélie back. I ignored their calls and their threats, and so, as I understand it, they went to see Giselle, and threatened her instead… She was not as emotionally strong, and she could not live with the guilt of what they were doing to me, and she hanged herself in her dingy flat in the Projects. She was five months pregnant, but with her history of mental health problems, the police did not look too hard into her situation.'

A single tear escapes Solange's eye, but evaporates before it reaches the bottom of her cheek; a solitary nod to the rival who lost the fight.

When Remy looks up at his family, his eyes are bursting with tears. 'I swear to you, they had nothing to do with you being taken, Aurélie. I was a stupid, stupid man, who did not know how good life was until it was taken away. This – your return, the publicity – it is a second chance for all of us. I have put my mistakes behind me, and I want to prove to you – to you both – that I can be the father and husband you deserve. Please don't let my past destroy our future.'

This isn't the confident, smarmy politician I met earlier in the week. I think for the first time, Remy has lowered his guard, and it is a question of whether his family can find it in their hearts to forgive him or not.

'Jasper Derwent,' Cavendish declares, breaking her silence. 'That name mean anything to any of you?'

It doesn't set any bells ringing in my head, and as I look around the room at Remy's and Solange's blank faces, it doesn't appear to be familiar to either of them either. Aurélie, on the other hand, looks less comfortable.

'That's the name of the man my team are currently searching for in connection with the DNA recovered from the cabin. Aurélie, I have some images I'd like you to look at, if you think you're up to it?'

Aurélie gulps and nods, but even I can see that name has stirred something inside of her.

Chapter Thirty-Seven

THEN

Poole, Dorset

Five days ago

The sound of the large door opening, followed by thundering footsteps, filled the air in the hole. The candle had died hours earlier, and although her eyes had been trained to find even the tiniest chinks of light in the enveloping darkness, there'd been little she could do, other than lie on the mattress and await his arrival. He was later than usual, and that stirred troublesome thoughts in her head.

Silence fell across the room again, which meant he had arrived at the interior door to her room, where he would take a moment to compose himself. This he did, as he had done more and more recently, before slipping the key into the lock and unfastening it. Light and a floral fragrance from a fresh candle filled the room, and he entered, immediately checking she was waiting for him on the mattress as he'd trained her to do; it wasn't like there was much else by way of soft furnishings anyway.

'Oh good,' he panted. 'You're awake. I have something for you.' He carried the candle to the table, lowering a cardboard box on top as well, raising the flaps. 'It's okay; you can come and look.'

She did as instructed, keeping her head bent low, avoiding unnecessary eye contact. Inside the box were two plates stacked upon one another, both covered in foil.

'I made us a warm dinner,' he continued. 'I thought it would be nice if we ate together tonight.'

She didn't speak, waiting patiently for his next instruction.

Lifting out one of the plates, he placed it at the table by her chair, before lowering the second plate to the visitor's chair. He removed the foil lids and the smell of garlic and cheese assaulted her nostrils, and had her salivating instantly.

He then reached into the box again, and removed a large thermos flask. 'Would you like some wine?'

She nodded, and took her seat when he indicated it was okay for her to do so. He opened the flask, poured a measure of burgundy into the plastic cup and handed it to her. Tilting the flask towards her cup, he brought them together, before pressing it to his lips and taking a long sip. She too took a sip, grimacing at the bitter acidity as it passed her dry, chapped lips.

It wasn't her first taste of wine, nor was it the first time he'd created such an intimate atmosphere for the two of them, but something was different this time. As much as she wanted to recoil and spit out the wine in case he had laced it with something, she played along, enjoying the warmth as it settled on the back of her throat. A second sip, and some of the acidity softened, and her gag reflex relaxed.

'Dinner smells delicious,' she dared to say, half-expecting his mood to change, but for once it didn't.

'It's cannelloni – a type of pasta – filled with spinach and ricotta cheese. It's only out of a packet, but it was reduced at the local shop. I thought… I thought it would be nice if we had one night when things are more normal.' He handed her a plastic fork, and encouraged her to tuck in.

The large tube of pasta was covered in a rich tomato sauce and melting cheese, but she wasn't sure whether to pick up the whole thing, or try and hack a piece off with the fork's edge. She watched him as he used his plastic fork to cut at a corner of his own tube, and she followed suit. The food was warm rather than hot, but her taste buds exploded with excitement as she savoured every ounce of flavour. She didn't wait to be told to continue, immediately pulling away a second forkful and placing it in her mouth.

Why didn't *all* food taste this good?

'How is the food?' he asked, and it was all she could do to swallow her mouthful quickly enough before confirming, 'It's delicious.'

'Good, good, I'm glad you're enjoying it.'

The candle's small flame flickered as they continued their meal in virtual silence, save for the occasional clatter when she would lower her fork to the plastic plate and reach for her cup of wine. It was the happiest and most relaxed she'd ever felt, and she longed to repeat the experience, but sensed there was another reason he had gone to all this trouble.

'Come to me,' he said, when they were both finished with their plates.

Ignoring the urge to lick the plate clean, she stood, moved around the table and sat gently on his lap, as he pushed his chair backwards.

'There's something I need to tell you, and I don't know how to find the words,' he said solemnly. 'I saw the doctor today, and... it isn't good news. I'm dying, my love. The doctor reckons I have weeks rather than months; some rare kind of blood cancer that has been slowly attacking my immune system; that's why I've been feeling so rough for the last few weeks.'

Having never experienced the feeling of loss and death, her mind didn't know how to react, and she had to stifle a giggle initially. Was this some kind of joke? Or another of his tests? Was he waiting to see if she would react with joy, and then punish her as a result?

'You should say something, my love. I'm dying, and we need to make a plan. You can't stay here with me anymore.'

She didn't want to hear anymore, and put her arms around his neck, burying her tearful eyes into his shoulder.

'We have talked about this before,' he continued, gently running his hand over her back. 'We always said the day would come when you would have to return to the real world; I just don't think either of us thought it would be so soon.'

'I – I – I don't want to go,' she stuttered. 'I don't want you to go, Jasper.'

'I know, my love, but it's out of my hands now, and I don't know how much longer I have. That's why we need to get the wheels in motion.'

There was no joviality in his tone, and as much as she didn't want to listen, she knew better than to argue.

'They won't understand what we have,' he said, holding her to him. 'I think the best thing for you will be to escape, or at least *appear* to escape. There are so many things I wish I could tell you about how you have melted this old man's heart, but they are empty words; I need to show you how important you are to me, and how I will always love you, and continue to watch over you from afar.'

'Please don't do this,' her muffled voice said into his skin. 'I don't want to leave; I want to stay here and take care of you in your final days. I don't want you to be on your own. You can trust me; I won't try and run.'

This was when he peeled her off him, and looked deep into her eyes. 'I wish it could be that way too, but it isn't feasible for you to remain here any longer. I need to be sure that you are taken care of when I'm gone. You don't have any money, nor any way to earn any, and once I die, you will be stuck here on your own.'

'Then take me with you,' she wept. 'We could be together for eternity.'

'I don't have the strength to do that to you, and besides, our daughter needs her mother.'

She instantly quietened.

'I lied to you before, my love. I told you she had died as our son had, but that wasn't true. I took her away from this place, and I put her up for adoption. She is alive and well, and I know how to find her again.'

She didn't move, a single tear escaping her eye. Why would he be so cruel to now try and make her believe that she had survived after all this time? Was it just one final act of cruelty, or should she take him at his word?

'I have made it my last mission to reunite you with her. She is safe, and living with a foster family in the local area. Once you have escaped, I will arrange to get her back to you, but it's going to take time. I'll need to make sure the police aren't looking for me. So, when you escape, you won't be able to tell them exactly what we have done here. As far as they are concerned you have remained my prisoner this entire time. Okay? They don't need to know about the day trips we've taken, nor about the valuable support you've given at the auctions. You also need to forget about the other girls, and some of the things you've witnessed and been involved in here. This is your chance to wipe the slate clean.'

There was so much she'd repressed over the years that she could no longer be certain what was real or what was memories of nightmares.

'They will see you as a victim,' he continued, 'and that plays into our hands. They will find this place, inevitably, but I have taken special care to remove any trace of you in the cabin upstairs. As far as they will find, you have been down here for the entirety of your absence from the real world. They will fall over themselves to take care of you – the care you deserve for being so loyal to me.'

She couldn't see into his eyes to estimate whether he was telling her the truth or just telling her what she wanted to hear as part of one of the games he used to play.

'But I want to tell them you are not a bad man,' she said, in case it was the latter. 'That you have loved and looked after me.'

'They wouldn't understand, my love; *nobody* will

understand what we have. You have to trust me: this is the best way. We will spend tonight together – one final night of love – and then in the morning I will be gone. I will leave the door ajar, and then you will need to make your way out. If you head straight through the trees you will come to a main road that will lead you towards the town centre where you will find care and understanding. When the time is right, I will contact you and take you to our daughter.'

Chapter Thirty-Eight

NOW

New Forest, Hampshire

I have a feeling there is something very wrong with the picture before me, but for the life of me, I can't see what it is. Aurélie and her parents have looked at the pictures Cavendish has shown them, one of which will have included their person of interest Jasper Derwent, and yet not a single one of them has reacted with any enthusiasm that the net is closing on him. I paid particular attention to Aurélie, searching for that moment her eyes would fill with dread and fear as she came face-to-face with the man who had abducted her, but her facial reactions have not changed once; the only conclusion I can come to is that she didn't recognise a single one of them, or she knew all four in some capacity. I don't know who else Cavendish will have shown the family, nor how recent the image of Jasper Derwent is; I suppose if it is a particularly old image, then maybe Aurélie wouldn't have recognised him? No, I don't believe that theory either.

'Mr Lebrun, I'd like it if you would accompany me to the station to review the statement you made in the immediate aftermath of your daughter's disappearance that day. In light of what you've told us this morning, I think it would be a good idea.'

He looks disgusted by the prospect of being frog-marched to the nearest police station. 'But what good will it do? They had nothing to do with any of this! After Giselle's suicide, they were no longer a problem.'

Even I frown at this statement, but maybe it's the language barrier that has caused the misunderstanding.

'I don't understand,' Cavendish challenges. 'You still owed them money, no?'

Remy is squirming on the sofa again, unable to even glance at his wife and daughter. 'What I didn't know at the time – what I couldn't have known – is that Giselle had been saving money for what she believed would be our new life together. She had close to twenty thousand Euro, which she paid to them the day she died. That halved my debt, and shortly afterwards the head of the group and most of his men were wiped out by another gang in a battle for territory. With his death went what remained of the debt I was slowly paying back.'

Cavendish narrows her eyes. 'Convenient. I definitely think we need to explore this claim a little further. I want to know the names of these so-called gangsters. I also want the name of the gendarme that investigated Giselle's suicide.'

'The Gendarmerie are responsible for crimes in rural towns; the Police Nationale handled her situation.'

'Okay, whatever,' Cavendish says, a little flustered, 'that will do. Let's go and talk about it somewhere more private.'

She hasn't formally said, but I sense that is our cue to leave too, though I'd like to stay and check Aurélie is feeling okay, as she's been pale as a sheet since Cavendish first mentioned Jasper Derwent's name. I'd also like her to share the dates and locations where she claims to have seen Anna. She stands, and declares she is going back to bed, before I get the chance to speak to her privately.

'Are you okay catching a lift back with these two?' Cavendish asks Jack, as she saunters over. 'You can leave your car parked at mine today, and collect it later if you like?'

Jack's cheeks redden instantly. 'Um… Yeah, sure. I mean… I'm sure I can catch a lift back with Rachel and uh… um… Emma.'

Wow! So not only is his car already at her place, but he can't even remember my name. I wish the ground would just open up and swallow me whole.

'If you need a place to crash again tonight, just let me know,' she continues, as if Rachel and I aren't huddled nearby. 'I had fun; it was good catching up.'

If Jack's cheeks darken any more I think his head may explode. 'Sure, I'll give you a call later, if that's okay?'

'You know it is; I'll probably be up to my eyes all day, but tonight… well, we could debrief over a glass of wine… or something else.'

I'm trying to force the image of the two of them from my mind, but I am suddenly queasy again.

'Sounds like a plan. Hey, would you mind sending me over what you have on Jasper Derwent? Maybe the three of us can look for any links to our other project.'

She takes a step forward and plants a wet kiss on his cheek. 'I already have. Call me later if you want to discuss anything.'

With that, she turns and leaves, and I don't know which of us will die of embarrassment sooner: Jack or me.

None of us speak again until we're back in Rachel's car. I'm in the front with Rachel, as I can't bear to look at Jack. I know there is nothing between us that should stop him pursuing a night of no-strings sex with an old acquaintance, but it wasn't that long ago he told me he'd like to see how things could develop between us. Whilst I told him nothing could happen while we were working together, that didn't mean I didn't secretly hope things might blossom further down the line. Right now though, he's revealed himself to be like any other man: led by his genitals.

'Do you want to hear the skinny on Jasper Derwent?' he calls from the back, avoiding the elephant in the car.

'Are you all right?' Rachel whispers to me.

I nod without meeting her gaze.

'Jasper Derwent is sixty-eight years old, and has a string of offences with minors to his name, but nothing since the early nineties,' Jack reads from his tablet in the back of the car. 'He was released from prison for offences related to images discovered in his home – pictures and videos; this was pre computers being a general home gadget – but as the Sex Offenders Register didn't come into operation until 1997, he's not on it. Arrested a couple of times, but no charges brought against him, later in that decade, but then nothing since 1999. According to this he undertook rehabilitation courses both inside and upon release from prison.'

'Can I see what he looks like?' Rachel asks, and Jack duly obliges by passing his tablet forward to me. I hold it out so that both Rachel and I can look, but Jasper Derwent isn't what I was expecting. Maybe it's the lingering image of Arthur

Turgood, but I always expect monsters like this to eek sleaze, but the face in the mugshot looks more like an estate agent or second-hand car salesman than the sort of person who sits in darkened rooms getting his kicks to child abuse.

I know I need to be more open-minded and that there isn't a stereotypical paedophile look – after all, Turgood's accomplices weren't as old as him, and both had wives and children of their own – but I just didn't expect Jasper Derwent to look so *normal*. In the picture, his head is a mop of chestnut curls, a long forehead, and strawberry-blond eyebrows. His chin is so clean-shaven, I can imagine he'd be the sort of man who would struggle to grow much facial hair.

I pass the tablet back to Jack.

'It's interesting that his record goes quiet post 2002 when Aurélie was snatched and held in captivity, so the timeline fits. Even if he *wasn't* the one holding Aurélie, the presence of his DNA in multiple places inside that cabin will take some explaining. His name hasn't come up in any of the cases we've looked at thus far, but it will be good to see whether any of his known associates cross-match with other names that have come up in our enquiry. I might need to head back to London to pursue this, though. If you want to hang around in Dorset for a few days more, I'm sure we can keep in touch via video call or telephone.'

I don't answer at first, my mind filling with imagined images of my elder sister trying to entice other potential victims from their parents, and I have to clamp my eyes shut to try and block them out.

'Emma? I said I might head back to London tonight to follow up on Derwent's connection to our enquiry. Is that okay?'

'Sure,' I reply, keeping my eyes closed.

'Oh, and that reminds me, some other news which is neither good nor bad: I received a call this morning from DCS Rawani, to advise Arthur Turgood passed away yesterday morning.'

My eyes snap open, and I turn to stare at Jack, astonished that this is the first I'm hearing of it. 'Wait, what? Turgood died?'

Jack nods. 'That's what Rawani said; peacefully in his sleep, which doesn't feel right, but I suppose it just means there's one less monster in the world. I know I shouldn't be so judgemental, but a part of me wanted to see him serve his sentence fully and then keel over the day of his release, knowing that he'd served time for his actions.'

My mind is racing with thoughts: with Turgood gone, so is our best chance of finding out *how* he obtained that video of Anna; but the key thought in my head is Freddie Mitchell.

'Someone needs to tell Freddie, Mike and Steve. They deserve to know their abuser is gone.'

'It's possible they already do know; under the Victim Contact Scheme, and given the circumstances, it would only be natural for them to have been informed of his passing.'

I turn back and rifle through my handbag for my phone. It's still on airplane mode so that the recording of the interview wouldn't be disturbed, but as soon as it connects to my network, I see I have missed three calls from Freddie, and that he's left me a voicemail. My heart sinks. I should have been there for him; if Jack had mentioned Turgood's passing sooner, I'd have been straight on the phone with Freddie.

Dialling the messaging service, I gasp as I hear Freddie close to tears.

'Hey... I've tried to call you a few times, but I guess you're busy living that celebrity lifestyle of yours... Anyway, I thought you should know that bastard Turgood is gone... so we can all move on with our lives once and for all... I want you to know, I'm okay, and that... I *will* be okay... When we last spoke you wanted to know about where they took us those times... I lied when I said I couldn't remember... I found it, Emma; I found it! And it only seems fitting that a place of such horror should go up in smoke the day that bastard reaches Hell... If you want to come and watch the pyrotechnics, look for Pendark Studios near Newbury.'

'What's going on?' Rachel asks, pulling into a layby. 'You look like you're going to be sick again.'

'I think Freddie may have done something stupid. We need to get to Newbury ASAP.'

Chapter Thirty-Nine

THEN

New Forest, Hampshire

With her dad, the detective and the others now gone, Aurélie remained cocooned in her room, under the guise of resting, when actually she still had hold of her dad's mobile phone, and had now sent a text message to the mobile number she had memorised five days ago. It was her only means of getting hold of Jasper, and although he'd told her *not* to message before a week had passed, there was no way he could know that their timeline had been hurried by the discovery of his DNA at the cabin. She'd been deliberately vague about how far she'd travelled to the hospital that day, and had done her best to throw the detective off the scent, but then that writer and her friend had stumbled across it. What were the chances!

They shouldn't have found the cabin initially until tomorrow, at which point the next phase of his plan would already be in place. He'd said to only message in an emergency, but the fact that his picture and name would now be on the lips of every law enforcement officer in the county was more than just a hurdle in the road; she had to warn him; he *had* to know.

Pacing the small room, her eyes darting to the phone's display on the bed every few seconds, she was beginning to question whether she'd made a mistake with the number. There had been four threes and two fives, or had that been three fours and five twos? Suddenly the string of numbers she'd pictured in her mind's eye were dancing about, and no longer in a discernible order.

Aurélie started at a knock at the door, followed by it opening a fraction, and her mother's tired face appearing in the crack. 'Would you like some tea?'

Aurélie looked back at the phone as the display lit up, and quickly hurried to the door. 'Non, merci. I am too tired for tea.'

Forcing the door closed once more, she hurried to the bed, scooping up the phone, and reading the message from the number she'd written to:

> *I miss you too, and thanks for the warning. You don't need to worry, as they won't find me in time. You have been so brave, but you need to hold on a little longer. When the time is right, I will be in touch.*

Her face crumpled. She'd wanted to read that he was calling to her; if he'd missed her, why didn't he want to see her as much as she him? Had he misunderstood her message? It was a cry for help, but maybe she hadn't been obvious enough. At least she'd got the number right. There was no harm in sending him a second message, as she would delete all trace of the conversation before she returned the phone to her father.

*I need to see you; I don't care about the plan anymore. I just want to
be with you NOW. Please? Tell me where you are and I will come.*

It was a little stronger than she'd originally intended, but
she didn't want there to be any room for doubt or
misinterpretation. She needed to see him one more time. The
phone's display lit up again almost immediately.

Canford Cliffs Pirate Ship Play Park. Come alone.

She had no idea where the park was, but an internet search
on her father's phone confirmed the address. It wasn't
walkable from the hotel, so she would have to have the
concierge call for a taxi for her.

Dressing quickly, she pocketed the phone in the denim
shorts her mother had bought at the hospital, along with the
cotton T-shirt with 'Badass' across the middle. Both items hung
from her tiny frame, but they were the closest-fitting items
they'd found in the hospital shop's limited range. Solange had
promised they'd go shopping for a new wardrobe as soon as
they were back in Paris, but Aurélie longed for the safety and
comfort of the dresses he'd made for her.

Solange was perched near the door when Aurélie dragged
it open, and looked embarrassed to have been caught listening
at the keyhole.

'I dropped a contact lens,' she claimed, but Aurélie didn't
have the time or patience to argue.

'I'm going for a walk. I need fresh air.'

'I can come with you if you like? Just give me a few
minutes to dress and do my makeup, and I—'

'I want to be alone,' Aurélie said, cutting her off.

Solange frowned, the botox struggling to keep the lines in order. 'Where will you go?'

'Only around the hotel's grounds. There's a garden, I think. I won't be long.'

Solange nodded distantly, buying the lie, and stepping aside to allow her daughter to leave through the door. Aurélie was convinced that her mother would have a change of heart and hurry after her, and was relieved to make it down the large, elaborate staircase to the lobby without interruption. Of course that didn't mean that Solange wouldn't be hurriedly dressing and following her shortly, so Aurélie would have to be quick.

An older couple were checking out at the reception desk, their suitcases standing on a tall trolley as they made small talk with the receptionist. There was no sign of any other staff she could ask to telephone for a taxi for her, but as her eyes settled on the hotel's entrance, she spotted a yellow taxi parked up, probably waiting for these two, who were in no hurry to actually depart. Taking her chance, Aurélie bowed her head, hurried out of the door and hopped into the back of the taxi.

The taxi driver stared back at her confused. 'Baker? I thought there were supposed to be two of you?'

'My husband will follow later. Please, let's be on the way.'

The driver started the engine. 'Bournemouth airport, isn't it? Where are your bags?'

'My husband is taking care of that, and no, I need to make a detour first.' She paused, showing him the address on the phone. 'Can you take me here first, and then onto the airport after? I need to collect something from a friend.'

The driver took a cautious look out of his window at the hotel, and not seeing any other passengers emerging, reluctantly put the car into first and pulled away, the gravel crackling beneath the tyres as they pulled away. It was only when they were back on the main road that Aurélie dared to breathe a sigh of relief.

A short walk from the beach, the Canford Cliffs Pirate Ship Play Park was exactly as Aurélie had imagined it would be: a climbing frame in the shape of a ship-wreck, swings, a sand pit and picnic tables in the shape of a skull and crossbones. Asking the taxi driver to wait at the kerbside, she promised him a big tip upon their arrival at the airport, leaving her father's phone with him as collateral. The fact that her pockets were now empty didn't cross her mind as she raced into the park, scanning the benches for any sign of Jasper.

The playground was far busier than she'd anticipated with children tearing around, screaming and laughing, bumping into one another, to the point where the entire space seemed to blur, and Aurélie could feel her knees weakening.

And that's when he caught her. 'Come, I'm sitting over there,' he said, his voice sounding odd without the usual echo, and hoarser than she remembered.

She buried herself in his embrace as he led her over to a small upturned log, barely long enough for them to perch together, and dangerously close to a wasp-swarming dustbin. And for the briefest moment, the rest of the world melted away, like someone had poured a bottle of water over a painting, colours merging and losing focus.

'Were you followed?' he asked, keeping his arm around her shoulders.

She shook her head, but kept it pressed into his neck. 'We don't have much time. The police are looking for you. I have a taxi waiting to take us to the airport, and—'

He peeled her off him, studying her face for any sign she was joking. 'The airport? No, that wasn't the plan.'

'I know,' she urged, placing her hand on his unshaven cheek, 'but we don't have a choice now. You and I, we can leave all of this behind, and just go. We can go to the airport, or catch a boat, or just drive far away from here. Please? It is too hard to do this without you.'

He reached for her hand and gently lowered it from his face, keeping his grip firm but tender. 'You're being irrational. We can't go to the airport; that's the first place they'd look for me, and I'll bet you don't have a new passport yet either.'

'No, but maybe we could bribe someone to help us,' she pleaded, determined not to let him go.

'It doesn't work like that, my sweet. Besides, I'm in no state to be leaving the country. I'm sick, and I don't know how much longer I have.'

The words she'd been dreading. 'So let's just drive somewhere; somewhere where nobody knows who we are. We could head north like we did once before. You have friends all over who could put us up for a few weeks…'

Couldn't he see the desperation in her eyes? So many times he'd questioned whether she really loved him, despite her telling him over and over, and now here she was declaring her undying love, and still he refused to believe. What more would it take?

'There's something you need to see,' he continued, his gaze drifting into the playground before them. 'I managed to track her down; there, look, that's *our* daughter.'

Aurélie didn't move, certain she'd misheard the words, and searching his body language for confirmation. Finally, she relented, and gradually allowed her neck to twist and her eyes to look where he was indicating.

'In the purple dress with her hair plaited,' he said. 'She's the spitting image of you at that age.'

The little girl threw her arms up in the air as she glided down the slide, landing in a heap at the bottom, before promptly standing and hurrying back to the ladder to repeat the experience. It was as if all time froze in that moment, as Aurélie came face to face with the child she'd never wanted, couldn't care for and yet now desperately wanted to scoop up and smother in affection. She couldn't see the resemblance, but then could any parent really see themselves in their child?

It felt like a dream, and if it was, then it was a dream Aurélie never wanted to wake from. Her mind whirred, trying to recall how she'd got here, looking for signs that this was all a mirage created by her imagination, but at the same time not caring, just wanting to savour every second of it.

'Her name is Crystal,' he said, 'and her foster mum brings her here most weekends. Isn't she the most precious thing in the world?'

Aurélie couldn't answer, her eyes misting and her voice unable to penetrate the enormous lump in her throat.

'Here, take these,' Jasper continued, reaching into his anorak and removing a handful of folded papers. 'When the time is right, you need to tell the police that she is yours, and to demand a DNA test which will definitely prove it. I don't know how long it will take, but they will have to let you have access, and if you stick to what I have told you about your captivity, then hopefully one day they will give her back to you. Tell me you understand.'

Aurélie couldn't picture a life where this sweet and innocent child would ever look up to her and call her 'Mum', and she didn't want to picture the scene without Crystal's father at her side.

'I can't do this alone,' Aurélie blurted, feeling the warmth of tears on her cheeks.

'You don't have a choice. Our daughter needs her mother, and you need her equally.'

'She needs her father too… I need you.'

Placing both his hands on her cheeks, he used his cracked thumbs to blot her tears. 'I want that more than anything too, but it is too late. You *can* do this; you are the strongest woman I've ever known, and I know our daughter will be safe with you.' He released his grip, and stood. 'Now, I must go. Don't stay here too long; if they're to believe your story, you can't be seen at this playground. You're not supposed to know she's still alive until much later. Remember?'

He moved off, heading to the opposite side of the park, beyond which signs indicated the beach car park.

Aurélie looked back out into the playground, searching for the little girl in the purple dress, who couldn't be much older than three, and eventually spotting her over in the sandpit. So close, Aurélie could almost reach out and touch her. Looking back at Jasper nearing the edge of the park, she made the only decision that made sense in her head.

Darting to the sandpit, she scooped the child up in an embrace and took off after the departing figure of Jasper, catching up with him just as the first cries of anguish erupted from the play area behind them.

'What are you doing?' Jasper demanded, stopping only temporarily before ploughing through the trees leading to the car park. 'This is madness!'

'No,' she retorted, hugging the terrified girl close, 'the three of us not being together is madness.'

Half a dozen burly dads were already cutting across the grass in pursuit, and there was barely time to get the child and Aurélie into the back of the car before they were bursting through the trees. Jasper floored the accelerator, beeping his horn and cutting around the slow driver ahead who was ambling for a space, before tearing out onto the road.

'This is crazy, Aurélie. The police will arrest us both, and then they will never let you see her again. My plan is up in smoke.'

'Only if they find us,' she called from the back, scanning the horizon for any pursuing vehicles. 'Drive us somewhere your friends will protect us. I know you are sick, but we need to make the most of any short time we have left together. Just drive, and drive fast.'

Crystal had started crying, the look of pure horror on her face bringing back unwanted memories in Aurélie's mind.

'It's okay,' Aurélie whispered gently. 'You don't need to be afraid. I'm your mama, and this man here is your papa; we will both look after you now. Please don't cry, angel.'

The child's tears and sobbing grew.

'Oh, Jesus, what a mess!' Jasper called out from the front. 'We should take her back. I'll let you out somewhere and just hand myself in to the police. You have the paperwork you need now. Them catching up with me was always inevitable, it's just happening sooner than I thought. Nobody knows you came to see me, and I can claim there was no accomplice. It'll be okay. I can fix this!'

'No!' Aurélie was surprised by the venom in her growl. 'We have our daughter, and we are together, that's all that matters. This is how it was meant to—'

But she didn't get to finish her sentence as the car mounted the kerb at speed, narrowly avoiding a child that had shot out into the road. The vehicle hurtled into the shop front of a closed Indian restaurant.

Chapter Forty

NOW

Newbury, Berkshire

I haven't stopped calling Freddie since hearing his message, but although his phone is ringing, he's not answering. He sounded so hurt in the message, and I am overwhelmed with guilt that I wasn't available in his moment of need. I shouldn't have put my phone on airplane mode; I should have known that asking questions about that time of his life would have stirred up bitter memories.

'Don't beat yourself up,' Rachel says beside me, 'you weren't to know.'

Glancing at the speedometer, I see she's doing more than eighty, and judging by Jack's grip of the door handle, he's not best pleased about it, though he hasn't said as much.

'I should have known,' I tell her. 'I wasn't surprised to hear his message, which means that somewhere in the back of my mind, I must have sensed that he was holding back when we spoke yesterday.'

'That isn't your fault, Emma. How many times have you encouraged Freddie to seek further counselling *since* the trial continued? Must be at least half a dozen, and those were just the times I was with you both. I don't mean to sound blunt, but Freddie's been running from his past for too long. Maybe – if anything – this coming out now will do more good than harm in the long run.'

'But what if he's done something stupid? You didn't hear how crestfallen he sounded in his message.'

Rachel scrunches her nose. 'How much trouble could he get into?'

The answer doesn't bear thinking about, and as we near the end of our journey along the A34, the feeling of dread is casting a greater shadow over us. The sight of thick black smoke in the near distance has me on the edge of my seat; I know instinctively that's where Freddie is.

There's only one road sign we've spotted for Pendark Studios, and the fact that there is a police barricade closing the road beyond it tells me all I need to know about how much trouble Freddie could get himself into.

'There's a serious fire up ahead,' the officer says, approaching the vehicle as Rachel lowers her window, 'so we're asking everyone to head back and follow the diversion being set up.'

Although the black smoke is high above us, the smell of burning soon fills the car.

'Can you tell us what happened?' Rachel tries. 'We were on our way to meet a friend at Pendark Studios.'

The police officer takes a step back, now taking a better look at all of us, as if committing to memory the faces he will later be asked to describe under questioning.

Jack exits the car, and shows his identification to the officer and they move away together, back to the officer's car, allowing Rachel to wind up the window and protect our lungs.

'It may have nothing to do with Freddie,' Rachel says, but neither of us believe a word of it.

Freddie's message echoes in my head: *a place of such horror should go up in smoke the day that bastard reaches Hell.*

'He's torched the place,' I tell her. 'Oh God, I should have phoned someone when I heard his message; maybe they could have stopped him.'

Rachel stares blankly back at me. 'Who would you have phoned? You couldn't know that Freddie was going to set fire to the building, and even if you'd suspected, it's unlikely the police would have had resources available to come out here and check, isn't it?'

Jack returns to the car, coughing and bringing more smoke in with him. 'The whole place is ablaze according to PC Aldwych. Apparently, a nearby farmer first saw the smoke and dialled 999, but by the time the fire brigade arrived about fifteen minutes ago, the fire had already caught hold and torn through the entire site. There was a man found at the scene, stinking of petrol, whom they have taken into custody. He's being looked over by paramedics as we speak, and then they will be taking him back to the police station for questioning. The man hasn't given his name, but when I explained that I may know who he is, and what the incident might relate to, PC Aldwych said I could go and speak to him. He's taken a note of our names, and is going to let us drive up to the next perimeter. He warned me the smoke is much thicker ahead, and that we should close all vents on the car.'

Rachel fiddles with the dial on the dashboard before

pulling around the officer as he waves us through. He's certainly right about the smoke getting thicker; Rachel has to slow to a snail's pace on account of the thick grey fog, until suddenly another police car, three fire engines and two ambulances come into view. A second officer approaches, and speaks through Jack's window, before advising us where to park up.

'They haven't arrested him yet,' Jack tells us as we follow the officer to the open side of one of the ambulances, 'which is why they've given us five minutes to speak to him, but that's the best I could manage. PC Aldwych only agreed to my request when I told him you'd name him in any book you write about the case.'

Freddie comes into view inside the ambulance, but he isn't the Freddie I know and love. With an oxygen mask strapped to his face, black stains on his denim jeans and jacket, and burns on his face and neck, he looks close to tears when he sees me there.

'We'll wait here,' Jack says, turning his back to offer some privacy. Rachel mirrors his action, creating a barrier of sorts, blocking out the carnage created behind me.

'Freddie,' I say as I move closer to the ambulance, but I don't know what else to say. He's been one of my closest friends for the last four years, but his history has always been the elephant in the room when we are trying to socialise as real friends do. We both know what he went through, but he's the one who has to carry the mental scars of living through it. I've always said I will probably never truly understand just how tough a life he's led.

The paramedic closest to him finishes her checks, and releases the blood-pressure strapping from around his arm.

'I'm not happy with the sound of your chest,' she tells him. 'We're going to take you into hospital to have you looked over; the police can reserve their questions until you're fit enough to answer them. Does anything hurt?'

He shakes his head, coughing violently in the process. 'She – this woman – is my friend. Can she travel with us?'

The paramedic narrows her eyes, before nodding and lowering a seat beside the gurney. 'You need to strap in. I'll let the police know what's going on.' She climbs down from the ambulance, sliding the door closed, leaving us alone.

Moving across, I push myself into the seat and pull the belt around myself, clicking it into place. 'Oh Freddie, what have you done?'

'I will never forget the castle on the horizon,' he says, though his words are muffled by the mask over his face. 'That's the one image I clung to for all these years; the castle backdrop; I think I used to imagine some knight in shining armour coming to my rescue, not that anyone ever did. Not until you, Emma.'

Glancing through the ambulance's windscreen where Freddie is indicating, I can now see the familiar turrets of the main spire of Highclere Castle. Yes, the one they use for exterior shots in the filming of *Downton Abbey*.

'After we spoke yesterday, I had a dream about the journey down here from the St Francis Home. I remembered passing signs for Oxford, and Newbury racecourse, and those turrets. When the woman called from the Victim Contact Scheme to tell me that bastard had snuffed it, the pieces of the puzzle slotted into place, and I had to come here. As soon as I saw it, I recognised the site as where they'd brought us over the years. I threw up in the visitors' car park; how ridiculous is that? How can an inanimate building have the power to make a person vomit? It's long been closed, I think, and looked more rundown than I recalled, but I have no doubt in my mind that this is where it all happened.'

I reach out and take his hand in mine, squeezing as tight as I can. 'I am so sorry I didn't receive your call. I should have been here.'

The first tear escapes, leaving a charcoal smear down his cheek. 'I shouldn't have left that message. I just didn't want you to wonder where I'd gone or what had happened to me. I wanted *someone* to know that I was safe. You're all the family I've got left now. Don't be mad with me.'

'I'm not mad with you, Freddie. I understand why you did it, I think, but I wish you hadn't. You've worked so hard on rebuilding your life, but now the police may press charges against you, and...' I can't finish the sentence because I don't want to imagine the bad road my friend has set himself on.

'At least they won't be able to cover it up this time. I had to make a big scene, so I couldn't be ignored – so that *you* couldn't be ignored.'

I'm not following what he's trying to tell me, and he must sense my puzzlement.

'I didn't just set fire to the building... I dragged out all the filing cabinets and records first. Five of the bastards! They were all locked, but I managed to break one open with a rock. Names, dates, addresses – it's all there, Emma. Every person who's ever hired the studios for whatever reason. I found Turgood's file... It says the purpose of his visit was "private movie". Don't you see? Every person that's ever hired the studio is named and shamed in those documents. You and that handsome boyfriend of yours can use that information to track down the people who forced your sister to perform too!'

I blink several times, unable to process what he's told me.

'It'll take some sorting out,' he continues. 'There are hundreds – if not thousands – of records to sift through, and not all of them will be dodgy, but somewhere in one of those filing cabinets is the name of the monster who videoed your sister, and all the other children on the videos recovered from Turgood's hard drive. They have no chance of keeping that quiet with the fire; but now it's up to you to do what you do best, Emma. You need to kick over every stone until you find the truth. All of this – you, me, Turgood, your sister, Aurélie Lebrun – it's all connected. You just need to join up the dots.'

The paramedic slides the door open, and the vehicle rocks as she jumps in. 'Are you still feeling well enough to travel?' she asks Freddie.

'Yes,' he replies, 'but my friend here isn't going to come with me now. She needs to stay behind; she has work to do.'

'No, Freddie, Jack and Rachel can deal with the fallout, I'll stay with you.'

It's his turn to squeeze my hand now. 'No, you're the only one I trust to keep those files safe. Your boyfriend needs to call in a favour with that DCS Rawani, and get those files back to London. Please, Emma?'

'What about you? Do you want me to have a solicitor meet you at the hospital?'

He smiles for the first time, and I see the essence of my friend returning. 'I'm a big boy; I can take care of myself. I *chose* to burn the place down, and I'm ready for any consequences coming my way. Think about it: victim returns to expose studio's dark history – it's the kind of headline that flogs newspapers. Make it happen for us.'

Unfastening my seat belt, I kiss Freddie on the cheek, promising I'll speak to the officer before I leave, and ask him to go easy on Freddie. And then I climb out and watch the ambulance pull away, taking with it the bravest man I've ever known.

Chapter Forty-One

THEN

Poole, Dorset

She didn't know how long she'd been hanging, suspended in mid-air by her seatbelt. The sound that woke her from the darkness was the whimpering of the four-year-old beside her, who was thankfully still secured by her own belt, and resting up against the crumpled door.

It took several moments for Aurélie to recall that they'd been in a car accident, but as soon as the realisation hit home, survival instinct kicked in, and she released herself, and pulled Crystal close, checking she wasn't injured, and promising everything was going to be okay. The car shook to the sound of rhythmic banging, and a moment later light poured in through the door above their heads, and a long arm dropped into the vehicle, followed by the face of a bearded man.

'Are you two okay?' he asked. 'There's an ambulance on the way. Can you move? If you can, I think we should get you out of here.'

He didn't look threatening, and Aurélie's priority had to be keeping her newfound daughter safe. Pressing her lips to Crystal's ear, she whispered, 'It will be okay. I'm going to pass you to this man, and then I'm going to get out behind you.'

Crystal shook her head, wrapping her shaking arms around Aurélie's neck; too many strangers and surprises had taken their toll, and now she was clinging to the least unfamiliar. Placing a protective arm around her daughter, Aurélie forced herself to stand on the door, despite the nagging pain in the side of her head. She used the man's outstretched arm for support and the vehicle's headrests as steps up and out through the open door.

A crowd had gathered nearby, and as she emerged – with Crystal dangling like some inappropriately sized necklace – two more men came rushing over to help them down from the car. Crystal refused to budge as a woman appeared from nowhere with a first-aid kit, offering to patch up any cuts.

Aurélie felt so light-headed and woozy that she had to plonk down beside the car and take a moment to catch her breath. Her first hour as a mother and she'd managed to put her daughter's life at risk, but she couldn't remember what had caused the accident, nor what they'd been doing in the moments before blacking out. And then the first stirrings of memory punctured her consciousness, and she remembered arguing with Jasper.

'Jasper!' she gasped aloud. Where was Jasper?

Trying to peel Crystal's hands from her neck, she eventually gave up, pushed herself upright and tottered around to the front of the car to try and look through the windscreen at him.

'Probably best not to look,' the bearded man warned, proffering a hand.

What did that mean? Why wouldn't she want to look...?

Pushing past the hand of warning, she choked on her own spittle as she caught sight of the red droplets hanging from the fractured glass, and the prone body poking through. She could only see the back of his head, but she recognised the long, grey, straggly hair and the crown poking through where his hair had thinned with time.

'Oh God,' she mouthed, as the realisation of what she was seeing slowly filtered into her consciousness.

'An ambulance is on the way,' the bearded man repeated, offering to take hold of Crystal again.

The girl refused to budge, until Aurélie whispered into her ear, 'Please, my darling, just stay with the man for a minute while I check on Daddy. Please? I will only be a second.'

Crystal reluctantly released her grip, and Aurélie lowered her to the floor, where the bearded man took her hand and held her out of sight of the windscreen.

Aurélie crept around the front of the vehicle, careful not to touch any part of it in case something dislodged and she caused further damage, until she came face to face with him. She couldn't stop herself gasping at the sight. His face was as grey as the clouds overhead, and she could see where a large shard of glass had ripped into his side, where the majority of the blood was pooling.

It would have been kinder had he not been conscious, but his eyes moved and lips parted into a smile when he saw her. 'I'm sorry,' he mouthed.

For so many years she'd imagined worse fates befalling him: a trip down the tunnel stairs resulting in impalement on some piece of farm equipment; her using the burning candle to scorch out his eyes; strangling him during sex until his eyes rolled back in his head. But now that she was faced with the moment – his life dripping away before her eyes – she didn't want it.

This man – this monster – who had robbed her of any childhood, stolen her innocence, set them on this route – why couldn't she embrace the natural hatred that should have cloaked every cell in her body? She knew she should hate him for everything he'd forced her to do down the years; for the way he had controlled every aspect of her life, including her eventual escape. All she felt now was her heart breaking in two at the prospect of never seeing him again, or hearing that croaky laugh in the rare moments of pleasure they'd shared.

Oh God, what was wrong with her? Why couldn't she feel hatred towards him? Nobody else in their right mind would be so prepared to forgive those early nights when he would force himself on her. Nobody else would forgive how he manipulated her into helping steal the innocence of other victims. How many girls and boys had she helped drag into this destitute life of assault and shame?

In the moment when she should have been revelling in his demise, all she wanted to do was reach out and touch his face one final time, and tell him to wait for her in the next life. She wanted to swap places with him, and if she'd had the courage, she would have snapped off a piece of that windscreen and dragged it across her own throat so she wouldn't have to be alone.

'You... need... to... go...' he said breathlessly.

'I can't do this without you,' she said, moving closer so that he would hear, now barely inches from where the blood was flowing like a waterfall. He didn't have long left, that much was clear from his face, and from the way his legs were jiggling as his brain began to realise its imminent doom.

'I… love… you… Aurélie,' he tried again.

In thirteen years he'd never used her first name, and now it would be the last word he would utter.

'I love you too,' she said, ignoring the revulsion in her head, and pressing her lips against his. 'I'm so sorry it's ending like this. I will see you again, my love.'

But as she straightened and looked back at him, she saw the life had left his eyes, and he was breathing no more.

The distant chorus of sirens snapped her out of the spell, and she swiftly moved back around the vehicle to where Crystal looked so confused by her immediate surroundings. The man with the beard released her hand, and she meandered over to Aurélie, uncertain which of the strangers to trust, and clearly missing her foster family. Aurélie took her hand and led her away from the scene, to somewhere quiet where she could try and explain what was going on, even though she could barely follow it as an adult.

Crouching at the kerb on the opposite side of the road where traffic had stopped following the accident, she wiped dirt from Crystal's cheeks. 'Some men will come for you soon. They are the police, and they will take you back to your family, okay? I did a bad thing taking you today, and I am so sorry to have scared you.'

Crystal buried her head in Aurélie's shoulder – her way of accepting the apology, Aurélie assumed. And there the two of them remained: a mother and daughter from different worlds sharing a bond of love that would never be broken. It had been impulsive to snatch Crystal at the playground and assume the three of them could make it out of the country, and now Aurélie would have to face questions about why she had done it, and jeopardise her chances of any normal kind of relationship with Crystal. At the same time, she couldn't ignore the probability that Crystal would surely have a better life if she never learned of the wretched past that had produced her. And maybe that was why she couldn't ultimately hate Jasper: he'd given her a daughter to fight for, a reason to keep going.

The consequences of what she'd done now terrified her, and she couldn't bear to think about the nature of the questions that would soon be levelled at her. And then she thought about the social workers who would be called to take Crystal away, and she didn't think it was fair for Crystal to have to deal with more strangers, and that's when she decided she would stop allowing other people to determine how her story would end.

'Do you like ice-cream?' she asked Crystal.

The little girl nodded, the first glimpse of a smile forming on her tired face.

'I think we should go and get some, don't you? I know a place where they sell the *best* ice-cream.'

And with nobody in the surrounding crowd really noticing, they slipped away, putting the past and sirens behind them.

Chapter Forty-Two

NOW

Weymouth, Dorset

'Do you think Jack will have much trouble securing the papers in those filing cabinets?' Rachel asks as she pulls up outside my flat.

'He didn't seem to think so,' I admit with a long yawn. 'He was on the phone to DCS Rawani when I left him at the ambulance, and Rawani isn't the sort of man who takes no for an answer. It wouldn't surprise me if the files didn't arrive at Uxbridge nick by the end of the day with a gift bow wrapped around them.'

'You look exhausted,' Rachel says, applying the handbrake. 'Are you sure you don't want me to come in with you?'

I smile gratefully, and pat her hand. 'That's kind of you, but I don't want to make you any later for your date with Daniella tonight. I said I could have caught a train from Newbury; you really didn't have to drive me all the way back, only to turn around and head for London.'

'Family before friends, remember? Besides, you're the perfect excuse for avoiding what probably won't be a telling off from my ex. She'll probably bring a restraining order with her, telling me to back the hell off.'

I offer a sympathetic grimace. 'It might not be nearly as bad as you assume; you don't know this isn't her attempt to win you back.'

'And I think you should stick to writing crime rather than romantic fiction, Emma. Know where your strengths are, and rely on them.'

There's a tone of indignant resignation in her voice, and no amount of gentle cajoling will convince her that tonight's rendezvous with Daniella will end any way but acrimoniously. I hope for both of their sakes she's wrong. Maybe there is more of a romantic side to me than I'm prepared to admit.

'Anyway, it's not like there's anywhere for me to properly park. The beach is manic here today.'

She isn't wrong, and staring out across the road to the beachfront, I can hardly see the shoreline for all the sun worshippers. What I would give for the innocence of not knowing how many monsters are out there preying on the innocent children splashing in the sea and building sandcastles. For all I know, there is someone on that beach right now looking the wrong way or planning to snatch a child in the same way Aurélie was snatched from Worthing thirteen years ago.

'Will you phone me and let me know how you get on?' I say to Rachel as I tug on the door handle.

'Of course I will,' she says, giving me a quick hug. 'If you need me to have a word with Jack too, you only have to say.'

'Jack?' I ask, puzzled. 'What about Jack?'

'Oh please,' she smirks, 'you've had a face like a bee has stung it all day. I saw how annoyed you looked when he turned up in the same car as Cavendish this morning. So what if they slept together last night? It doesn't mean he isn't sweet on you. You said yourself that you were keeping things professional while you carried on your investigation, so you can't hold it against him if he gave in to an old flame offering herself – he is a guy, after all.'

Has my face really reflected my mood all day? I thought I'd done a better job of keeping my annoyance hidden; I wonder if he too witnessed it.

'He's definitely still sweet on you, Emma, and as much as you don't want to admit it, you're sweet on him too. It's only a matter of time until the two of you admit how you feel about each other. You'll see.'

Flashing her a frown, I climb out and wave her off before turning to move to my flat. I hadn't noticed that Cavendish had been sitting at a table of the café just along the road, but she is now making a beeline for me, and I don't like the scowl she's wearing. She couldn't have overheard our conversation, but something has riled her.

'Where've you been?' she demands without a hello.

'Newbury, as it happens. Jack and I think we may have made a breakthrough with our investigation into the videos found on Arthur Turgood's laptop.'

'Oh really? So you haven't spent the afternoon with Aurélie Lebrun then?'

It's an accusation rather than a question, and one that instantly puts me on the back foot.

'No; I haven't seen her since we left the hotel this morning. Why, has something happened?'

She eyes me suspiciously, as if trying to read my mind. 'A four-year-old girl was abducted from a playground in Poole earlier today, by a man in his sixties and a woman in her early twenties. The vehicle they fled the scene in was later found crashed and the male driver, who died at the scene, was identified as Jasper Derwent. Witnesses placed Aurélie at the scene with the child, but they slipped away before the emergency services got there.'

I'm hoping my gaping mouth and obvious shock at this revelation convince her that this is all news to me. I have so many questions, but I don't know where to begin.

'I need to find Aurélie as soon as possible, and I am asking you directly: has she been in touch?'

'No,' I snap. 'Do you really think I would harbour her after something like that? Check my phone if you don't believe me.'

To my surprise, she holds her hand out, expecting me to hand the phone over. With nothing to hide, I acquiesce.

'Very well,' Cavendish sighs, after an extensive search of my messages and call history. 'If she does reach out to you again, I want you to call me immediately. My primary concern is the safety of the child in her possession, and then we will deal with how she came into contact with Derwent and why she didn't inform us.'

I accept my phone back, and drop it into my satchel. 'Do you think she's been in contact with Derwent this whole time?'

Cavendish narrows her eyes. 'What makes you say that?'

It's a fair question, and I can't quite place my finger on why I asked it. 'There's been something about this whole thing from the start, don't you think? All so staged, like someone was putting together one of those Sunday-night serial crime dramas on the television.'

Cavendish considers the statement, but doesn't disagree. 'Will you phone me if she makes contact?'

'Absolutely, but I'd have thought I'd be the last person she'd come to; we didn't exactly end things on the best terms earlier, after she accused my sister of conspiring with the enemy.'

'Mmm, I thought you looked cross when I last saw you. I thought it was because Jack was with me last night.'

It's clearly a dig, an effort to get a rise out of me, and it takes all my restraint to hold back.

'Who and what Jack gets up to in his spare time is none of my concern.'

'Good, because I wouldn't want there to be any animosity between us because of my relationship with him. We have a lot in common, and we've known each other for a long time; it was inevitable that we'd be drawn to each other again. You see that, don't you?'

My cheeks are burning with anger, and it wouldn't surprise me if smoke was billowing from my ears like in a cartoon. 'As I said, Jack's love life is none of my concern; he's merely a colleague.'

'Yeah, that's pretty much what he said too. Good. So you'll call me if Aurélie turns up?'

I nod again, relieved that the interrogation is over. I remain where I am until she's pulled away before fishing into my satchel and removing my house keys. I have only one thing on my mind right now, and it's frozen and living in the freezer. I have every intention of devouring the entire container of salted caramel swirl this evening, finishing it off with a large glass of Rachel's expensive wine.

I've just put my key into the lock when a voice saying my

name causes me to spin round instantly. There before me is
Aurélie, clutching the hand of a young girl who is eating an
ice-cream cone.

'Please, Emma,' Aurélie says, 'I need to talk.'

Placing the mug of tea on the table before her, I sit in the chair
opposite, and blow on the rim of my own mug. The child –
Crystal apparently – is still devouring her ice-cream cone with
the television in the living room distracting her.

'You do realise I need to phone the police,' I caution. 'DS
Cavendish literally ordered me to do that, seconds before you
said my name.'

'I know,' she nods, 'but I wanted to explain myself to you
first; you deserve that.'

Crystal seems content in the living room, and from a brief
examination she doesn't appear to have suffered any harm. I
desperately want to phone someone to let her foster parents
know she is safe and well, but the terror and upset in Aurélie's
eyes convince me to hold back.

'I never met your sister,' she says after a beat. 'I made that
bit up. The girl in the picture that you showed me was never
present at the auctions. The actions I described to you –
keeping the other children in order, helping to talk children
into coming away from their parents – those were my actions,
not your sister's. I'm ashamed of everything I did in the last
few years, and I have no defence. I knew in my heart that what
I was doing was wrong, but I was eager to please Jasper. I
knew that if I obeyed, then I wouldn't be hurt, and I would
have done anything to survive. That's the bit that nobody can

understand until they've been in that situation: collaboration is the only means of survival. My ancestors did it in the 1940s, and I witnessed first-hand what would become of me if I dared to resist. Your Jemima Hooper: I saw what happened to her because she dared to escape. I tried to warn her – I really did – but she refused to listen.'

I should probably be recording the conversation, but I have a feeling I will never forget a single word of what she is telling me; it will haunt my dreams forever.

'The girl in the other room – Crystal – she's your daughter?'

Aurélie nods. 'Apparently so. Jasper said I was to insist on a DNA test to prove it, but I don't think I will make such a request; what life can a broken woman like me offer her? I have spent most of my life in the shadows, but she got the clean break I never did, and I don't have the heart to drag her back in. I'm grateful I've had the opportunity to spend a few hours in her company, but hopefully she won't recall much of this experience as she grows up. It is better if she doesn't know the horror that led to her place in this world; I owe her that much.'

'You shouldn't blame yourself for everything that's happened,' I say sympathetically. 'It is a widely acknowledged fact that people who sustain the level of trauma and pressure that you have can become susceptible to suggestion. Stockholm Syndrome is a psychological response to that: when hostages or abuse victims bond with their captors or abusers. A psychological connection can develop over days, weeks or months. It's hardly surprising, considering the years of captivity and abuse you suffered. Over time, some victims can develop positive feelings toward their captors. Did that happen between you and Jasper Derwent?'

Aurélie nods again, this time tears escaping.

'You can't blame yourself for this, Aurélie. It is a coping mechanism to yield to the abuses and demands of your captor. A level of understanding develops between victim and abuser; their goals become your goals, and their feelings of negativity towards authority figures like the police become your own feelings of negativity. You have suffered an enormous psychological trauma, and you will need help to overcome it and find a way back, but DS Cavendish and the police authorities will be able to provide that for you. And even if they don't, I'm sure your parents will offer any and all support you need.'

I pass Aurélie a box of tissues, and she duly wipes her eyes and nose. 'I wish there was more I could do to help you find your sister, but Jasper was the only name I knew. Men came and went, but I never saw any faces. When I would help him, he would always make me stay out of the way when he spoke with other people like him. I was *his* and his alone, and he would not share me with anyone else.'

'I need to phone DS Cavendish and let her know that you are here, and that Crystal is safe. Okay?'

She nods, and asks to use the bathroom. I point it out while dialling Cavendish's number. 'You were right,' I say into the phone when it connects. 'She showed up.'

'I knew it! Is she still there now?'

'Yes, and so is the little girl. She's perfectly well, eating ice-cream and watching television.'

'And Aurélie? Where is she?'

'Using the facilities.'

'Are you sure? Is there a window in the bathroom? Are you sure she isn't escaping?'

I drop the phone, as the panic rises in my throat, and tear back through the kitchen towards the bathroom. The door is locked when I depress the handle, but the lock can be opened from the outside with a coin, and I use one of my fingernails to turn the mechanism. The window is wide open, but Aurélie is sitting on the edge of the bath sobbing.

'Why do I miss him?' she asks. 'He raped and beat me for years; he forced me to help him abduct other children, and to threaten them when they got out of line. He turned me into a monster, and yet I can't stop crying for him.'

Joining her on the edge of the bath, I wrap my arms around her. 'The human spirit is a curious one. I can't tell you that everything will be okay, but I *believe* you will find a way through it if you let the experts help you.'

We remain there on the edge of the bath until Cavendish arrives and promptly takes her into custody. Two women in jeans and T-shirts from Social Services lead a very confused-looking Crystal to a nearby car, and I see her waving goodbye to her birth mother as she is placed into the back. Having witnessed the effects of losing a child in my own mother, I sense the road ahead for Aurélie will be far from easy going, but I don't doubt she will be supported every step of the way.

I'm grateful for her admission that she never met Anna, but Aurélie's words will ring in my ears for evermore: *collaboration is the only means of survival.* Whilst there is no evidence that Anna yielded to the pressures of captivity, *if* she is still alive now, then there's every chance she is as broken and twisted as the woman before me now. I detest the possibility that Anna's hands could be as dirty as Aurélie's but the sooner I accept it, the better chance I'll have of forgiving her.

Chapter Forty-Three

NOW

Uxbridge, London

Three days later

'There must be over a hundred company names and addresses here,' I say, staring at the umpteenth file from the cabinet, crammed into the tiny room at Uxbridge police station. It is the hottest day of the year so far, and the desktop fan plugged in beside me is loud, but doing little to generate anything close to cool air.

The filing cabinets that Freddie managed to drag from Pendark Studios before he set the site alight are lined up against the far wall, and although all five of them have now been forcibly opened, we are only halfway through reviewing the files in the second of them, and my eyes are already tired.

'It's a shame they didn't keep copies of the films on file too, as that would have made it a lot easier to trace back who had done what,' Jack admits. His tie is off and he's rolled up his sleeves as far as his bulging biceps will allow. His face and patchy beard are clammy, and it genuinely looks like he is melting in the swelter.

Neither of us will give up and go though. These cabinets represent an enormous puzzle, and somewhere within the files is the truth about who took Anna, Jemima Hooper and Aurélie Lebrun. We could do with a dozen extra men and women to support us, but right now we are alone in our battle.

Jack adds his latest file to a pile on the floor. The files in the cabinets were stored alphabetically, but we have decided to rearrange them into chronological order. So far, the earliest files we've found relate to 1974, and the latest 2017. If you'd asked me, before all this happened, how many 'private movies' would have been made in that forty-three-year period, I couldn't have hazarded a guess, but I certainly wouldn't have estimated hundreds. That's not to say the 'private movie' reference numbers we've found so far all relate to pornography – or child pornography at that – but it's certainly possible; there's a reason why further detail about the nature of the films is hidden; 'private' covers a multitude of sins.

The hope is, by arranging them into chronological order, we might somehow be able to tie them back to dates when children went missing. For example, we know that Jemima Hooper was away between 2015 and 2016, so she could be linked to one of the more recent files. It's interesting that Pendark Studios went out of business in 2017, when my investigation into Freddie's abuse at the St Francis Home was gathering momentum, but it's probably just coincidence.

Our attention is diverted by a crisp knock at the door,

followed by the arrival of DCS Jagtar Rawani, who has ultimate operational control over activities undertaken for this area of West London. His turban is immaculately tied as always, and if I had to guess I would say he trims his beard every day to keep it looking so carefully sculpted. In fact, despite his suit jacket and straight tie, he looks as though he has just stepped out of an icebox.

Jack leaps to his feet, searching for his own tie, and jacket, but Rawani gestures to him to sit. 'How are you both?' he asks, closing the door behind him.

'In our element, sir,' Jack answers for both of us. 'Have you come to lend us a hand?'

Rawani doesn't laugh. 'No, but there is something I need to speak to you about, regarding all this.' He pauses, and takes in the filing cabinets in the tightly packed room. 'To both of you, actually. It seems your work here hasn't gone unnoticed. As you know, since the specialist Sapphire team was disbanded two years ago, investigations into sexual assaults were pushed out to local forces to handle, and that will remain the situation for the time being. However, the work the two of you have been doing here, and with the team reviewing the metadata of the video footage recovered from Arthur Turgood's computer, is now considered a critical investigation.

'The National Crime Agency, who are responsible for heading up investigations into Serious and Organised Crime, have pulled together a small team to specifically pick up the baton from the two of you. They will take operational control with immediate effect, and someone will be here to collect the cabinets before the end of the day.'

I look over to Jack, waiting for him to interrupt and refuse to accept the news, but although he looks as shocked as I feel, he remains tight-lipped. It genuinely feels like this project is being stolen from us, which irks me, and yet at the same time I need to consider what is best for the victims of the crimes these files allude to. It could take Jack and me years to review and digest all the information; a larger team with better resources could move things along quicker. I can't be so selfish.

'I wanted to personally come down here and thank you both for your exceptional efforts,' Rawani continues, looking specifically at me. 'I know it feels like you've barely scratched the surface of all of this, but I'm confident that the backing of a specialist team will uncover more of the conspirators involved. If – as you both suspect – there is an illicit network of sex traffickers at work along the south coast of England, it is going to take more than two of you in a cramped office to connect all the dots.'

Jack looks at me now apologetically; I know he doesn't have any choice but to follow the instruction of his senior officer, who in turn is merely passing on a message he's received from on high.

'It's been nice working with you,' Jack says to me now, and I can see the disappointment reflected in his eyes. 'I guess this means I'll be back on cold cases from tomorrow?' he asks the DCS.

'No,' Rawani replies flatly. 'I insisted they needed someone to fill in the new team on progress. As of tomorrow, you'll be working with the NCA out of their office in Vauxhall. It will be on a secondment basis, but that secondment will be indefinite to begin with.'

Jack opens and closes his mouth, trying to find the right

words. 'But what about Mila? I need to be able to look after her twice a week.'

Rawani cuts him off with a raised hand. 'I have spoken to the DCI taking charge, and have explained your personal situation. The role should not get in the way of that. Save for the additional commute, your circumstances won't dramatically change. Oh, and of course it is a plain-clothes office, so you'll have to do something to improve your wardrobe.'

He says it so deadpan that I can't tell if Rawani is making a joke at Jack's expense. Neither of them smirk, so I choke down my own.

'You'll be part of a team of twelve initially,' he continues, 'though there is capacity to extend that to twenty, depending on early progress in the investigation. The team is well funded and there is an expectation that the investigation will dramatically improve the success ratio of missing child cases. There are too many unsolved out there, and centralising the work with the discoveries you have made about the film studios and possible network should help to reduce that number. I know Mr Mitchell is facing charges for criminal damage, but that fire really helped kick up this hornets' nest. I would never condone his behaviour, but the added impetus is priceless.'

I picture Freddie in my mind. He phoned me last night to say that the CPS are looking to press charges, which could result in a short custodial sentence, depending on the magistrate's viewpoint. I've offered to come and give a character reference, but he's outright refused. He's out on bail and continuing to serve at the hostel, so I will continue to nag at him until time runs out. He can be frustratingly stubborn, but whatever happens, he'll be back. He's come too far to give up on the promise of a brighter future.

Rawani turns to me next. 'I'm sorry, but I wasn't able to get you a buy-in to the new team, Miss Hunter. I know you have a personal interest in all of this, but you will now need to step away. I want to personally thank you for all your time and effort; it's certainly appreciated by me.'

Twelve to twenty experienced detectives working to uncover this network is more than I could have hoped for. Sure, I'm disappointed that I won't get to share in the uncovering of the monsters behind it all, but I can see now it is for the best. I suppose what I'm most disappointed about is that I won't be working so closely with Jack anymore. Despite whatever went on between him and Cavendish in Poole, he's still someone I regard as a friend, and I'll miss his goofy grin, his bad taste in dad jokes and his encouraging remarks about my writing.

'Thank you,' I say to Rawani. 'It's been an eye-opening experience, but I have a ton of personal responsibilities that will keep me busy for the foreseeable future anyway. There's the writing of Aurélie's story, plus the mounting requests within the Anna Hunter Foundation.'

Rawani looks relieved neither of us have made a fuss, and leaves the room without another word. In fairness, I think I'll also miss that efficiency; he's very much someone who looks to progress from A to B by the quickest route possible.

Jack turns to me now with his eyebrows raised. 'Well, I didn't see that coming.'

I shrug because I don't know what else to do. 'I'm sure it'll all be for the best. Besides, it'll be good to spend an extended period back in Weymouth; since Rachel and Daniella rekindled their romance, it's been a bit cramped in her flat. I really don't think Rachel appreciates just how thin the walls are at her place.'

Jack closes the open file on the table before him. 'I promise I'll keep you posted on how the investigation is progressing; especially anything that comes up involving your sister. You have my word.'

I force a smile as I feel tears forming in the back of my eyes. 'Thank you.'

Jack holds my stare. 'And I was thinking I might bring Mila down to Weymouth for a day at the beach at the weekend if you fancy joining us?'

What about Zoe Cavendish?, I want to ask, but I'm not brave enough.

'Yeah, that sounds nice.' I pause, and frown. 'Wait, are you only inviting me so that I can get on the beach early and reserve you a good spot?' I mean it as a joke, but I can't read his face.

'Well, I mean, that would be an added bonus, what with you living on the doorstep. It's not like you'd even need to get up all that early.' The goofy grin breaks out across his face again. 'I need to check with Mila's mum Chrissie first, but, if she agrees, is it okay if I call you?'

'Sure,' I say, packing my things into my satchel. 'You'll want to be down before nine though, or you'll never get a parking space.'

Jack remains seated. 'Is everything okay? Between us, I mean? I know I shouldn't have tried to kiss you last week, and I thought we'd got over that, but… I just sense you're cross with me since we returned from Poole, and—'

'Everything's fine,' I say, without looking at him, pushing

Cavendish's face from my mind. 'Listen, I'd better get going. If I'm lucky I can pack my things and catch a train back to Weymouth tonight. Are you okay to finish putting all of this back before your new team comes to collect it all?'

He begins to stand. 'Of course. I'll show you out.'

'No, you stay; I can find my own way back to the front desk. They all know me here now anyway.'

I don't look back as I leave the room, willing my stupid tears to stay put. I manage to get out into the warm sunshine before my chest tightens and I can't hold back the sobs any longer. For twenty years I believed that Anna's disappearance that day had been bad luck, she'd been in the wrong place at the wrong time; but all of this suggests that there was far more going on than I ever could have realised. If only the police investigation team had known about the ring, maybe they would have made different decisions, or would have checked in different places. If there hadn't been a preliminary focus on my parents' possible involvement, and they'd listened when Mum had said Anna wasn't the sort of girl to run away, then just maybe I wouldn't have grown up mourning her.

I barely make it to the tube station before my thoughts become too much and I fall to a bench inside the station and just let it all out. The last thing I'd need right now is for some paparazzi to appear and snap my picture, but I actually think the sound of my wailing is keeping the public from approaching me. Jemima Hooper was taken from her parents, physically abused and killed. As much as I don't want to believe that Anna suffered in the same way, I can't block out the voice in the back of my head.

I can't give up. I've come too far to simply accept that I'll never discover the truth about what happened to Anna. I will find out the truth no matter how many hours it takes, nor how many tears I will shed.

I'm coming for you, Anna. I'm coming for you.

THE END

Emma Hunter will return in *Discarded*...

Acknowledgments

I'll start by thanking my brilliant editor, Bethan Morgan, who is so great at what she does. It was her feedback and plot suggestions that took the original pitch from an obscure idea to the six books planned for the series. She taught me how to flesh out Emma's character, to build on her nuance and motivations, and how to truly bring her to life. Emma has become like a best friend or sister to me, and I'm going to be so sad when our adventure finishes.

Bethan 'gets' Emma and her close friends and is always there to fine-tune character voice and to point out when one strays into another. I also love it when she leaves little comments on the manuscript where she's enjoyed a particular passage or use of phrase. It gives my low self-esteem a real boost to know that I'm not writing a load of old nonsense.

This series is going from strength-to-strength, and the whole team at One More Chapter deserve a huge amount of credit for all the work that has gone in to crafting it. Thanks to Lucy Bennett for her work in producing the series' covers; to

Tony Russell, whose copyediting is always relatively painless; and to Simon Fox who kindly completed the proofread to pull out those all embarrassing spelling mistakes. Finally, no book release is complete without the fervent effort of the publicity team, so big thanks to Melanie Price and Claire Fenby for all they've done to raise awareness of the series and encourage new readers to pick up the books.

Writing *Trafficked* required me to reach into parts of my psyche and imagination that were perilous to venture to. As a father, the thought of either of my children being taken from me is too painful to consider, but that's precisely the fear I used when writing about the Lebruns. I figured that if something was powerful enough to scare me, then it would likely pack a similar punch with my readers. For those who found it tough to read, I'm sorry and will warn that there are tougher challenges facing Emma in the remaining three books.

I'd love to know what you thought about *Trafficked*, and whether you think Emma and Jack will find the happy ending they both so desperately deserve. I am active on Facebook, Twitter, and Instagram, so please do stop by with any messages, observations, or questions. Hearing from readers of my books truly brightens my days and encourages me to keep writing, so don't be a stranger. I promise I *will* respond to every message and comment.

Away from publishing, I wouldn't be a writer if it wasn't for my beautiful and always supportive wife Hannah. She keeps all the 'behind the scenes' stuff of my life in order and our children's lives would be far greyer if I was left in sole charge. I'd also like to thank my mother-in-law Marina for all the championing of my books she does on social media. Thank you as ever to my best friend Dr Parashar Ramanuj, who never shies away from the awkward medical questions I ask him. Thank you to Alex Shaw and Paul Grzegorzek – authors and dear friends – who are happy to listen to me moan and whinge about the pitfalls of the publishing industry, offering words of encouragement along the way.

And final thanks must go to YOU for picking up and reading *Trafficked*. You are the reason I wake up ridiculously early to write every day, and why every free moment is spent devising plot twists. I feel truly honoured to call myself a writer, and it thrills me to know that other people are being entertained by the weird and wonderful visions my imagination creates. I love getting lost in my imagination and the more people who read and enjoy my stories, the more I can do it.

ONE MORE CHAPTER

YOUR NUMBER ONE STOP

FOR PAGETURNING BOOKS

One More Chapter is an award-winning global division of HarperCollins.

Sign up to our newsletter to get our latest eBook deals and stay up to date with our weekly Book Club!
<u>Subscribe here.</u>

Meet the team at
www.onemorechapter.com

Follow us!
@OneMoreChapter_
@OneMoreChapter
@onemorechapterhc

Do you write unputdownable fiction?
We love to hear from new voices.
Find out how to submit your novel at
www.onemorechapter.com/submissions